MW01148411

FRIED CHICKEN CASTAÑEDA

Suzanne Stauffer

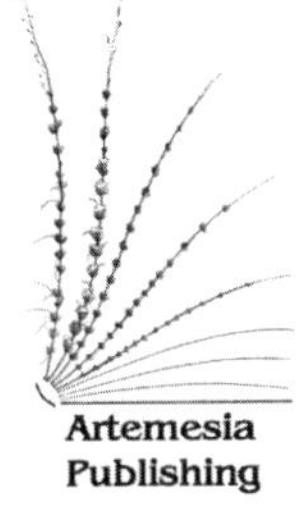

ISBN: 978-1-963832-05-1 (paperback)
ISBN: 978-1-963832-24-2 (ebook)
LCCN: 2024951570

Printed in the United States

Artemesia Publishing
9 Mockingbird Hill Rd
Tijeras, New Mexico 87059
www.apbooks.net
info@artemesiapublishing.com

Content Notice:
This story is set at a time when racial slurs and derogatory phrases were used in many common and ordinary situations. The author and the publisher acknowledge that these statements were wrong to be spoken at the time and are wrong to be spoken now. We have kept the use of these phrases in the context of the story and the historical setting.

To my dear friend, Kent, without whose unwavering belief and encouragement this would never have been finished. And to my editor, who prevented a rift in the space-time continuum.

Chapter 1

January 1929

Cleveland, Ohio

"PRUDENCE? PRUDENCE? SHIFT'S OVER. I'm here to relieve you." The woman's low whisper was loud in the quiet of the public library reading room. Prudence Bates jumped slightly and shook her head to clear the cobwebs. She had been daydreaming again. This time, she had rescued the mayor's daughter from kidnappers who were holding her for ransom. She had been in the middle of an interview with the *New York Times* about how she'd solved the case when she was interrupted. Her dark, bobbed hair swung around her cheeks, then settled again in a smooth cap, as she turned to face the woman at her side.

"Oh, I'm sorry, Pat. I didn't hear you come up."

Pat laughed. "You looked like you were a million miles away." She glanced around the library reading room. "How has it been this morning?"

"Oh, the usual." Prudence nodded toward the tables where several men and women, one heavily pregnant, were perusing newspapers and magazines. "Old Mr. Brown is checking the stock reports, Mrs. Johnson is looking at the latest fashion magazines, and Mrs. Jacobs is reading *Parenting*. Paul Martin has this month's issue of *Popular Mechanics*. He's still working on that wireless set. I guess he's almost finished, as he asked for a book on Morse code." She sighed and repeated, "The usual." Was it any wonder that she spent most of her time at the reference desk daydreaming? It was the same thing day after day. Same people. Same questions. No one ever asked for help identifying a rare poison or locating a missing relative or decoding a secret message. No questions about art or literature or culture. Nothing that challenged her abilities as a librarian or took advantage of her education and interests. She pushed the chair away from the desk and relinquished it to Pat, relieved that her two-hour morning shift had ended.

"Morse code?" Pat asked. "For a ham radio?"

"He explained it to me, but I'm afraid I wasn't really listening. I'm sure he'll be glad to explain it to you, if you ask him." They both laughed softly.

"Oh, I almost forgot," Pat said. "Miss Eastman would like to speak to you."

Prudence looked at her quizzically. "Me? About what?" What could the library director want to speak to her about?

Pat shrugged. "She didn't say why. Just asked me to let you know." Pat settled herself at the desk and Prudence headed for Miss Eastman's office. She couldn't imagine why Miss Eastman wanted to see her. Surely there hadn't been any complaints from the patrons! Had there? The library wasn't cutting back on staff, as far as she knew. Could Miss Eastman be moving her to another department? Not that she'd mind moving, as long as it wasn't to the Business Collection, but they were short-staffed. She hoped it wasn't another shelf-reading or weeding project. She sighed as she remembered walking along the shelves in the reference section, making sure that the books were in Dewey Decimal order and deciding whether books with damaged spines should be repaired or discarded. It was necessary work, but... it wasn't what she'd thought she'd be doing when she'd decided to go to library school.

Linda Eastman was seated at her desk, reading through a stack of papers. Her long gray hair was twisted into a soft bun on the crown of her head, but her raw silk suit was as stylish and sophisticated as Prudence's own. She looked up when Prudence knocked lightly on the open door.

"Pat said you wanted to speak with me?"

"Yes. Do come in and have a seat," she indicated the chair next to her desk. Prudence sat and looked at her expectantly.

Miss Eastman clasped her hands on top of her desk and turned toward Prudence. "I have a special assignment for you, one that I hope you'll enjoy." Prudence nodded and kept her expression neutral. "But, first, let me refresh my memory. As I recall, your undergraduate degree is in anthropology?" Prudence nodded.

"Yes, I thought so. And, correct me if I'm wrong, but you are a native of Cleveland, are you not?" Prudence nodded again, wondering where this was going, but hesitated to demand answers from the library director "Have you ever been to the American Southwest?"

The question surprised her. She shook her head. "Actually, Miss Eastman, I've never been farther west than Chicago."

Miss Eastman nodded. "I thought that was the case. Well, this is a chance for you to broaden your horizons, in a way. A Miss Anita Rose, of the Fred Harvey Southwestern Indian Detours, is speaking on the Detours in the community room here tomorrow night. I'd like you to attend, with an eye to using the information as the basis for programs that the library could offer. And I am putting you in charge of developing those programs." She sat back and waited for Prudence's response.

"Programs?" Prudence looked confused. Miss Eastman couldn't mean that the library was going to promote the Harvey company.

Miss Eastman smiled and shook her head. "Art, history, geography... all of these topics are popular. And as someone who has no experience of the Southwest, you will be able to develop programs that will appeal to others in the same position. With the added bonus of developing your own knowledge at the same time."

Prudence nodded. "Yes, ma'am." It would be more interesting than listening to Paul Martin ramble on about his wireless radio set, if nothing else.

Miss Eastman gazed at Prudence with a slight frown. "Forgive me for intruding, but... is everything well at home? Recently, you've seemed... distracted and lacking in... animation."

Prudence felt herself blushing in shame. She hadn't realized that her feelings were so conspicuous. She took a deep breath. "Oh, no. Everything at home is fine. I..." She paused, searching for the right words. "I suppose it's just that..." She trailed off. She could not bring herself to tell the director that she found her work at the library boring.

"Everything feels so routine after two years?" Miss Eastman smiled in sympathy. Prudence nodded.

"Then this new assignment will change that." She smiled again and turned back to the papers on her desk.

Prudence stood uncertainly, then said, "Yes, ma'am. I'm sure it will," and headed to her desk in the reference librarians' office. The Southwestern Indian Detours program was not especially enticing. It was sure to be a sales pitch, but, on the other hand, what did she have to lose? It was certain to be at least as interesting as evaluating books for the Business Collection for Miss Freeman. And Miss Eastman might be right. Developing the programs might alleviate some of the recent boredom and general dissatisfaction with her personal and professional life, if nothing else. She'd have to make an effort to act as if it did, in any case, now that she knew that her feelings were obvious to the library director. The first thing she needed to do was learn more about the Harvey Company. And maybe she'd suggest that Wally accompany her to the program and kill two birds with one stone. Mother had been asking why he hadn't been over for dinner recently and this had the advantage of being a work assignment, not a social event, so he might not get the wrong idea. Although he probably would. Like most people, he saw what he wanted to see.

* * *

AS PRUDENCE glanced through the illustrated tour brochure she'd picked up at the door, she was drawn to the vast, spare landscape of mountains and mesas and pueblos depicted in the drawings and photographs, so very different from the lush, green plains and woodlands of her native Ohio. Even before Miss Rose began speaking, Prudence felt the call and the romance of the American West which had lured so many in years gone by.

Out of the corner of her eye, she could see Wally looking at her from the next seat, but she refused to turn her head. Not because he was hard to look at. He might even be considered good looking, tall and broad and rather well set up, given the summers he had spent working on his father's farm through high school and college. Well-groomed as well, if rather conservative and conventional. Plenty of girls in Cleveland would be more than happy to sit next to him and to look at him, and she could name most of them. She and Wally had grown up in the same neighborhood and graduated in the same high school class. He'd even graduated from Western Reserve the same year she had earned her bachelor's degree. Now, he was working his way up in the advertising department at the White Motor Company, where he was unambiguously "Mr. Walter Carver." But, to her, he was just Wally from down the street and yet one more aspect of her life that bored her with its familiarity.

Miss Rose stood at the front of the library auditorium wearing a dark blue velvet tunic with long sleeves that was fastened around her waist with a belt of heavy silver conchos and a pleated whipcord walking skirt. A heavy silver and turquoise necklace hung around her neck and on her head she wore a soft, wide-brimmed hat with an unusual looking badge pinned to the front of it. A portable motion picture screen was set up behind her and a magic lantern and motion picture projector were set side-by-side halfway down the center aisle.

"Welcome to this presentation on the Fred Harvey Southwestern Indian Detours. I am Anita Rose, representative of the Fred Harvey Company. I hope that you all picked up a brochure as you came in. If not, please feel free to take one as you leave." She held up the rather thick booklet, then walked down the aisle to the magic lantern. She turned it on, nodded toward the back of the room, and the lights were shut off.

The first slide showed the logo of the Fred Harvey company. "I am sure that all of you are familiar with Fred Harvey of Harvey House fame." She paused while many in the audience murmured agreement. "What you may not know is that Fred Harvey founded the first Harvey House in the Topeka, Kansas railroad depot in 1876 on a handshake." A photograph of the Topeka depot was displayed on the screen.

Prudence found her attention wandering. She had read about the rise of the Fred Harvey company and its chain of hotels and restaurants, and while an American success story, the dry facts were less than gripping. However, her attention was suddenly caught as Miss Rose began showing photographic images of the Harvey Hotels in New Mexico, changing the glass slides as she named each one, "beginning with the Castañeda in Las Vegas, New Mexico in 1898, followed by the Alvarado in Albuquerque in 1902, the El Ortiz in Lamy in 1910, and the El Navajo in Gallup in 1923. And, just four years ago, the La Fonda in its namesake city, Santa Fe, was acquired by the Railway. I mention these particular hotels because they are the hotels from which the Indian Detours set out and to which they return."

Prudence was entranced with the projected images of the hotels, each architecturally unique, set in the rugged Western landscape. The slides had been hand tinted in hues of burnt orange, rust, sage, purple, and tan. The factual information she had absorbed had not prepared her for the natural wonders displayed on the screen in front of her. She could almost feel the desert sun beating down on her head and the hot, dry wind brushing her cheek, a sharp contrast to the frigid January air outside the library. She was not the only member of the audience who was awestruck by the images, as evidenced by the whispered comments she could hear around her.

Even Wally seemed impressed. He nudged her with his elbow and whispered, "That's some pretty spiffy scenery and ritzy hotels." She shook her head impatiently and motioned to him to be quiet. Miss Rose was still speaking.

"And, so, we come to the Indian Detours. As most of you know, passengers on the transcontinental trains often face layovers of many hours, if not overnight. In 1925, the Fred Harvey company had the innovative idea of offering short "detours" to local sites of interest via automobile to such waiting passengers. These tours were led by specially trained Couriers, young women who had completed an intensive training course." The image of a group of smiling young women, all pretty and all dressed in a similar costume to Miss Rose's, replaced that of the La Fonda hotel. One of them looked familiar.

"I myself am a graduate of that first class of Couriers in April 1926," she said, rather smugly, and paused for applause. The next slide was a closeup of the badge on one of the women's hats. "This badge, the thunderbird of Indian mythology, is the logo of the Harvey Detours. It was a very proud day when I was given the right to wear it."

"The Detours have grown to include one, two, three, and four-day journeys with stops at the Taos Pueblo and Artists' Colony, the Old Governor's Palace in Santa Fe, and Indian pueblos such as Tesuque, Santa Clara, and Puyé," as she spoke, the slides changed to depict each of the locations and buildings she mentioned.

"While at the pueblos, Detourists have an opportunity to observe the Indians in their native habitat, wearing their native clothing, and performing their native dances," she continued, exhibiting slides of exotic looking people dressed in colorful, primitive clothing.

At this point, she shut off the magic lantern and started the motion picture projector. Almost immediately, the screen was filled with images of Indian men wearing breechcloths, moccasins, and painted masks or feathered headdresses, stamping around a circle and turning, bowing, and jerking in time to the drums and rattles being played in the background. They appeared to be chanting, as well, as their lips were moving.

When the film stopped a few moments later, she shut off the projector and turned the magic lantern back on.

"Detourists are also able to purchase intriguing and exotic native jewelry, rugs, and pottery directly from the craftsmen themselves." These slides showed the same exotic people, using primitive tools and techniques to work silver, weave rugs, and shape pottery while seated on the ground or at low tables.

Prudence missed Miss Rose's next comments as she imagined herself dressed in the soft, heavy velvet blouse with the weight of conchos around her waist and squash blossoms hanging from her neck, standing amid quaint adobe dwellings, watching exotically dressed Indians performing their native dances to the rhythmic beat of their traditional instruments, against a background of majestic mountains with brilliant white snow caps reaching up to the sky. Eager Detourists clustered around her, asking her to explain the meaning and history of the dances, which she did with ease and expertise.

Once again, Prudence forced her attention to return to Miss Rose. "I am pleased to announce that we are now offering, as of this year, five-day Detours from Santa Fe to the Grand Canyon," the image of the Grand Canyon, stretching into infinity, seemed too large to be contained within the confines of the motion picture screen. She paused to allow the audience to fully appreciate the natural wonder, then continued, "Which include overnight stops at the Alvarado, the El Navajo, and the El Tovar. The tour will include visits to various Hopi Indian villages as well as the famous Painted Desert of Arizona." The colored image of the Painted Desert also elicited gasps of awe as it leapt on the screen. Miss Rose paused again to allow the audience to absorb the spectacle. Then she changed the slide to one of ruined adobe buildings huddled under the shelter of an overhanging cliff.

"And it would be remiss of me not to at least mention our eight-day Sierra Verde Circle Cruise that makes a nine-hundred-mile circuit of northwestern New Mexico and southwestern Colorado, and includes such highlights as Mesa Verde National Park, Chaco Canyon National Monument, and the forest, mountains, rivers and Indians of this strange and exotic Navajo country." Her final slide depicted a Navajo family, the husband with his dark hair in a traditional bun, the wife in a velvet tunic much like that worn by Miss Rose and a long, gathered skirt, and two young boys, their dark hair cut short in the Western style. The adults stared at the camera impassively, but the boys smiled shyly. They stood in front of an eight-sided log structure with a blanket for a door and a small corral made of brush to one side penning in a few sheep and goats. In the distance, a mountain range tipped with snow reached toward a cloudless sky.

After a few seconds, Miss Rose turned off the magic lantern and called for "Lights, please." She stepped to the front of the room and smiled at the audience. "So, as I'm sure you all realize, the Detours are no longer merely an opportunity to while away an hour or two while waiting for your connection, but have become destinations in and of themselves, as alien and exotic as any foreign country. But with the benefit of never having to leave the United States, never having to learn a foreign language, and being served at every meal with the specialties that have made Harvey House chefs renowned throughout the country. And now, are there any questions from the audience?"

Prudence could scarcely contain herself. Her hand shot up. "How does one become a Courier?" she asked, almost before she was recognized.

Miss Rose smiled. "As I noted, Couriers complete an intensive one-month training course presented by recognized experts in the history, politics, sociology, anthropology, geology and art of the area that provides them with the knowledge to lead the tours. Only those who pass the final exam are hired, so you can be confident that they are competent to answer any and all questions that you might have on your Detour." She looked out over the audience and continued, "Beyond that, our Couriers are all college-educated girls, at least twenty-five years old and with experience in working closely with the public, so you can all rest assured that they will provide you with the very best in service."

She smiled again at the audience at large. "Nearly all of them speak at least one other language, and many speak two, so that they may converse with our foreign Detourists and recent U.S. citizens in their native tongue."

"When does the next training course begin?" Prudence asked quickly.

Miss Rose looked surprised, then nodded slowly as Prudence's meaning became clear. "In June, but for obvious reasons, we prefer young ladies who have the personal knowledge that comes from having lived in the Southwest." She looked away, out over the audience, ready to take the next question.

"And where is it held?"

"In Santa Fe at the La Fonda. You can write to the address on the brochure for an application." She gazed over Prudence's head. "Now are there any questions about the Detours themselves? Yes, sir?"

"Uh, yes, could you tell us more about those buildings, the ones under the cliff?"

"Ah, yes, the cliff dwellings of Mesa Verde National Park..."

Prudence set her jaw. She was a college graduate—twice over. She had a bachelor's degree in anthropology and another in library science from Western Reserve University. Anything the Fred Harvey company could teach, she could learn. She was as close to twenty-five years old as made no difference. She might not have personal knowledge—yet—but she had desire and determination and intelligence. They had seen her this far. They'd see her through this.

She joined in the applause when Miss Rose had finished answering the final question. After she had bowed her thanks and left the auditorium, Prudence snapped open her compact, touched up her lipstick and powder, and tucked a few stray hairs back into her cloche. She stood and Wally helped her on with her coat. Looking at him over her shoulder, she asked, "Would you like to come to dinner? Mother said to invite you. She's fixed a nice pot roast just in case."

"With gravy?"

"Of course! And carrots and potatoes. I'm sure she'll have made something nice for dessert, as well. She knows all your favorites."

He laughed. "It's not even Sunday! How can I say no?"

As they stepped outside, she snuggled more deeply into her coat and turned the fur collar up around her ears. Wally tugged his fedora firmly on his head against the icy wind blowing off of Lake Erie. They walked quickly to where he had parked his automobile, then drove the few blocks to her house. Prudence resisted telling him, yet again, that they could have easily walked. He was so proud of owning a motor car, even if it was last year's model. And, if she were honest with herself, it was much more pleasant riding in the warmth of the car than walking in the freezing wind.

They hurried through the gate in the white picket fence, up the walk and the stairs, across the porch, and through the front door. Prudence called out, "Mother! We're home," as they hung their coats on the hall tree and Wally placed his hat on the shelf above. Prudence headed up the stairs to her bedroom, while Wally started back toward the kitchen. He was met by Mrs. Bates, wiping her hands on a towel. Not as tall as her daughter, she was a comfortable woman whose greying hair was pinned up in the "cottage loaf" pompadour of the previous generation and whose house dress was covered in a "Mother Hubbard" apron.

"Oh, Wally, it's good to see you. Is Pru getting changed?"

"Hi, Ma," he said, bending to kiss her cheek. "Yes, she is.'"

Mrs. Bates shook her head and laughed. "Well, don't just stand there. Come on back to the dining room. Would you like something hot to drink? I have coffee ready, or tea."

"Coffee would be great, but first, what can I do to help?" They carried the serving dishes of food from the kitchen to the dining table, which was set for three, then Mrs. Bates returned for the coffee pot and to leave her apron in the kitchen.

Her mother was pouring coffee into Wally's cup when Prudence entered. Her dark, bobbed hair was brushed until it shone and she had changed into a set of silk lounging pajamas, with wide flowing legs and a kimono jacket, and comfortable embroidered house slippers.

She set the program brochure on the table between her plate and her mother's.

Mrs. Bates poured a cup of coffee for herself and Prudence. "Wally, don't wait on ceremony!" she laughed. "I know you must be hungry. Serve yourself some pot roast. Pru, please start the carrots. Here you go, Wally, have some potatoes." The dishes made their way around the table, then there was silence for several minutes, broken only by the clink of silverware on china and muffled sounds of chewing.

"Tell me about the program, dear. Are you going to go on one of those—detours? Is that what they're called?—for your vacation this year? It's a bit far away..." She picked up the brochure and leafed through it.

"Oh, Mother! It was marvelous!! The illustrations in the brochure only hint at the wonders of the landscape. Such vast expanses! The horizon—there doesn't seem to be a horizon. Just empty desert and range after range of buttes and mesas and in the far distance, mountain peaks that look as if they are floating. And the colors! She showed us colored slides of the scenes in the brochure. So striking in the sunlight—such dark, rusty red and burnt orange bands with streaks of verdigris and gold. And at sunset, they are all purple and gray and black. And the Grand Canyon! Mother, words cannot describe…"

Wally laughed. Prudence shot him a stern glance across the table. "Our Pru is thinking of abandoning us to become an Indian Detours guide, Ma." He ignored the dirty looks she was giving him.

Her mother looked startled, then laughed uncertainly. "Oh, Wally, you're such a prankster." She looked at her daughter. "He is making a joke, isn't he?"

Prudence glared at Wally from under her eyebrows. "Yes, Mother, he's joking. I'm not abandoning anyone."

She turned to face her mother. "It would only be for a year… or two."

Her mother's face crumpled. "But, I had hoped, now that you've finished with college…" She looked in Wally's direction. He grinned wryly and looked at his now-empty plate.

"We've been over all that, Mother," Prudence muttered through gritted teeth. "I'm not ready to settle down just yet."

"You're not getting any younger, dear. And what about your job at the library? Working for that nice Miss Freeman and Miss Eastman."

Prudence took a deep breath and waited until her surge of irritation had tempered. She wondered if her mother even realized that the two women she held up to her as role models had never married and Miss Freeman, at least, had traveled extensively. "They would be the first ones to tell me to follow my dream, Mother. Miss Freeman would say that travel broadens the mind, and that I would be a better librarian at the end of it. Miss Eastman is always encouraging us to expand our horizons. I have a suspicion that is why Miss Eastman asked me to attend the program. There are times that I feel that they both think I'm terribly provincial, never having left home."

She leaned forward, and continued earnestly, "And this would be a chance to see all those Indian tribes I only read about in my anthropology books and in their natural setting. You remember how much they fascinated me when I was in college and how much I wanted to go out West to do field work with them when I was a student. Don't you see,

Mother, how important this is?" She did not add that the only reason she had not gone was because her mother had thought that she would be gone too far for too long.

Her mother sighed. "I thought you were all through with that, now that you've got such a nice job at the library and such a nice future ahead of you. I really don't understand..."

Wally grinned. "I think it's because she likes the clothes. You know how our Pru likes clothes."

Prudence rolled her eyes, while mentally thanking Wally for changing the subject, and answered her mother's confused and questioning look. "She was wearing the Courier uniform, and, yes, I liked it. It's—well, rather exotic—a velvet blouse of the type that the Indian women in that area wear, heavy silver and turquoise jewelry, a pleated walking skirt, a soft hat, and walking shoes, of course. Stylish and practical. But if the clothes were all I wanted, I could easily order a set made for me here. I want more than that."

Her mother sighed, but before she could speak, Wally interrupted. "She said they only hire girls who grew up there. How are you going to get around that?" He leaned back in his chair, looking smug.

"Well, MISTER Carver," she snapped. "She said they "prefer"—which means they make exceptions. So, all I have to do is convince them that I am one of the exceptions. I AM a librarian. I CAN read. And between now and June, I'll be able to read just about everything written on the American Southwest—that I haven't read already. And what the Library doesn't have, I can get on interlibrary loan." She paused, then her eyes lit up. "In fact, I'm going to spend the next six months organizing a series of lectures for the library on the subject of the American Southwest. I'll know more about the Southwest than even the Harvey Detours instructors by the time I'm through."

Wally opened his mouth to respond, but stopped when Mrs. Bates shook her head. "She knows her own mind, Wally. You know as well as I do that no one can change her mind for her once she's set on something."

His lips twisted into a wry smile again, as he nodded. "Yeah, Ma, yeah, we both know." He sat up straight. "Maybe

I can put a good word in for you. We do have the contract for some of the HarveyCars and they buy trucks from us. Someone in purchasing might be able to pull a string or two."

"Walter Carver," Prudence stared at him across the table. "I don't know whether to kiss you or smack you. Why didn't you say something earlier?"

He shrugged. "I was hoping to talk you out of it. Besides, I don't know how much good it will do, but I'll ask around. It's not as if we're working with Fred Harvey himself, or I should say, Ford Harvey. He took over when the old man died about 30 years ago. Or even with the head of the Detours, Major Clarkson. Our contact is someone in their transportation department." Prudence grinned at him. "Don't go getting your hopes too high, missy," he warned.

Mrs. Bates slid back from the table. "Now, who wants pie?" She smiled at Wally. "It's peach, your favorite. Made with canned peaches, I'm afraid."

"And I won't be able to tell the difference, if you made it," Wally proclaimed.

After dinner, Prudence and Wally insisted that Mrs. Bates leave them to clear up. As she washed the dishes and Wally dried, they continued their discussion from dinner.

Wally began, "Look, Pru... I know I've asked this before and..."

She turned to him as she handed him a clean plate, "Wally, you know what my answer will be."

"I know, but like I told you—you're the only girl for me. You've been the only girl since we were six years old."

"And I'm very fond of you, Wally. I always have been. I'm just not ready to settle down to a white picket fence, a couple of kids, and pot roast every Sunday." She sighed and looked pensive. "Dad told me just before he died that the only regrets he had were for the things he didn't do. He and Mother married so young, and then he worked so hard to provide for us. If it hadn't been for us, he probably would have joined up in 1917, just to see Europe. He planned for them to travel when he retired and was saving toward that. He'd bought the house and started Mother's annuity when they got married, and he got steady promotions and things were going well for us financially, but he got sick and the travel money went into a trust fund for my education. I don't want to have the same regrets, Wally. I've still got some money left in the trust fund. The house is paid for and Mother's annuity is plenty for her to live on and I will always be able to support myself as a librarian, so I'm going to use it in a way that I know he would have wanted me to."

She stopped and stared out of the kitchen window, then continued in a different tone of voice, "Come with me, Wally!" She turned toward him, her eyes sparkling, "Come with me! Just for a few months! We could have an adventure together."

"Now, Pru... that's not very practical. I'd have to give up my position at the motor company and I'm due a promotion before the end of this year. Besides, what would people say?"

"Oh, who cares what people would say?" She rolled her eyes. "Besides, we'd be in the company of other Detourists and Couriers. It's not as if we would be going off into the wilds together, just the two of us. As for your job, you're young, and you're good at what you do. A few months wouldn't be the end of your career... and think how much fun we could have!" She smiled enticingly at him, inviting him to change her opinion of him.

He shook his head and changed the subject, trying to console her by offering her a bribe, as if she were a child who had been denied a treat. "Friday night, how about we go to that new speakeasy on Short Vincent that I've heard good things about?"

She smiled regretfully and looked back down at the sink. "All right. It's been ages since we've been dancing." How many chances was she going to give him to show that he was—that he could be—the kind of man she wanted to spend the rest of her life with? Or even that he understood her and what she wanted?

They talked about the speakeasy as they finished the dishes, then Prudence walked him to the door. Wally slipped on his coat and took his hat in his hand. "Look, Pru," he said, in a low voice, "I know you want to do this and I know you've made up your mind, but, if you won't think about us, think about your mother. You're all she has. Leaving her all alone to go gallivanting after Indians..."

Prudence glared at him. "I won't be "gallivanting after Indians," as you put it," she hissed. "I don't even know any Indians. I'll be expanding my horizons. And when have I not thought of Mother? I wanted to go to one of the Seven Sisters, but instead, I went to Western Reserve, because it was close to home. I earned a master's in library science because Western Reserve offered one and I could get a job here in Cleveland and I got one. I'm twenty-five years old, Wally, and I've never been farther from Cleveland than Chicago, and then only for a couple of nights. I wanted to be an anthropologist and study primitive tribes, like Margaret Mead, not just read about them. It's too late for me to do that, but I could do this."

She paused for breath. She refrained from adding that she had maintained a close friendship with Wally in part because her mother doted on him and he cared about her mother almost as much as she did.

"Ah," Wally nodded. "So that's what's got you all het up. That woman's book that came out last year."

She gritted her teeth. "It certainly brought it all home to me how little I've done that I really wanted to do. And now I have this opportunity—possibly my last opportunity—and all you can say is "think about your mother." When do I get to think about myself?"

He looked down at the hat he held in his hand. "I never realized you resented your mother so much, Pru."

"I don't "resent" my mother!" Prudence hissed through clenched teeth. "I love my mother and I'm grateful for everything she's done for me. I just don't see why that has to mean that I can't have a life of my own!"

"Now, Pru," Wally put out a hand to her arm. "We only want what's best for you, you know that."

"And this IS what's best for me!"

"Are you sure?"

"The only way to know that is to do it, Wally. At least I have to try. And it's not as if this is a permanent change. It's only for a year or two."

"Even if it means leaving your mother all alone for that year or two?"

"Mother is not "all alone." She has her ladies' club and her church group and the neighbors." She paused in exasperation. "And she has you. You know you're like a son to her."

He looked at the ceiling. "Like a son to her, Prudence, not a son." He shook his head in exasperation. "I could be a son to her, if you'd just say the word. Agree to marry me and you can go off on your adventure, leaving your fiancé to look after your mother. That's the proper way to do it. And I won't even ask you to set the date until after you get back."

She moved closer and put her arms around his neck. "I might consider it," she said and pulled him closer, pressing up against him, lifting her face toward his.

He brushed a chaste kiss on her lips, then pulled his head back and pushed her gently away. "Now, Pru," he chided, "We both know you're not that kind of girl. So, what's it to be?"

"No, Wally, it's no. Not even for Mother." And never for someone who couldn't see her as a woman, not a girl and a rather staid and colorless girl, at that.

He shrugged. "You'll change your mind one of these days, Pru. Well, I guess you know that I'll look after her, regardless, and I'll still be here waiting when you get back." He settled his hat on his head and opened the door. "Night, pumpkin. Don't take any wooden nickels." He grinned as he left.

She stared through the glass at his back as he walked down the sidewalk. "Not that kind of girl? You don't know me at all..." she muttered to herself. "That was your last chance, Wally Carver. Now I'm going to go out and find someone who is 'that kind of boy.' Or better, that kind of man." And if she didn't, well, Wally would still be there waiting for her when she got back. She hoped she'd be able to do better, but if not, she knew that she could do a lot worse.

Chapter 2

Tuesday - Wednesday

May 28-29, 1929

Cleveland to Chicago

PRUDENCE AND HER MOTHER formed a little island of calm amid the rush on the platform at the Cleveland train station. The stream of passengers moving toward and away from the trains and the porters with their laden luggage carts following them split around pair. Prudence stood gazing over the heads of the crowd toward the entrance as her mother fluttered around her. "Do you have your ticket, dear? And your overnight bag? Oh, I do wish you'd let me pay the extra for a room, instead of a Pullman coach. It would have been my little treat, and much safer," Mrs. Bates fussed, picking a piece of lint off the collar of Prudence's traveling suit, tucking a stray strand of hair under the brim of her hat, smoothing the front of her coat.

"Yes, Mother, it's right here," Prudence held up the folder with her train tickets. "And here," she indicated her overnight bag at her feet. The rest of her luggage was already on the train. "I'll be perfectly fine in a Pullman. There's no need to go to unnecessary expense. Besides, I want the same experience as my future clients. My training as a Courier begins the moment I get on the Santa Fe Railroad train in Chicago."

"Yes, dear," her mother murmured in a distracted tone. "Where are you going to get your hair styled? And buy clothes? Are you certain that they have running water?"

Prudence laughed. "Yes, Mother, they have running water and beauty parlors. Goodness, it is 1929! As for clothes, I'll be wearing my uniform most days. And I'll have plenty of time in Las Vegas to buy new ones if I need them before I get to Santa Fe, and I'm sure there are dressmakers in Santa Fe, as well."

"Now, you're sure you know what to do once you get to Chicago?" her mother worried. "I do wish you had let Wally go with you as far as Kansas City. He could have helped you with the transfer in Chicago. I hate to think of you wandering around that great big station all on your own."

Prudence smiled tolerantly. "Yes, Mother. I know what to do and I can manage all by myself. I'll have dinner at the Harvey House at the station, then take a cab to the hotel. I already have a reservation there, so there's nothing to worry about. I've checked my luggage through to Las Vegas, so I don't need to worry about it, either. I do wish that you would reconsider inviting one of your cousins for an extended visit. There's no reason for my room to sit empty."

"Oh, I don't know ..." Mrs. Bates dithered. "It would be so strange to have someone else living in the house and what if you change your mind? I would hate to turn someone out if you wanted to come home again right away."

"Oh, look, there's Wally," Prudence waved, and Wally hurried toward them.

"So, you're really going?" He asked, taking both of her hands in his.

She nodded.

"Oh, Wally," Mrs. Bates looked at him sadly. "I wish you could have talked her out of it. Or at least traveled as far as Kansas City with her. I worry about that layover in Chicago."

"I tried, Ma," Wally shook his head, "But she wasn't having any of it."

"And I wish that the two would not speak about me as if I were not here," Prudence remarked sharply. "And as if I were a child."

Wally turned toward her, grinning. "Whereas you're a big girl, all grown up, with her very own money."

Prudence just stared at him. This was not the time or the place for that argument. She was spared having to respond by the announcement that the Chicago train was arriving.

They turned toward the track as the train rumbled into the station. For several moments, there was the noise and rush of arriving passengers disembarking, struggling with bags and boxes and suitcases, and of porters removing baggage destined for Cleveland from the baggage car and trundling it to the baggage claim area. As soon as they had finished, others began loading luggage headed for Chicago and points west into the baggage car in its place.

The conductors signaled to the waiting passengers that they could begin boarding. Prudence showed her ticket to the one nearest to her, and he directed them to the correct car.

She took a deep breath and forced herself to smile to hide her nerves. She leaned down and hugged her mother, "I'll be fine, Mother," she repeated. "I'll wire you when I get to Chicago, about dinnertime."

Her mother returned the hug. "Wire me from Chicago and from Kansas City and every chance you get," she said. "I won't sleep not knowing you're safe."

"I'll wire you from Chicago, but the train only stops for ten minutes in Kansas City. I won't have time, but I'll let you know the minute I get to Las Vegas, I promise."

She turned to Wally, who wrapped her in his arms. "I'll miss you, Pru."

"And I'll miss you, Wally," she replied. "When I think of it, anyway." He laughed. She wasn't sure that she was joking.

"Take care of Mother for me. See if you can talk her into inviting someone to stay with her, at least for a little while," she whispered, then turned and walked up the steps into the railcar.

She easily found her seat—the seat numbering system held no mysteries for a qualified and experienced librarian—retrieved Agatha Christie's newest, *Partners in Crime*, from her bag, then stowed it in the luggage rack overhead and sat down. She tucked her clutch purse between her thigh and the side of her seat, opened the book at the first page and tried to read, hoping to calm the butterflies that had begun to flit around inside her stomach. She stopped pretending to read when she realized that she had read the same page three times and still had no idea what it said.

She folded the book on her lap and closed her eyes.

Was she doing the right thing? As she'd said to Wally, she'd never been farther from Cleveland than Chicago to the west and Pittsburgh to the east. Mother didn't like staying away from home for more than one night, except for their annual two weeks in the summer at Geneva-On-The-Lake. They always stayed at the same inn, the one that Father had selected all those years ago. In fact, they had the same rooms and stayed for the same two weeks.

Prudence had tried to convince her mother to visit New York City just once, but she was terrified of "the noise, the crowds, the crime and all those strange people. Chicago is exciting enough for me." Prudence had not reminded her mother of the many mobs that were based in Chicago. Now Prudence was jumping feet first into a strange country with a lot of strange people. And while she was both anxious and excited at the prospect, she felt a twinge of guilt at causing her mother so much worry. She reminded herself that she was sure that her father would have approved. She would telegram and write to her mother regularly, to assure her that all was well, but she knew that she would regret it for the rest of her life if she did not take this opportunity that had fallen in her lap.

She could hear other passengers speaking in low voices to each other, punctuated by quick laughs and, occasionally, a sharp reprimand to a child. She opened her eyes and looked around the car as nonchalantly as possible. She had been grateful that the seat next to her had remained unclaimed, but now she thought she might welcome someone to talk to, or to talk to her and take her mind off of her worries. She noticed that, while there were a few men alone who looked as if they might be traveling to Chicago on business, most of the passengers were in small groups of two or more. She guessed that the groups of young women her age were on their way to shop at the Chicago department stores, perhaps attend a show, stop at a speakeasy, and spend a night or two at a hotel on a "girls' getaway." She smiled as she remembered several such excursions when she was in college, excursions she had been careful not to mention to her mother. These days, most of her girlfriends were married with children and far too busy for such events, even if they could have afforded it.

Others were obviously family groups, with a father, mother, and one or two school age children, with just the occasional toddler or infant. She allowed her imagination free rein, picturing them visiting grandparents on farms in the Midwest or going even further, to the mountains and beaches of California. She wondered whether any of them might be stopping in New Mexico or Arizona. They wouldn't be going on a Detour, as those were restricted to adults, but they might be visiting the Grand Canyon or the Indian pueblos on their own.

Finally, there were the middle-aged couples without children. Many of them were in groups of four, friends traveling together. Their clothing, accessories, and grooming proclaimed them solidly middle-class, with plenty of disposable income. Prudence was sure that some of them were on their way to one of the longer Detours, certainly the three-day Las Vegas to Albuquerque tour that she was taking next week and possibly even the eight-day Circle Cruise. Looking at them, Prudence again felt a surge of doubt. Did she really want to spend eight days in the company of such people? The women looked censorious and difficult and the men... she'd already caught one of them giving her the glad eye. Still, she dealt with people like them regularly at the library, and that did not offer the compensation of that wild, beautiful western landscape and the fascinating and exotic natives who lived in it.

Before she was aware of it, they had arrived at Union Station in Chicago. The groups of young women were first off the train, laughing and running toward the exits. Then came the middle-aged couples, many of the women looking as disapproving as Prudence had expected them to. She waited until the family groups had gathered up their belongings and their children and left the train before disembarking herself, tucking her book back inside her overnight case.

She looked around her and realized that she had no idea where the Harvey House was. She and her friends had always headed for the exits and the speakeasies and her mother always wanted to go straight to the hotel to "freshen up." She was about to ask for directions when she noted the signs pointing towards, among other things, the Harvey House restaurant. She smiled, picked up her bag, and strode off in the direction indicated. She had identified the location before she could even read the sign over the door by the steady stream of customers entering and leaving the establishment.

As she waited to be seated, she marveled at the speed and efficiency of the renowned Harvey Girls. In their ankle length black dresses, with the high neck and long sleeves, and their starched white bib aprons and big white bows at the back of their heads, they looked like they had stepped out of one of the photos in her mother's album from when she was young. As soon as the diners left a table, it was cleared of glasses, dishes and cutlery, the white starched tablecloth was whipped off and replaced with a clean one, and new table settings laid. Even more surprising was the quality of the food. She ordered the specialty of the house, Pork Chops Bavarian, and it was easily the equal of anything she'd had in any fine dining restaurant in Cleveland. The meat was so tender, it literally fell off the bone, and she could not get enough of the hot sauerkraut, flavored with onion, garlic, bay leaf, and fresh tomatoes. The accompanying potatoes had been cooked with the meat and sauerkraut and had soaked up the juices and the flavors. She wondered if this meal would be matched in the more far-flung Harvey Houses. She refused coffee, as she was already concerned about getting a good night's sleep.

She asked the waitress for directions to the Western Union office and sent a wire to her mother assuring her that her trip had been safe and uneventful. She passed a Harvey House lunchroom on the way to the Western Union and marked it down as a place to eat the next day. She followed the signs to the taxi stand, where she was amused to see cabbies buying sandwiches at a convenient Harvey sandwich shop. She headed to the cab that was at the front of the line, and one of the men rushed up, sandwich in hand, to open the door for her. He put her suitcase in the trunk of the cab and getting in the front, turned toward her, "Where to?" He took a bite of his sandwich and set it on the seat next to him.

"The Palmer House, please."

He looked impressed but not surprised. After he finished chewing and had swallowed, he said, "Nice hotel. You stayed there before?" He started the engine.

She nodded. "Yes, it's our usual hotel when visiting Chicago." He put the car in gear and waited for a break in the traffic.

"Where ya' from?" He merged into the line of cars and headed toward the river and the Palmer House.

"Cleveland."

He nodded. "Nice town. Stayin' long?"

"Just overnight. I'll be catching the California Limited tomorrow. I'm on my way to Santa Fe, New Mexico."

He nodded but didn't respond as he was negotiating the turn onto the bridge over the river. "Been there before?" He picked up the thread of the conversation.

"No, it will be my first trip. I've done a lot of reading about it and I'm signed up for a Fred Harvey Southwestern Indian Detour."

He nodded. "Get a fair number of passengers who tell me they are goin' on one of those. Can't see the appeal, myself. What's New Mexico got that Chicago ain't? And, Chicago's got plenty that New Mexico ain't got. From what I hear, it's mostly empty desert. Nah, I'll take the Windy City." He looked at her in the rear-view mirror. "No offense, miss."

She laughed. "None taken. I can certainly appreciate the appeal of Chicago. I'm just looking for... a change of scenery, I guess."

The cab stopped in front of the Palmer House. "Thirty-five cents." She handed him two quarters. "Thanks, lady." He got out, went around and opened the door for her, then removed her suitcase from the trunk and set it on the sidewalk next to her. "Enjoy your trip."

She picked up her suitcase and headed into the Palmer House. It seemed silly to waste a bellboy's time for just one small overnight case. As always, she stopped to admire the magnificent lobby, with its garnet-draped chandeliers, Tiffany lamps and, above all, the Rigal ceiling fresco. The cabbie's words rang in her ears, "What's New Mexico got that Chicago ain't?" She was willing to bet that New Mexico had nothing like the lobby of the Palmer House, but... it would have its own attractions and its own charms, ones she had yet to experience.

The clerk at the registration desk was efficient, pleasant, and entirely impersonal. Prudence took the elevator to her room, again carrying her bag herself. She looked around the luxurious room, with its plush carpets and drapes, Tiffany lamps, and French impressionist paintings. The chandelier hanging from the ceiling was a smaller version of those in the lobby, and the bathroom was as luxurious as the bedroom. It included a deep tub that almost demanded that she take a long, hot soak.

She turned on the taps and sprinkled in a good amount of the bath salts provided by the hotel. She left it to run while she unpacked her pajamas and other items she'd need for the night. By the time she had cleaned her teeth and washed her face, the tub was full. The water was deliciously hot and nearly to her chin when she slid down into the tub. It was deeper than the tub in her bathroom at home and one of the things she always liked about staying at the Palmer House. She felt the stress of the day melting away in the fragrant hot water and hoped that she would sleep well that night.

She was relieved that her trip had been uneventful so far, and while she sincerely hoped that the remainder would be more interesting, she worried that there might be delays, that her luggage would be lost, and that other passengers would be difficult or annoying. Despite what she had told her mother and Wally, she worried that the Harvey Company would reject her application. If they did accept it, she worried that she would fail the test at the end of the training period. And as excited as she was at the prospect of seeing the vast expanses of the American West and the native peoples, she admitted to herself that she was already feeling rather lonely. She realized with something of a shock that this was the first time in her life that she had stayed alone in a hotel. She began to feel more sympathy for her mother, who hadn't spent a night alone in the house in more than twenty-five years. She would renew her suggestion that her mother invite a friend or relative for an extended visit. The thought salved her conscience.

When the water had cooled, she stepped out and dried

off on one of the thick Turkish towels and stepped into the silk pajamas she had laid out on the bed, turned off the lights, and slid into the bed. However, even the hot bath did not really help. She dozed fitfully, disturbed by dreams of missed trains and lost luggage and loud, obnoxious men who kept pinching her and trying to kiss her. Finally, at five o'clock, she gave up any pretense of even trying to sleep. She got up, washed and dressed, carefully applied her makeup, repacked the few items she had removed from her overnight bag, and headed down to the hotel dining room for breakfast. She lingered over coffee afterward. Her train didn't leave until later tonight, so she was in no rush to get back to Union Station.

Breakfast finished, she checked out of the hotel. This morning's desk clerk was as efficient and impersonal as the one of the night before, which suited her mood.

She got a cab back to Union Station from the taxi stand in front of the hotel, but whether it was his personality or the early hour, this cab driver was not at all talkative, merely asking her designation and then telling her the fare when they arrived at the station. She was relieved not to have to make conversation.

The cab dropped her off at the front entrance of Union Station. She left her bag at the baggage check and walked across the river to the Art Institute to spend the day immersed in its many collections, savoring the experience. This would be her last opportunity for some time to appreciate these masterpieces of Western culture. She stood for several moments gazing up at the Beaux-Arts building, fixing it in her memory and took a turn through the gardens surrounding it.

When the museum closed that evening, she walked back to Union Station, and, once she had got her bearings, she headed for the Harvey lunchroom she had noted the night before. Despite being called a "lunchroom," the restaurant served food all day. The only difference between it and the restaurant that she could see was that it was smaller and lacked table service. She selected one of the few available seats at the long counter that curved around the room. The counter was constantly filled with customers. As soon as a diner finished and left, the seat was taken by another. Prudence assumed that, like her, they were passengers on trains leaving later. When she was asked for her order, she couldn't help but request the Harvey Girl Special Little Thin Orange Pancakes and coffee. She wanted a light meal before she got on the train and they sounded delicious. The Girl who took her order did not seem at all surprised that someone had ordered breakfast at this hour. She simply nodded and headed back to the kitchen to place the order and another Harvey Girl hurried up with a pot of coffee and filled her cup.

As she waited for her pancakes, Prudence amused herself with observing the Harvey coffee cup code in action. It was one of the ways that the restaurants in stations along the line were able to serve passengers quickly enough for them to finish their meal before it was time to reboard their train. From what she had read, a coffee cup right side up in the saucer, as hers had been, meant hot coffee. Most cups were in this position. There were a few which were turned upside down in the saucer, which meant an order for hot tea. Upside down and tilted against the saucer, iced tea, although she did not see any cups in that configuration this late in the afternoon. Finally, upside down and off of the saucer entirely signified a glass of milk.

The pancakes when they came were thin and warm and filled with zesty grated orange peel, bits of fresh orange pulp, and the flavor of freshly squeezed juice. If every meal were the equal of this, she'd have to start a slimming regimen. The famous Fred Harvey coffee proved to be deserving of its reputation as the best coffee to be had.

Supper over, she still had several hours before her train left so she wandered through the station, marveling at the Beaux Arts Great Hall and regretting the number of times she had been in the station, but never taken the time to appreciate it. She gazed at the clothing and other items for sale in the windows of the many shops and perused the reading material in the bookstore, noting several new mysteries by new authors, and counted at least five more Fred Harvey eateries, not including the soda fountain in the drug store. She smiled to herself when she remembered using the phrase "the Harvey House restaurant" just the day before. Neither she nor her mother had had any concept of the number of Harvey eating establishments there were in Union Station. The name was everywhere! The Harvey Company seemed to have a near-monopoly on food service for the Santa Fe Railway.

As large and impressive and interesting as the station was, she still had at least an hour to wait after she had thoroughly explored it. She found her platform, then went into the nearest Harvey lunchroom and ordered coffee and a cheese Danish. After all the walking she had done this morning, she felt justified in treating herself. As she tried to kill the remaining time, her worries of the night before revived. Was she doing the right thing? Would she be able to convince them to give her a chance? Would she adapt to life in the "Wild West?" Would her mother manage on her own? Should she turn in her ticket for a return to Cleveland? It wasn't too late... Her thoughts were interrupted by the announcement that the California Limited was ready for boarding. She had to make a decision. It was now or never, whatever decision she made.

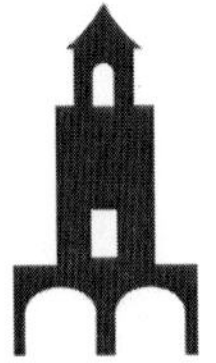

Chapter 3

Wednesday - Thursday,

May 29-30, 1929

California Limited Day One

SETTLING INTO HER SEAT next to the window, Prudence wondered who her traveling companion would be for the journey. She hoped it would be another woman. How awkward if it were a man! Unless, of course, he were the right kind of man. She smiled to herself as she envisioned a handsome and charming cowboy sitting across from her, regaling her with tales of rodeos and ranching in the Wild West.

Looking around, she saw that, as before, most passengers were traveling in couples or families. Maybe her mother had been right. Maybe she should have allowed Wally to accompany her as far as Kansas City. He'd been willing to take that much time off of work, but... no. He'd had his chance to join her in an adventure and now he was everything she wanted to get away from. He would only have spent the trip trying to convince her that she was making a mistake and trying to make her feel guilty about leaving her mother to "fend for herself."

The seat opposite her was still vacant when the train started to move. When the porter, a tall young Black man in the recognizable Pullman uniform, came to make up the beds, she asked him whether anyone had booked that seat.

"No, ma'am," he replied. "Not until Kansas City."

She thanked him, retrieved her overnight bag and headed to the end of the car to wash her face and brush her teeth and change into her pajamas and robe. That mission accomplished, she returned to find her berth ready for her. She slipped between the curtains that screened her berth and settled herself for sleep. Despite being exhausted, or perhaps because of it, she was kept awake by the sounds of other passengers heading to and from the bathrooms, chatting as they changed their clothes and settled in for the night, and by the subtle sounds of people breathing around her. Even though everyone was sleeping in a separate berth, nearly all of the other passengers were occupying a bunk that was above or below one where a family member also slumbered. Some were completely surrounded by loved ones. She, on the other hand, was alone among strangers. She mentally shook herself. She had wanted adventure, and she was on her way to getting what she wanted. This was no time for self-pity! Eventually, everyone quieted, and the coach lights were dimmed. She allowed the motion of the train and the regular, rhythmic sounds of the wheels to lull her off to sleep.

* * *

PRUDENCE HAD just returned to her seat from breakfast and opened *Partners in Crime* when the train pulled into Kansas City Union Station. There was a flurry of activity, as departing passengers gathered their belongings and hurried off, to be replaced by new passengers joining the train. Prudence continued to read, but out of the corner of her eye, she saw a pair of tooled leather cowboy boots, topped with blue jeans, stop in the aisle. She repressed a little shiver of excitement. A real cowboy! Although she kept her eyes on her book, she couldn't help but take quick side long glances as the man slid into the seat across from her. Cowboy boots, blue jeans, and a sheepskin jacket. Maybe her Western adventure was starting now.

He settled back and let out a sigh. As Prudence looked up, he said, in a rather high voice, "Mary Howard, pleased to meet you," and reached out a hand. Prudence shook her hand as she responded, "Prudence Bates." She felt a brief moment of disappointment. She had so hoped "he" would be that tall, dark, handsome stranger of her imagination.

Mary Howard was wearing men's blue jeans, but there

was no doubt she was a woman. The buttons of her satin blouse were mother-of-pearl, the yoke was embellished with rhinestones and dripping with silky fringe, and the edges of the cuffs peeking out from the sleeves of her jacket were bordered with rhinestones. Her lips were a dark red and nature had certainly been given some assistance with her cheeks and eyes. In fact, her makeup rivaled Prudence's own. At the same time, her short, curly hair was topped by what Prudence could only think was a cowboy hat. She was confused by a woman who traveled on the train in men's pants, but was so well-groomed otherwise. She knew that western wear was a new fashion for men and women, but the magazines she read showed women in split skirts and cute little hats with wide, flat brims and a chin strap, wearing fringed leather vests or jackets—and none of them wore a belt with such a huge, shiny buckle. She had to struggle not to stare at it.

"So, are you going far?" Mary asked. Prudence suppressed a smile at what seemed to be the standard method of initiating a conversation on the Santa Fe Railroad.

"Las Vegas."

Mary nodded. "I'm going as far as La Junta myself, then changing for Denver." Prudence noticed that she gave the station an American, rather than Spanish, pronunciation. "My… partner… and I have a ranch up there. It's a working ranch, but we're looking at taking in some dudes—or dudesses, I guess you'd say—in the summer, to help to make ends meet. I inherited it from my father, and he did pretty well by it, but it just doesn't make the kind of money it used to, so… I've been meeting with some people in Kansas City about maybe backing the dude ranch." She laughed and indicated her clothing. "That's the reason I wore my barrel racing clothes, so I'd look 'authentic' to them." She lifted the belt buckle, "Won this two years ago at the Cowboys' Reunion Rodeo in Las Vegas." She laughed again, "But, I don't usually wear satin and rhinestones when I'm working with the cattle."

Prudence laughed with her, while wondering whether Mary would have worn more traditional women's clothing if she hadn't been meeting with "some people in Kansas City," or would she still have been in men's jeans, boots, and hat, with a more sober man's shirt.

Mary leaned forward and jerked her chin toward the book in Prudence's hand. "Mind if I ask what you're reading?"

Prudence turned the cover toward her. "It's Agatha Christie's newest." She smiled a little self-consciously. "I'm afraid that I'm a bit of a mystery story fanatic."

Mary nodded. "I thought it might be Greek poetry. My friend and I like to read poetry in the original Greek." She observed Prudence closely.

Prudence shook her head, confused. Why would Mary think that? "No, Greek is not a language that I speak or read." As she said it, she suddenly remembered a similar conversation in college and what it had meant. "But, I had a very good friend in college who was a devotee of Greek poetry. She invited me to a few readings at a club in Cleveland, but... I'm afraid it really has no appeal for me."

Mary nodded, settled back and crossed her legs. "It's not for everyone. So, what takes you to Las Vegas?"

Prudence explained about the Indian Detours.

"Hmm!" Mary looked interested. "So, they meet these dudes at the train station and ferry them around to the sights?"

Prudence nodded. "Some of the trips are just a few hours; some are several days; a few are more than a week."

"Uh-huh." She pursed her lips in thought. "I guess they provide food?"

"Yes. Usually, a picnic lunch and dinner at a Harvey House. The longer trips include breakfast and hotel accommodations, as well."

"Hmmm. Not too many hotels up where we are, but... might think about setting up some army tents, maybe cots... cook over an open fire... give them a real taste of the Wild West." She grinned. "Take 'em out in buckboards, if they can't ride. So many women can't." She leaned forward, "Do you think this is something your friend and her friends might be interested in?"

"I don't know, it's not something we ever discussed but... I think if the company were... congenial, they would be, yes. They all seemed rather... unconventional and willing to try new things."

Mary nodded. "Somethin' to think about." She opened the leather portfolio she had laid on the seat next to her when she sat down. "Well, I'll let you get back to your book." She held up a sheaf of papers, "And I'll go over these stock reports."

Prudence was deep in the adventures of Tommy and Tuppence when she heard the call for the first lunch seating. She inserted the bookmark and looked across at her seatmate.

Mary shook her head. "I'm down for the second seating." Prudence nodded, tucked the book into her handbag and her handbag under her arm, and headed for the dining car. The dining car attendant, a dignified Black man with greying temples, escorted her to a table for two and left her with a menu. Prudence smiled as she began perusing yet another Fred Harvey menu.

A slim young woman with chin-length wavy bright red hair and a sprinkling of freckles across her nose slid into the chair across from her. "Hi," she said, cheerfully. "I'm Sally Johnson."

"Prudence Bates." It was too much to hope that the attendant would have sat a tall, dark, handsome stranger across from her. Prudence noted that Sally was wearing a rather loud floral print dress that was obviously homemade and clashed with her hair.

"Are you going' far?"

"Las Vegas, in New Mexico."

Sally grinned. "I'm headed for Santa Fe, myself. Will you be stayin' there long?"

From someone less friendly and outgoing, the questions would seem intrusive, but Sally seemed genuinely interested. "Just a week. Then I'll be going to Santa Fe, as well." Prudence answered her next question before she could ask it, "I'm going to train as an Indian Detours Courier. Are you familiar with the Indian Detours?"

Sally laughed. "I should say so! I'm a Harvey Girl at La Fonda."

"No! What a coincidence!"

"Not really," Sally smiled. "We Harvey Girls get a free ticket on the Santa Fe every six months. Some of the girls go out to California or head for home, but a lot of us go to

Chicago every chance we get. I just love the picture palaces and speakeasies! And the YWCA's a nice, cheap place to stay. Two girls, by themselves, on this train—one of 'em's bound to be a Harvey Girl."

"Do you like being a Harvey Girl?"

"Oh, I like it fine. Mr. Harvey's a real stickler, but pay is good, food is really good, we get to meet all kinds of people. Of course, at the end of the day, all I want to do is kick off my shoes and get off my feet! Run, run, run." She laughed again. "I'm only doin' this until I meet Mr. Right, of course. And a Harvey House restaurant is the perfect place for that. And they make the Mr. Wrongs behave themselves. No pinching in a Harvey House." She laughed.

Prudence chuckled along with her. "Have you ever thought of being a Courier?"

"Nah," Sally shook her head. "Don't have a college degree, do I? And all that studying' you have to do to be a Courier! Not for me. I'd much rather spend my free time at the moving pictures or dancing at the speakeasy..." Prudence was relieved that Sally did not seem to take offense at her assumption that she was college-educated.

"Have you ladies decided on what you would like for lunch?" The waiter asked, deferentially.

"Oh, my goodness," Sally grinned up at him. "I've been talkin' this lady's ear off and she didn't even have a chance to look at the menu. I'll have the daily special."

"Yes, Miss Sally," the waiter jotted something on his pad. "And coffee?"

"Oh, yes, of course, coffee!" Sally leaned forward, "I always get the special. It's bound to be good and it makes me feel just a bit darin', orderin' somethin' without knowin' what I'll get."

"I'll have the same," Prudence handed the menu to the waiter, "I'm also feeling adventurous."

A man at another table shouted, "George!" and snapped his fingers. Their waiter turned and walked slowly in that direction.

"Yes, sir?" he asked.

"Empty this ashtray, would you?" Despite the phrasing, it was a command, not a request.

Sally scowled and shook her head. "That makes me so

mad when they do that!"

"Do what?" Prudence thought that emptying ash trays was one of his responsibilities.

"Snap their fingers and call him 'George.' His name is not George. It's Luther."

"Then why...?"

"Rude people call all of the porters 'George,' after George Pullman," she explained, "As if they are all interchangeable parts of the train. They're the same ones who call all Indian men 'chief' and all Indian women 'squaws.' You'll see what I mean when you start workin' the Detours."

Prudence could hardly contain her excitement at meeting someone with a personal connection to the Fred Harvey Company. As they waited for the meal, she quizzed Sally about the La Fonda and the Castañeda, about the Indian Detours training, about the people who were merely names to her. Sally was a fount of inside information and harmless gossip about the hotels and their staff, the groups of Couriers-in-training, and the Detours that left from La Fonda, even though she knew very little about the actual Couriers training itself. Prudence found herself wishing that Sally were her Pullman car seatmate, but they were in entirely different cars and, when she thought about it, she doubted that they really had very much more to talk about.

The special, when it arrived, proved to be beef rissoles served with potatoes and beef gravy and green beans. Although it was a dish that might be found on many a home table, the addition of fresh herbs, nutmeg and grated lemon rind elevated the breaded and fried meatballs above the ordinary. The thick, rich beef gravy, as well, would put any housewife's efforts to shame, except maybe her mother's. Prudence felt a twinge of homesickness at the thought.

"Well, that's it for me." Sally yawned and dropped her napkin on her empty plate. "Had a late night. I'm headin' back for a bit of a snooze. Maybe we'll see each other at dinner."

"I hope so," Prudence responded. "We'll certainly be seeing each other in Santa Fe." She finished her coffee, left an extra-large tip as an apology for the other passengers' boorish behavior, then returned to her seat. Mary Howard's seat was empty, and eager to discover what her namesake,

Prudence Beresford, was up to in the next story, she sat back and opened her book. She wondered if she should introduce herself as "Tuppence" in the future, but decided that most Americans simply would not understand it.

She had only been reading a short while when Mary Howard returned from the dining car. She picked up her portfolio and said, "Reckon I'll head on up to the club car, take a look at today's newspapers." Prudence smiled and nodded and returned to her book.

She had made good headway in her reading when the first dinner service was called. Her companion at that meal was a pleasant, grandmotherly woman who regaled her with tales of the grandchildren she was going to visit in California. Prudence smiled and nodded at the stories and the photographs that she showed her, and agreed that her grandchildren were quite darling. Her years working with the public in the library were serving her well.

It was a relief to return to her quiet seat and open her book again. At this rate, she'd have finished it well before bedtime, but she'd planned for that eventuality and picked up *The Roman Hat Mystery* by a new author, Ellery Queen, in the Union Station bookstore. And *The Grey Mask* by another new author, Patricia Wentworth. That was in addition to the Margery Allingham and Dorothy L. Sayers that her colleagues had given her as goodbye gifts. They knew of her fondness for amateur detectives of all kinds, but especially the aristocratic ones.

"Excuse me, miss," the porter interrupted her just as she'd begun reading. "I hate to disturb you, but it's time to make up the beds."

"Not at all," she said. She realized why so many passengers had chosen the final dinner seating. Their beds would be ready for them when they returned, while she had to move to a vacant seat farther down the corridor. On second thought, she realized that she would have the ladies' restroom all to herself. She retrieved her overnight bag and headed to the end of the car. When she returned, wrapped in her dressing gown, Mary was standing near their berth, a small leather bag in her hand.

"Guess it's my turn to clean up. I'm leaving in just a few hours, so I won't be changing," Mary explained, "Just catch a few winks before we get to La Junta. I'll say goodnight now. You look like you're ready to drop."

"It was a pleasure to meet you," Prudence responded. "Yes, it's been a long day." She slipped between the sheets in her berth as Mary walked away. She was too tired to sit up and read, as she usually did, and, besides, she'd done more than enough reading for one day. She was aware of Mary climbing the ladder on her return, and the small sounds she made as she readied herself for a few hours of sleep.

Once again, she was kept awake by the sounds made by the other passengers. She found herself thinking of Sally Johnson and smiled at the memory of her companion at the lunch table. No doubt she was tucked away in her berth, dreaming happily of Mr. Right. And her dinner companion was likely eagerly looking forward to reuniting with her daughter and son-in-law and meeting her grandchildren. As with the night before, it was soon quiet and the porter dimmed the lights. The motion of the train and the regular, rhythmic sounds of the wheels once again lulled her off to sleep. She was vaguely aware of Mary descending the ladder in stocking feet, by the sound of it, several hours later, but quickly returned to sleep, worn out by two days of travel.

Chapter 4

Friday

May 31, 1929

California Limited Day Two

IT WAS DARK WHEN Prudence awoke, her body still on Ohio time. She decided to take advantage of the availability of the restroom while everyone else was still sleeping. The first light of dawn was emerging over the horizon when she returned, washed and dressed, with her hair and makeup fixed as best she could in the small mirror of the tiny bathroom. She nodded a quiet "Good morning" to the porter, then made her way to the observation car. It was too early for breakfast, but more than that, she wanted her first views of her new home.

The train had climbed the eastern side of the Sangre de Cristo Mountains while she slept and made the descent into New Mexico through the Raton Pass. Prudence walked to the front of the observation car and stood watching in awe as the landscape was revealed to her. The light of the sun rising over the mountains from the east struck the western mountains in front of her. Everything on the left side of the train was in the shadow of the mountains over which the sun was climbing. The shadows stretched across the plain in front of them and slowly crawled backwards as the sun rose. Everything on the right side was bright with the golden light, the evergreens turning a luminous golden-green and the boulders glinting. She wished she had spent time learning the names of the different trees and shrubs and other plants that grew here. All she knew was that everything was so different from home here in the high desert of the Colorado Plateau.

She imagined what it must have been like earlier when the engine entered the tunnel at the crest of the Pass, and then, in one breathtaking moment, emerged and started down trees and rocks rushing past. She was overwhelmed by the vista spread before her. It was so vast, she felt her own insignificance even more than she did when she looked at the stars in the night sky. A flat plain stretched ahead, ringed with mountain ranges that marched off into the distance, the light glinting off of the blindingly white snow that even now clung to the highest peaks. The color of the mountains changed from blue to purple as the rays slowly climbed down their flanks. In the east the mountains were black silhouettes against the brilliance of the rising sun, which was painting the few high, thin clouds gold and apricot and orange. She could just catch the silvery glint of water in a river far below, flowing between scattered groves of trees and clumps of shrubs in every shade of green from shining leaf green to muted sage. The land was sere and brown, interspersed with the green of a planted field or a pasture. Some small town was visible in the distance, an unnatural cluster of buildings that looked like blocks a child had set down in the middle of a floor.

The mountains seemed to be holding up the sky, and as the train continued its journey and the sun continued to rise, the illusion only became stronger and the sensation of entering into a secret country grew. Prudence marveled that a land and sky so vast and endless could, at the same time, feel so enclosed and protected.

"It never ceases to amaze me," a deep voice said behind her. "No matter how many times I travel this route."

Prudence turned and looked up at the speaker. He was taller than she, with short dark hair, what she could see of it underneath his cowboy hat, anyway, dark, slightly narrow eyes, skin several shades darker than hers, and a somewhat round face. He was wearing a plaid shirt, blue jeans, and cowboy boots and carrying a small duffel bag. She couldn't help but notice how fit and trim he was and how well his blue jeans fit him. At first, she thought he was Oriental, but then he smiled and introduced himself, "Jerry Begay."

He set the duffel at his feet and moved forward to stand beside her at the window. "I usually have the view to myself at this hour. Not many people are willing to get up quite so early just to watch the sun rise on the Sangre de Cristo mountains."

She recognized the Navajo surname and felt a definite frisson of excitement. Not only a tall, dark, handsome cowboy, but an Indian as well. And such a wonderfully masculine voice. She couldn't have asked for more, although she was a little disappointed that his hair was not tied in a traditional bun.

"Prudence Bates." She turned back to the vista. "I've read about it and even seen paintings and photographs, but... none of them do it justice. I had no idea of the scope. They really didn't prepare me."

"Is this your first visit to New Mexico?"

She nodded.

"I thought it might be." She looked at him quizzically. "Your clothes and your shoes. We don't see many women in such high fashion and such flimsy shoes out here. You'll break an ankle in those high heels." He grinned.

She grinned back. "Yes, well... sounds like a good excuse to do some shopping, once we get to Las Vegas. And, of course, I'll have my Courier uniform once I finish my training for the Indian Detours."

His brow wrinkled and he stared out of the window, then changed the subject. "Breakfast?" he asked, turning and sweeping his arm toward the stairs, "The dining car should be open now." He picked up the duffel and moved to the head of the stairs.

Prudence nodded and followed him down to the still empty dining car. Once they were seated, Jerry put his duffel and hat on the seat next to him. After they placed their order for coffee and Santa Fe French Toast with bacon for Prudence and sausages for Jerry, he leaned back and said, "So, tell me about yourself, Prudence Bates."

"Well, I'm twenty-five years old. I'm from Cleveland, Ohio. I have a bachelor's degree in anthropology and a master's degree in library science," he raised his eyebrows, "and for the past three years, I've been a librarian at the Cleveland Public Library." She paused, expectantly. Jerry looked at her quizzically. "Go ahead," she said. "Say it."

"Say what?"

"What they always say. 'I didn't know you had to go to school to be a librarian' or 'You can get a degree in that?'"

"Well, I didn't know. I can't say that I've ever given it much thought, but... I don't see why people would find it hard to believe. I wouldn't have the faintest idea of where to start if I were suddenly put in charge of a library. No, actually, my question is, why library science?"

She smiled broadly. "I'm sorry to sound so... prickly. Why library science? I hope I don't sound pretentious, but, I want to make a difference in the world, to make it a better place. And I truly believe that knowledge is power. And I do love being a librarian. It's satisfying helping people to find the answers to their questions. I especially enjoy recommending books to patrons and discussing the books with them, but... something's been missing. It's become so... ordinary... routine... predictable. The questions are all starting to sound the same! So, here I am on my way to Santa Fe to work as a Courier for the Indian Detours. Different job, different country, different people. I'm not quite sure what to expect, and that's exactly what I'm looking for—the unexpected. Although," she paused in surprise, "I suppose I'll be doing much the same thing, providing people with knowledge and answering their questions, but in a very different setting."

The waiter, a Black man like all of the dining car staff, set their coffee in front of them and placed a pitcher of cream on the table. Jerry picked up his cup, took a swallow of black coffee, and asked, "Family?"

"Just my mother and some cousins on my father's side somewhere. My father died about ten years ago. He'd been sick for a while..." She trailed off. She busied herself with adding cream and sugar to her coffee.

Jerry wrinkled his brow. "I know it's none of my business, and forgive me if it seems presumptuous, but, if it's just you and your mother... who's there with her?"

"You sound just like Wally," Prudence muttered. She'd come more than a thousand miles only to meet with the same criticism.

"I'm sorry? I didn't catch that."

"Oh, nothing." She sighed and looked down into her cup, then up at Jerry. "I went to college in Cleveland so that she wouldn't be alone, and I didn't go on any anthropological field trips so that she wouldn't be alone. I went to graduate school in Cleveland and got a job at the Cleveland Public Library, so that she wouldn't be alone. Time is passing and I just..."

"Just want to live your own life." She nodded. "That's understandable."

Prudence stared at him. "Thank you," she said softly. "And, really, she isn't alone. She has her ladies' club and her church group. She's lived in the same house since before I was born, so she knows all of the neighbors; they are in and out of each other's houses all day. And I won't be gone all that long. Just a year or two. I've suggested that she invite a friend or relative to stay with her while I'm gone. I do hope she does."

Jerry nodded. She changed the subject. "So, what about you? Tell me about yourself."

"I'm thirty years old, from someplace you've never heard of on the Navajo reservation. I have a bachelor's in history and a master's in education." He paused as Prudence stared at him in surprise. "Some of us do, you know. Not many, but a few." He took another sip of coffee.

She blushed in embarrassment. He set his cup down. "And now it's your turn to say it." She looked at him in puzzlement. "That you didn't know that a master's degree was necessary to be a teacher."

She nodded in comprehension. "I know that it isn't. A degree from a normal school or teacher's college is all that is required in most states. So, why a master's degree?"

He chuckled. "I should have known that a librarian would know that. The answer is simple, really. I hadn't decided to be a teacher until I was nearly finished with my undergraduate degree. No point in getting two bachelor's degrees. And it will be useful if I want to move into administration."

"And now my question is, why education?"

He smiled and leaned back. "Ah, well, that's a bit of a long story. I was sent to an Indian boarding school as a child where I learned to speak, write, and think in English. They cut my hair, gave me an English name, and forbade me to speak Navajo. My relatives say that I speak it like a five-year old. My accent is good, but my grammar is rather simplistic and my vocabulary... seriously lacking." He smiled wryly. "I'd go home during the summer, but I'd just be starting to re-adapt when it would be time to return to school." He toyed with his cup.

"I wondered why you speak such good English," Prudence said. He raised his eyebrows. "I mean... well... um..." she stammered and trailed off. First Sally, now Jerry. Had she said anything to offend Mary Howard? "It must have been hard for your parents, too."

Jerry nodded. "In any case, they don't do that anymore, not to little kids. Anyway, once I reached high school, I started looking for excuses not to go home, usually a summer job on a farm. The transitions were just too difficult and.... well...." He shrugged. "Then, after I graduated, I was one of the lucky ones. A teacher I was close to recommended me for a scholarship to the University of Oklahoma." He shrugged. "They say college helps you to find yourself. It helped me to realize that what I really wanted to do with my life was make a difference to my people. Eventually, I decided that the best way to do that was to become a teacher on the reservation." He looked at her. "Like you, I truly believe that knowledge is power. This will be my second year." He smiled. "My pupils try to teach me to speak Navajo like an adult and I try to teach them what the white man wants them to know."

Prudence picked up her cup, took a swallow, and asked, "Family?"

Jerry grinned. "Extended. Very extended. Father, mother, a younger sister and two younger brothers, all single for the moment, aunts, uncles, cousins, grandparents... As I'm sure you know, if you studied anthropology, the Navajo kinship system is rather complicated, so let's just call it extended. And, before you ask, yes, I have a Navajo name, but it's a secret name only known to the family and only used for specific purposes."

"I wasn't going to ask..." Prudence began, but paused as the waiter placed their breakfast order in front of them. The aroma and sight of the food reminded Prudence that she had not eaten in more than twelve hours and was hungry! Jerry apparently felt the same, as they both tucked into their meals with an appetite. Only after their initial hunger was sated did they pause in their eating.

"I've been wondering about something," Prudence said, "According to the schedule, the train stopped at the town of Raton early this morning." Jerry nodded. "Raton means mouse in Spanish. I wonder why they named the town that?"

"After the Raton Pass," Jerry responded slyly.

"And why is it called Raton Pass?" She rolled her eyes.

"After the Raton Range." They both laughed.

"No idea, really. That's just what it's always been called" he finished.

Prudence looked around at the sparsely seated tables. "I know it's early," Jerry looked at his watch and grinned. "All right, it's about six o'clock in the morning, but I'd expected to see more people eating breakfast. After all, it's been nearly twelve hours since dinner."

"The ones leaving the train at Las Vegas are waiting to eat at the Harvey House there," Jerry explained, "So, there's no reason for us to rush through our meal. They won't need the tables any time soon." He leaned back, coffee cup in hand, "Tell me about your home." He took a sip of coffee and waited expectantly.

"Cleveland? Have you been to Cleveland?

"No, I haven't been anywhere east of Kansas City, yet."

"Well… I think the first thing you'd notice is that it's green."

Jerry laughed. 'Yes, I imagine I would find Cleveland green, but, what I really meant was your house. Where you live."

"Oh. Well, it's what most people would consider a 'modest' house. It's built of yellow brick, two stories tall with an attic. There's a covered porch with a white railing that matches the white picket fence in the front." Jerry nodded and kept his eyes fixed on her face as she talked.

"Let's see—there's a brick walk from the gate to the porch, with a flower bed on either side." She smiled a bit nostalgically. "I just planted the summer annuals before I left. I used to help my father with it and it's been one of my responsibilities since he died." She stopped and took a sip of coffee, then cleared her throat. "We have perennials planted all along the fence. On the left of the walk, in the middle of the lawn, is a birdbath in a circle of rosebushes. On the right is a red maple tree." She stared off into space for a moment. "It must be all of fifty years old now. I know it's older than I am. One of my earliest memories is my father pushing me in a swing hanging from a branch. I haven't thought of that in years." She coughed again. Jerry reached across the table and squeezed her hand. She smiled at him.

"And now," she continued, "we walk up the four steps to the porch."

"Which has a swing," Jerry finished her sentence. She laughed. "How did you know?"

He grinned. "From the movies. Houses with porches always have swings."

"Well, there is, and a rocking chair next to it."

"Of course. How could I forget?"

"And there's a wicker table and two wicker armchairs on the other side of the steps."

"Where you sit drinking cold lemonade on warm summer nights." They laughed together.

"There's also a glass storm door and a wooden door with a glass fanlight at the top. Inside, there's a rather small foyer, with the stairs to the second floor going up on the right, a hallway going back on the left, and a door on the right at the foot of the stairs. It leads to what used to what used to be Father's den, then my study when I was a student, and is now... I guess you'd call it the office." She paused again to take another sip of coffee. "There's more."

"So, let's hear it. I'm enjoying imaging you in your native habitat."

"Well, if you go down the hallway to the left of the stairs, there's a door to the living room, with the dining room beyond it. There's a small storage closet under the stairs, and, before you come to the kitchen, a little lavatory that used to be a broom closet. And then, the kitchen, with a door to the back yard. That's all for the first floor."

"What's in your back yard?"

"Oh, nothing much, really. Just the garden shed and a

lawn. The clothesline, of course. It's fenced all around. There used to be rose bushes along the fence, but... we tore them out when Father got too sick to care for them." She hadn't realized how many memories of her father were associated with the house and the yard.

"I'm sorry." He reached over and squeezed her hand again. She smiled weakly.

She sat up straight. "So, second floor?" He nodded. "Just the two bedrooms and two bathrooms. There used to be four bedrooms, but my parents remodeled it when they had the bathrooms and lavatory put in. Two big bedrooms, each with its own private bath."

He leaned back and looked at her with careful consideration. "Sounds like quite an idyllic place to grow up."

"Yes, I suppose it was. I'd never thought of it that way. It was just home. What about your home?"

"Nothing like yours! I was born in a hogan on the reservation. It's just one big room, with a smoke hole in the middle of the roof. That's our kitchen in the cold months, as well as our heat. The door, a handwoven blanket, faces east, to welcome the morning sun. No windows, just the one door. A couple of shelves on the wall to hold our belongings. Our hogan was—is made of unpeeled logs set in an octagon." He laughed. "That's a word I learned in school. My parents would never call it that."

Prudence opened her mouth to ask a question, then closed it. Jerry smiled. "Go ahead, ask any questions you like. I promise I won't be offended."

She nodded. "Well, what about... privacy?"

"It's not something that we value the way you white people do, other than what is necessary to preserve modesty. Besides, if we want to get away from everyone, all we have to do is go outside. Our nearest neighbors are miles away. We do create private spaces inside for sleeping and such by stretching blankets across the corners, but, as the family gets bigger... the entire floor may be covered with blankets at night. We have to be careful not to step over people if we have to get up in the night. Which leads to your next question. The... necessary facilities... are in a separate building outside. They are private." He grinned.

"Outside, there's a corral for the sheep, of course. We

also have a summer shelter built of poles and brush that is much cooler for sleeping, or we just roll our blankets out under the stars. Cooking is also done outside in the summer. My mother and sister have their looms set up there, as well." He sighed. "Imagine a kitchen and a dining room with the sky for a ceiling and the mountains for walls and all the space you could ask for. Imagine a yard that stretches for as far as you can see in all directions, bordered by the four Sacred Mountains."

He paused, then began again. "I don't live there now, of course." Prudence looked at him quizzically. "It's too far from the school. I live in a government-provided shoebox of a house, with four walls and a roof. I've got a bedroom, bathroom, kitchen, and living room, which is more than enough for one person. It even has electricity and running water. But, I still have that yard and that view."

Prudence had slowly become aware that some of the other diners were staring at them and whispering, and that some muttered under their breath as they passed by the table on their way through the car. Before she could respond to Jerry's last statement, a man bumped into their table, jostling the coffee cups, and continued without apologizing.

"Sorry about that," sighed Jerry.

Prudence looked at him quizzically. "You didn't do anything."

"Just sat at a table with a white woman," he said. "And I'm sure some of our fellow passengers think I shouldn't be sitting in this car at all. In some parts of the country, I wouldn't be."

She looked shocked. She was shocked. "You mean you really didn't know?"

"How would I? There aren't many Navajo in Cleveland. We reserve our prejudices for the colored folk and even then... there's no legal segregation. Social, but not legal, although... it's not illegal, either. To be honest, I've never given it much thought."

"Hmm. Well, in this area, Indians, and Mexicans and Orientals, for that matter, are part of the colored folk. Unless they are Spanish, of course." He grinned wryly.

"I don't understand."

"Are you sure you want the lecture?" She nodded. "I'll keep it short. The Spanish are descendants of the Europeans who came over from Spain in the sixteenth and seventeenth centuries, more or less. They didn't intermarry with the natives—or, at least, they don't admit it if they did. Very proud of their pure Spanish blood, some of them, especially the descendants of the old dons, the ones who had the Spanish land grants. Mexicans—well, of course, all citizens of the country of Mexico are Mexicans, but here in the Southwest, it refers to people with both Spanish and native ancestry who speak Spanish as their first language. You with me so far?"

She nodded. "Yes, but... if the Spanish didn't intermarry with the natives, how did... oh." She felt herself blushing.

"Exactly. Now, Indians—I'm speaking of the Indians in the United States—we have mostly native ancestry, but we tend not to make any distinction between those who have mixed ancestry and those who don't. We are, however, low man on the totem pole, so to speak," he grinned at his own joke, "and there are plenty of "Mexicans" in the Southwest who have no Spanish ancestry whatsoever. Being Mexican may be lower in status than being white, but it's better than being Indian. It's one way that we're losing our heritage. Their children and grandchildren grow up thinking that they are, in fact, Mexican and with no knowledge of the history or traditions of their people."

He stared into his coffee cup. "So, there you have it. The quick and dirty version, anyway." He finished his coffee and leaned forward, his arms on the table. "Let's not let it spoil what has been a very pleasant morning."

"You know," she said, "People would say that we have nothing in common. We grew up in completely different circumstances and our lives seem to have taken opposite directions. You're going back to your family after years away, while I'm leaving mine for the first time in my life. And yet..." She smiled into his eyes and grasped his hands. He smiled back and gripped her hands.

"And yet..." They leaned forward toward each other.

"Would either of you care for more coffee?" the waiter asked. He stared meaningfully at Jerry, who dropped his eyes and let go of Prudence's hands. He sat back in his seat while Prudence fussed with her clothing, brushing away imaginary crumbs.

"No, no, thank you," Prudence answered in some confusion. Jerry shook his head and still refused to meet the waiter's eyes. The waiter nodded and walked away.

"What was that all about?" Prudence asked.

"Those people," Jerry jerked his chin toward the diners at the other end of the car, "would do far worse than jostle the table if I were to kiss you. Just holding your hands might be enough for a beating." He leaned forward. "The waiter was right to remind me."

Prudence stared at him, aghast.

Jerry muttered, "Close your mouth and change the subject."

Prudence looked around wildly. "Tell me more about those mountains over there. What did you call them? Sangre de Cristo?"

"Yes, and you'll have plenty of opportunities to learn all about them in Santa Fe when you do your training. The Harvey company is nothing if not thorough. This is your stop coming up."

He beckoned to the waiter for the check as the speed of the train began to slacken. "My treat," he said, reaching for his wallet in his back pocket. She started to protest.

He held up a hand. "Even a teacher can afford to stand a pretty lady breakfast once in a while," he continued.

She smiled. "Thank you, kind sir. Goodness, I'd completely lost track of time. Are you getting off here?"

He shook his head, "I'm on until Gallup." She looked at his duffel on the chair beside him. "Just cautious," he said. He stood, put his hat on his head, picked up his duffel, and walked with her down the aisle toward the Pullman cars. "Do you need any help with your valise?"

"Nuh... why, yes, thank you." The porters had restored the car to its previous configuration and set the passengers' luggage and other belongings on their seats. Prudence pulled on her gloves and hat. Jerry lifted her overnight bag and followed her toward the end of the car. She thanked the porter and tipped him generously as she exited the train. Jerry followed her onto the platform and set her bag at her feet.

Prudence was excited to see blankets spread out along the platform, covered with jewelry, pottery, and other small items, presided over by Indian men and women. They were selling the items to passengers who had left the train to look at their wares. Others were walking the length of the train, calling to the passengers crowding the windows, and passing up various items in exchange for cash. The men were wearing blue jeans and loose cotton shirts, belted with a cotton sash or a leather belt. Some wore a high-crowned hat, while others had tied a cloth headband around their heads. Some had their hair cut short, like Jerry's, while others' hung in long braids down their shoulders, and many wore handcrafted necklaces and bracelets, similar to what they were selling. The women wore loose, gathered cotton dresses or skirts with a loose overblouse with a wide sash belted around the waist. The younger women's skirts were knee length while the older women's fell to their ankles. Some wore their hair loose over their shoulders while others had it tied up in a knot at the back of their head. They also wore handcrafted jewelry.

"Oh, I've been hoping to buy authentic Indian jewelry..." she trailed off when she saw the look on Jerry's face. Anger, but also sadness and even... was it shame? She remembered how he had changed the subject when she told him that she was going to train as a Courier.

Jerry turned away and smiled at her, with an effort. "Well, it was nice meeting you, Miss Prudence Bates."

"I certainly enjoyed our chat. If you're ever in Santa Fe, look me up," she said, a little amazed at her boldness.

"I'll do that," he smiled in return. She picked up her overnight bag and headed toward the imposing entrance of the Fred Harvey Castañeda Hotel.

Jerry jumped back on the train just as it began to pick up speed. The horses hitched to the Indians' wagons on the other side of the tracks were the only ones to witness first a small duffel being thrown from the train, then the figure of a man in a cowboy hat and cowboy boots, denim pants and a plaid shirt leaping from the train, rolling down the embankment, then heading in a crouching run back along the tracks toward the equipment sheds, stopping briefly to pick up the duffel bag.

Chapter 5

Friday

May 31, 1929

Las Vegas, Day One

AS SHE WAITED AT the registration desk in the line of passengers who had left the train at Las Vegas, Prudence watched with envy as the Couriers, easily identifiable by their dress, gathered their groups of Detourists and shepherded them into the dining room. She knew that while their charges ate, the Couriers and drivers would be loading the HarveyCars with the leather drink bottles and the zinc-lined boxes of ice that would help to cool overheated Detourists. The Couriers would arrange for trunks to be sent on to the station where their Detourists would be rejoining the train, and the drivers would be loading their hand luggage.

Prudence reflected that, while the Castañeda was a well-designed and impressive hotel for a railroad hostelry, to someone accustomed to the imposing classical architecture of the Midwest, it was rather rustic. The colonnades, bell tower, and red tile roof certainly lent it an exotic air, reflecting the earlier Spanish architecture of the region, but it was only two stories tall, which would barely qualify it as a hotel in Cleveland. For the first time, she felt that she really was in the "Wild West" of the American frontier.

She gathered that the bedrooms were all on the second floor, as the restaurant, lobby, and registration desk appeared to fill the first floor. She requested and was given a room overlooking the Sangre de Cristo mountains to the west. It also had the benefit of being farther from the train tracks and not directly over the kitchens or restaurant. She followed the porter up to her room, carrying her overnight bag herself. He set her smaller bag on the bed and the larger on the luggage rack, thanked her for the tip, and left. The room itself was spacious, if a bit primitive, with a shared bathroom down the hall. It did, however, have a sink with running water and a mirror, so she could freshen up to some extent.

After unpacking her bags, she wrote a quick note to her mother and to Wally on picture postcards she had bought at the desk. She'd send a wire, as well, so that her mother didn't imagine the worst. Then she changed into her walking shoes. Jerry really didn't know much about women if he thought that the shoes she wore on the train were her only footwear. After two days on the train, she needed some exercise in the fresh air. She headed down to the lobby and addressed the young woman with shining chestnut hair at the registration desk.

"Excuse me, Miss…?"

"I'm Clara."

"Nice to meet you, Clara. I'm Prudence. I wonder if there are any good walks around the city. I'm on my way to Santa Fe at the end of the week to train as a Courier for the Indian Detours," she explained, "They told me that they prefer girls who have personal knowledge of the area, so I want to learn as much as I can about each of the cities where the Detours originate. I've read about the history of Las Vegas, and now I want to see the places I read about."

"Well, there's the Old Plaza over in Old Town. You'll have read about that, I'm sure. It's the part that was built by the Mexicans before the railroad. It's still mostly Mexican. The Plaza itself is quite pretty and there's the Plaza Hotel. It was built around 1880 and is known as "The Belle of the Southwest," so that's worth seeing. On this side of the river, in New Town, there's the Castañeda, of course," she grinned. "The Meadows, across the way. That's what 'Las Vegas' means, you know, 'The meadows.' Then there's the Duncan Opera House. And you wouldn't want to miss our Carnegie Library."

Prudence wondered if it were obvious that she was a librarian.

"It's a scale model of Jefferson's Monticello," Clara explained, as she reached under the counter for a street map of Las Vegas. She marked the route and the locations of various sites, explaining that if she got lost, she could "just ask anyone" the way to the Castañeda. Prudence also asked her to mark the location of the post office and the nearest telegraph office.

"It's our new post office," Clara explained, as she did so, "Just finished last year." She smiled as she looked down at the desk at a small yellow sign. "The nearest telegraph office is here at this desk." She handed Prudence a blank telegraph form, waited while she wrote her brief message, calculated the cost, and promised that it would go out within the hour.

On her way out the door, skirting the hand luggage of the Detourists stacked neatly near the desk, Prudence noticed a flyer advertising a dance that night at the YMCA. That took care of her plans for the evening. She'd get plenty of "personal knowledge" at a local dance.

There was a line of HarveyCars at the back of the hotel clearly identifiable by the thunderbird logo emblazoned on the sides. Prudence noted the White Motor Company logo on the rear. She'd have to remember to tell Wally. The cars left every morning at nine o'clock for the three-day "Detour" between Las Vegas and Albuquerque by way of Santa Fe. The drivers and Couriers must have been in the hotel kitchens, collecting the drinks and ice, as there was no one with the touring cars. She opened the door of the one nearest her and peaked inside. Twelve large, cushioned leather seats that swiveled, so that passengers could easily see from the windows on both sides, in addition to the driver's seat in the front. Windows that opened to allow cooling breezes and closed to keep out the dust. The utmost in touring luxury. In a few weeks she would be sitting in this seat next to the driver, conducting her very own Indian Detour. She shivered in anticipation.

She headed north on the aptly named Railroad Avenue toward National Avenue, turned left on National and followed it for two blocks, and there was the city's tiny Carnegie Library, a miniature Monticello seated in the center of a grassy park, although the grass was already looking a little dry in this arid climate. While it was charming in a doll's house furniture sort of way, she felt no compulsion to visit it. She was not, after all, on a busman's holiday and it could not possibly compete with the collections and services of the Cleveland Public Library. As she stood there, an elderly man walked toward the door. He stepped aside as the door opened and a group of children exited, followed by two women, their arms filled with books. The women nodded to the man, who returned the greeting before entering the library. When the children reached the sidewalk at the end of the paved pathway, they began running and laughing. One of the women shouted at them to "Be careful." Prudence had to admit that, while it might not be the equal of the Cleveland Public Library, it certainly seemed to serve this community.

In another two blocks, she came to the New Mexico Normal University. Not exactly an architectural marvel, but its presence did speak well of the city, even if it only offered degrees in education. The only people she could see on the campus were grounds' keepers, mowing and trimming and weeding. Summer was always a quiet time at a college campus, but she was a bit surprised that there didn't seem to be any students or faculty. Did they not teach summer courses? She wondered if the library were open, but was not curious enough to try to find it.

Looking down the long, straight avenue, she could see the park at the center of the Old Plaza ahead. In another two blocks, she crossed over the Gallinas Creek. She felt proud as she remembered that "gallina" was the Spanish word for "hens." The lecturer in the program on New Mexican cuisine had said that "pollo" was the word for the meat and "gallina" was the word for the bird, so it could be translated as "hen" or "chicken."

From her study of maps of New Mexico for the library programs, she remembered that if she followed the Creek, it would soon join the Gallinas River. The Gallinas flowed into the Pecos, and the Pecos into the Rio Grande, famous in song and story. Creeks and rivers were certainly not alien to a woman from Ohio, but no one had ever written any tall tales that featured the Cuyahoga, and the only thing on the other side of the Cuyahoga was more of Ohio.

When she reached the Old Plaza, she gratefully sat on a bench in the shade of a tree and caught her breath. The elevation was some six thousand feet higher than she was used to. She was also quite thirsty, as the air was considerably dryer than that of the Midwest. With luck, she'd have adapted before she started leading Detours! She wondered what had happened to the electric trolley whose tracks she could see in the streets around the Old Plaza and sincerely wished that it were still running, as the tracks seemed to head in the direction she had come from.

The Plaza was not precisely what she had expected. It was much smaller than she had thought it would be. It did feature a gazebo and paved paths through a grassy center, and was bordered by trees and shrubs, but there were none of the flower beds or sculptures that she was used to seeing in public parks and no bandstand. Looking down National, she could see a large red sandstone church. According to the street map that Clara had given her, it was Our Lady of Sorrows Catholic Church. If she weren't already hot, tired, and thirsty, she would walk the additional block to view the stained-glass windows and interior but... she was hot and tired and thirsty.

The plaza itself was ringed with other historic buildings from the past century, most of them continuing to serve as shops of various kinds—drug stores, dry goods, and mercantiles—as well as offices of professional men. Women in dresses, hats and gloves, carrying shopping baskets, and men in business suits and fedoras strolled or bustled along the sidewalks, singly or in groups, carrying on the work of their day. And, of course, there was the three-story Plaza Hotel itself. The "Belle of the Southwest" it might be, but, like the Castañeda, it would be considered ordinary, at best, in Cleveland or Chicago. It certainly offered no competition to the Palmer House.

She sighed and wondered what she was doing here, in this tiny town with its pretentious scale-model replicas of truly great architecture. It wasn't at all what she'd imagined. Where was the excitement, the adventure, the exoticism? She leaned back against the bench and, as she did, she saw, over the top of the Plaza Hotel, the Sangre de Cristo mountains away in the distance, and she remembered what had attracted her. The sheer magnitude of the landscape. The mountains reaching upward farther than the tallest skyscraper in Chicago, dwarfing any man-made structure. The wide, open spaces that made the cities of the east feel narrow and crowded. The pristine air, filled with the clean, sharp fragrance of the native plants. The mesas rising from the flat desert floor. And the people who had made this land their home for uncounted centuries, adapting to it rather than fighting against it, living in harmony with it.

And, despite all that, she was still thirsty. She laughed at herself. She was still thirsty, it was nearing lunch time, and the hotel was bound to have an acceptable restaurant. She crossed the plaza and entered the hotel. Although small, the lobby truly was worthy of the title "Belle of the Southwest," with its crystal chandeliers, deep pile carpet, and twin sweeping staircases. The Castañeda was impressive and even luxurious, but the Plaza was elegant and refined. The bar to the right of the lobby and the restaurant to the left both exuded an atmosphere of Golden Age gentility.

There were only a few diners in the restaurant at this relatively early hour. She asked for and was given a table by the window, where she could enjoy the sights of the plaza and the passing pedestrians. The menu was also rather pedestrian, when compared with the Harvey menus she'd become accustomed to over the past several days. The day was a warm one, so she opted for chicken salad and pineapple upside-down cake.

As she ate, she slowly realized that, while the diners were all white, the staff of the restaurant were Mexican. At the Harvey House, the few staff she had seen and all of the guests standing in line to register had been white. Clara had said that the Old Town was "mostly Mexican," but it had not dawned on her that what she meant was, not just that few white people lived there, but that most of the Mexicans—and Indians, she assumed—in Las Vegas lived and even worked there. She wondered where they ate, if not here. At home, of course, but those who were in the area working and shopping would want lunch or just a bite to eat and something to drink, and it didn't appear that they were welcome in the same places as she was.

She looked across the plaza to where there was a steady stream of customers entering and leaving the drug store on the corner, which undoubtedly had a lunch counter. Although she couldn't see faces clearly, she could see that nearly everyone had dark hair. She must have Jerry on the brain because that man who just left could have been him. But, of course, that was impossible as he was still on the train going to Gallup. She smiled wistfully.

Lunch concluded, she headed back to the Castañeda by a different route. This time, she was far more aware of how different the landscape was from that of Cleveland. The empty lots and alleyways in the commercial areas were hardly distinguishable from the rangeland that surrounded the city, being dirt plots in which sage brush, creosote, rabbit brush, and other such plants grew unhindered. Far from taming the land, even white people were forced to… live in harmony with the land? No, not quite. White people seemed to resist such concepts. To establish an uneasy truce? Clearly some of them had, setting out boundaries beyond which they simply allowed nature to take her course. And some, it seemed, persisted in the effort to make the desert blossom as the rose.

The few lawns that she passed were struggling in the heat and aridity and very few people had planted flower beds of any kind, although those who had clearly tended them carefully. Most homes had at least one spreading shade tree in the front or the back. She recognized a few ashes and a few oaks, but others were unknown to her. Laundry was drying on lines in the back yards of most of the houses. She saw several housewives shaking throw rugs and hanging them over porch railings, while others were sweeping the front steps. A baby in a playpen under a tree staggered to its feet and, holding onto the top rail, managed to walk itself to one corner. It reached out to grasp the perpendicular rail but lost its balance and sat heavily on its diapered bottom. Its mother came running as it set up a loud and lusty howl.

A gang of boys and girls were running through adjacent backyards, laughing and shouting and playing… was it cowboys and Indians? Some of them were wearing cowboy hats and toy gun belts and they were all shooting cap guns at each other, but whether the ones without cowboy hats were Indians or stagecoach robbers, she couldn't tell, although she didn't see anyone with a bow and arrow. What she could tell was that they all had more than a passing familiarity with western movies and especially serials. Boys who were "shot" staggered backwards, threw their hands in the air, and shouted, "Ya' got me!" before collapsing on the ground.

Several dogs were also running alongside the children, darting in now and then. One jumped on a boy who had been "shot" and began licking his face. The boy opened one eye and said, "Stop lickin' me! I'm dead." The dog paid no attention, but licked even more and wagged his tail even harder.

After a few moments watching them playing, she continued her search for the Post Office. She found it in the same boxy redbrick building as the Court House. A horse-drawn wagon was drawn up to the front of it. Inside, it included the expected post office boxes, but only had one window. An Indian man, dressed similarly to those who met the train, was picking up mail from one of the post office boxes. Prudence tried not to stare. The contrast between the man's native dress and his calmly flipping through a stack of stamped letters and bills—well, she'd wanted exotic and unexpected! There was no line at the window, so she was able to quickly purchase the required stamps and mail her postcards. The wagon was gone when she left the building.

She continued toward the intersection of Sixth Street and Douglas. She was feeling less disappointed in Las Vegas, but she still smiled to herself at the idea that she could somehow get lost. Not only were the directions easy to follow, the landmarks were obvious, and there were so few streets, it would be hard to get confused. It was difficult to believe that Las Vegas had been one of the largest cities in the Southwest not so many years ago or perhaps that said more about the size of cities in the Southwest.

The Duncan Opera House stood on the northeast corner of the intersection. It was an excellent example of what she was coming to think of as Southwestern Railroad style, Italianate Romanesque in design, but Southwestern in construction, utilizing the locally available limestone, sandstone, and occasionally adobe, and somewhat stunted and even disproportional, but it was a change from the usual red brick boxes with rectangular windows. She was relieved that Las Vegas was merely the starting point of the Detours, not one of the stops, as it would be difficult to find enough of interest to satisfy a group of sophisticated tourists.

Her attention was drawn to her left down Sixth Street by a group of people who were clustered near what she thought was City Hall. She could just hear their voices but could not make out what they were saying. An official-looking van had just pulled up and parked next to what looked like a police car. Two men got out and pushed their way through the crowd. Other people were walking in that direction, so she headed that way as well. As she got closer, she could distinguish words and phrases.

"It's disgusting! Drinking themselves to death right here in town."

"Why don't they stay on the reservation where they belong?"

"Or on the other side of the river!"

"This is becoming a regular occurrence!"

"Why don't the police do something to stop it?"

A man in a uniform raised his hand, "Stand back, people. Give them room to work." The crowd parted and Prudence could see three forms lying on the ground. Two were shrouded by blankets, and one of the men from the van was pulling a blanket over the remaining body. They laid canvas stretchers next to each body, then lifted each onto a stretcher, and carried them one by one to the van. The bystanders continued to mutter about "drunken Indians," and some raised their voices. "If the Harvey Company didn't invite them here..."

A large, bearded man standing in the open door of the building next to City Hall stepped forward. Prudence could read the letters "YMCA" over the door. Someone in the crowd shouted at him, "And if you people didn't give them handouts, they'd go back to where they belong."

Others in the crowd shouted in agreement.

The man responded, "Where's your Christian charity?

These poor souls deserve our pity, not our condemnation. If one of us weren't selling them illegal whiskey..." he stopped as the van's engine was started.

People turned to watch as the van drove off. The man in uniform stepped forward, "Let's break it up, folks. Go on about your business." He walked up to the man from the YMCA.

"Sorry about that, Myron. Some people are always lookin' for someone to blame."

"No apology necessary, Jim," Myron responded. "They, too, are deserving of charity and forgiveness. I only pray that they find it in their hearts to offer the same to others. Was it the same cause as the previous deaths?"

Jim nodded. "Seems to be. Won't know for sure until the doc has a look at them, but they had a bottle. These seem to be random killings. The only thing they have in common is that they are all Indians. Someone tryin' to make a fast buck, sellin' hooch that's been cut with wood alcohol."

"It is inconceivable to me that anyone could be so utterly wicked and place such a low value on human life. Preying on the weak and vulnerable. This is surely the work of a very disturbed individual. I shall pray for whoever it is."

"Can't say I disagree with you, but we've both seen what greed can do."

"As the good book says, the love of money is the root of all evil."

The men shook hands, and Myron went back inside the building. The police officer returned to his car and drove away.

Prudence turned and headed back toward the Castañeda, deep in thought about what she had just witnessed. She assumed that those were the bodies of Indians under those blankets. Was the crowd right? Had they drunk themselves to death? As far as she knew, it was illegal to sell alcohol to Indians, but, then it was illegal to sell alcohol to anyone. Was the police officer correct and they had been sold poisoned alcohol? What did the crowd mean "a regular occurrence?" How often were Indians dying in this way? And did the Harvey Company bear some of the blame? This sleepy little town was suddenly a lot more complicated than she had thought.

She was relieved when she spied the Castañeda across the highway. She was physically and emotionally tired and looking forward to a quiet afternoon. She also spied someone lounging against the side of the hotel, smoking a cigarette, a man in the now-familiar uniform of blue jeans, plaid shirt, and cowboy hat. As she watched, another man in a sport coat and homburg came out of the hotel, looked furtively up and down the street, then walked quickly to the corner of the building. He and the man lounging there conferred for a minute, and something changed hands. The man from the hotel slipped whatever he had received into his pocket, then returned as quickly as he had come. The other man leaned back against the side of the hotel. He crushed his cigarette against the bricks and dropped the butt on the ground.

She shrugged and continued walking toward the hotel. Obviously bootlegging wasn't restricted to the Midwest. She might ask someone for the location of a speakeasy later, now that she'd done her duty and absorbed more local history than she had intended. She shoved aside the question of whether this would also make her complicit in the deaths of the Indians by supporting the bootlegging industry.

Prudence stopped walking when she saw the side door of the hotel open and a young woman in the uniform of a Harvey Girl come out and start talking to the young bootlegger. She seemed to be pleading with him, shaking her head and raising her hands in supplication. Prudence could hear that her voice was raised but could not make out the words. While the girl talked, the young man reached into his shirt pocket and removed a pack of cigarettes. He slowly and deliberately shook out a cigarette, put it between his lips, returned the cigarette pack to his pocket, and removed a paper folder of matches. With equal deliberation, he pulled a match free, struck it, lit his cigarette, then shook out the match and dropped it on the ground. As the girl pleaded, he took a drag on the cigarette and slowly blew smoke in her direction. She turned away in disgust and re-entered the hotel. He finished the cigarette, then flipped the butt derisively in her direction and settled back against the wall.

Prudence continued past on the opposite side of the street, only crossing after the side of the building hid her from the young man's sight. She noticed idly that she had been right about the trolley's route. The tracks ended at the hotel, but they came up Railroad Avenue from the south, the opposite direction from which she had gone that morning.

As she entered the lobby, Clara greeted her. "Did you enjoy your walk?"

"Yes, thank you. It was quite educational. I ate lunch at the Plaza Hotel, as well," she answered politely. She decided not to mention the disturbing scene that she had witnessed earlier. It would only embarrass Clara and put her in an awkward position. There was also no point in mentioning the bootlegger for the same reason.

"The restaurant there is not bad. Not quite up to Harvey House standards, of course." She grinned. "Did you find the post office? It's a real improvement on the old building."

Prudence nodded and answered the unasked question. "Yes, it's very impressive and modern."

"If a bit small by bit city standards. Still, a poor thing, but our own." Clara laughed. "And the library?" Prudence nodded again. "We're rather proud of it. It took some doing to qualify for the Carnegie grant. My aunt's ladies' literary society donated books and money to open it, as did the YMCA and even the Santa Fe Railway. My father was on the first board of directors." She smiled nostalgically. "I used to love to go to the library as a child, to listen to stories and get books to take home and read. I still do check out books as often as I can. I'm hoping to take over the library when Miss Watkins retires, if she ever does."

Prudence felt a sense of shame at her dismissal of the Carnegie library building. "How wonderful! I wasn't going to mention it but… I'm a librarian, myself. Or, at least, I was, at the Cleveland Public Library."

"Why did you give it up?" Clara asked, as she polished the counter.

"Oh, I haven't given it up," Prudence replied. "I'm just looking for a change for a while. I'll still have my master's degree, so I'll be able to get another position without too much trouble when I'm ready to go back to it." She laughed. "In fact, my supervisors at the library have been encouraging me to learn more about the world outside of Cleveland. They say it will make me a better librarian, in the long-term, give me a broader outlook. Public librarians do have to serve the needs of the entire community, after all, and people do have such varied needs."

Clara nodded. "I suppose that's one of the things that attracts me. I'd get to work with everyone in Las Vegas, helping them to find the answers to all different kinds of questions, as well as find a good book to read. Teaching is all well and good, but it's rather restricting, having to specialize in one grade or one subject and work with just one age group. The only thing is, I can't afford to go away to earn a library science degree and there are no programs here, but, then, Miss Watkins doesn't have any formal training, either, and she does all right. And I, at least, will have a college degree, even it is in education."

"Some libraries pay for their librarians to attend summer training schools, like the one at the Chautauqua Institute. You might keep that in mind. I think there might be something in Los Angeles or Salt Lake City." She deliberately said nothing about the need for such training. She'd already insulted Clara enough in her thoughts that morning and she felt uncomfortable as she remembered how she'd complained to Wally about being pressured to earn the masters degree. She'd never thought of it as a privilege before.

"That's good to know. Actually, I've been thinking about applying for a job at the university library. They have part-time positions for students, and it would at least give me some exposure to the basics. I'm sure there's more to being a librarian than just checking out books and putting them back on the shelves. And I'm sure not having to learn it all through trial and error or make it up as you go along saves time and frustration."

Prudence smiled. "That was certainly my experience! I'd never have come up with anything as detailed and orderly as the Dewey Decimal system! Well, it's been lovely talking with you." As she walked up the stairs, she wondered whether she would even have earned a bachelor's degree if she had not had the benefit of the trust fund that her father left her. Where would the money have come from?

Upstairs in her room, her sense of shame deepened. She had been dismissing these people as unsophisticated, uneducated rubes with rustic, backward ways and viewing herself as some kind of modern-day Lady Bountiful, condescending to take an interest in them. But, Clara, at least, was under no illusions that Las Vegas was anything other than what it was. And she loved it for precisely that reason. Prudence now understood that the personal knowledge that the Harvey Company preferred was not restricted to objective information, but included an understanding of and love for the peoples and the cultures of the area and the challenges they met on a daily basis.

With several hours until dinner, she found herself at loose ends. A moving picture? She'd noticed two movie theaters on her walk, but hadn't paid attention to what was playing. Would either of them have a matinee? And if they did, would it be a picture she had not yet seen? Probably not. She sighed. She had plenty of reading to do, and it was time she settled down and got to it. At least there was a comfortable-looking armchair in her room.

She hadn't been reading long when she began to feel the effects of the night on the train, as well as the change in time and altitude, and decided to have a brief nap before dinner. She slipped out of her clothes and into the waiting bed. In just a few breaths, she was asleep. Sometime later, in the middle of a dream which involved a giant mouse racing a train through a mountain pass, she was awakened by the tantalizing aroma of frying onions and roasting meats calling to her from downstairs.

She dressed, refreshed her lipstick and face powder and tidied her hair, then headed down for dinner. Her life right now seemed to be a succession of meals interspersed with periods of waiting for meals. That would change soon enough when she reached Santa Fe.

The restaurant was crowded and busy. She paused in the door, watching the Harvey Girls in their black dresses and white aprons, moving in a choreographed dance throughout the room, sliding between tables with plates and trays of glasses held high, changing tablecloths and place settings, and never putting a foot wrong. She became part of the dance, as she was almost waltzed to her table, seated and presented with a menu. A glass of water appeared almost from the air. The menu was far more interesting and unusual than that at the Plaza Hotel. After due consideration, she selected the Fried Chicken Castañeda, the specialty of the House.

As she waited for the waitress to come to take her order, she observed the other customers seated near her. They all appeared to be like herself, comfortably middle-class, but closer to middle-age or even older. The men were well-fed and prosperous looking, their wives equally so, if more rigidly corseted. Her attention was caught by the phrase, "Indian Detours," and she realized that these diners would be her customers in the not-too-distant future. She caught herself staring at the table which was discussing the Detours, and quickly looked away before they could notice. They must have arrived on the Chief this morning and would leave with the others the next day. They were exhibiting to each other the jewelry they had purchased from the Indian vendors on the train platform. The women compared the necklaces, bracelets, and rings they wore. The men had exchanged their cloth neckties for braided leather cord ties with large turquoise stones set in the slides and seemed to take great delight in comparing the size of the stones. One of them, a man in a familiar-looking sport coat, said something about a "ten-gallon hat." Prudence sincerely hoped that he was not planning on buying one for himself, but feared the worst. Their meal over, the men leaned back in their chairs, lit cigarettes and inhaled deeply. One of the women took a long cigarette holder out of her handbag and inserted a cigarette into it, then held it out for the man next to her to light.

"Sorry about the wait," her waitress said as she hurried up. Prudence was intrigued to see that she was the same Harvey Girl she had seen arguing with the young man earlier. What had that been about?

Her meal came promptly, and as she ate the rich chicken dish, any doubts about the quality of the Harvey food in the more remote locations vanished. The tender slices of chicken breast had been coated in a thick sauce, then dredged in breadcrumbs and fried. They were served with a subtly spiced tomato sauce and fresh French peas. No wonder the Castañeda was famous for it.

She also thought more about the incident between her waitress and the young man that she had witnessed outside the hotel and how she could find out what it had all been about. When the waitress returned for her dessert order, she attempted to engage her in conversation.

"Goodness! I couldn't possibly eat dessert after this. It's quite delicious, but so rich and filling. Don't you think so?"

The young woman nodded, but resisted the overture of friendship. "Yes, ma'am. Most of the ladies say so."

Of course, she couldn't even seem to criticize the Harvey menu. "Well, then, I'll just have my check."

She signed for her meal, then tried again, taking a different tack. "By the way, I'm thinking of going to the dance at the Y this evening. Do you recommend it?"

"Oh, yes, ma'am. All the kids will be going and there'll be a pretty good dance band. I'll be getting off work early enough to go myself." She paused. "Not much for refreshments, though. Usually just lemonade. Oh, and no smoking."

"It sounds ideal! What should I wear? I've never been to a dance at a Railroad YMCA before. Oh, my name is Prudence Bates," she said, and waited expectantly.

"I'm Martha Morgan. Pleased to meet you." She thrust out her hand and Prudence shook it briefly. Martha's long dark, shining hair was tidily confined in a loose twisted knot at her neck. She smiled and her brown eyes were friendly as she looked Prudence up and down. "I'd say what you have on is just fine. Nothing too fancy. Just a nice, friendly local dance." She started stacking the dirty dishes on the table, as Prudence stood to leave the restaurant. "Hope to see you tonight, then."

It was dusk when Prudence headed down Douglas Avenue to Sixth Street toward the YMCA, passing the modern Meadows Hotel, the Castañeda's competitor for the automobile traffic on the CanAm highway, that two-thousand-mile throughway that linked the deserts of western Texas to the lakes and forests of northern Canada. Looking down the street, she saw couples and small groups of people entering the YMCA building, where only hours before, three people had lain dead on the sidewalk. She mentally shook herself. It would not do to be morbid!

The men wore their usual uniform of plaid shirt, jeans, boots, and cowboy hat, although the shirt and jeans looked newer and cleaner than their daily wear. Most of them were wearing braided leather or cord string ties with silver slides with a turquoise or other stone inset. The women's brightly-colored A-line cotton skirts, blouses, and boots made Prudence feel both over-dressed and out-of-place in her navy silk drop-waist dress and spectator pumps. A few of the women were even wearing jeans with the kind of satin blouse that Mary Howard had worn on the train. She was glad that she had asked Martha for advice about what to wear, or she really would have been dressed inappropriately. Well, this was meant to be a learning experience, and she was already learning. Several of the men and a few of the women extinguished cigarettes on the ground before they entered the building.

The dance was held in a large room on the ground floor. A small band was setting up at one end of the room. A table along one wall held glasses and punch bowls full of lemonade. Chairs lined the remaining space along the walls. She wondered if she'd spend the evening there, a wallflower for the first time in her life.

"So, you made it!" Martha came up behind her. She had brushed out her hair so that it curled around her shoulders and changed her somber Harvey uniform for a vivid red blouse, flashy print bandanna, indigo skirt, and tooled leather cowboy boots. She wore a heavy silver and turquoise necklace and silver bangles on her wrist. "Let me introduce you to a few people."

The band began tuning up as Martha introduced Prudence to her group of friends. She recognized auburn-haired Anne, with her chin-length wavy bob, as another of the waitresses at the Castañeda and noted that Clara had added marcel waves to her hair for the occasion. They were all wearing more makeup than they did at work, which made Prudence less self-conscious about her own.

"And that's Liz over there" Martha indicated a tall young woman with expertly shingled blonde hair standing near the punch bowl. Even from that distance, Prudence could see that her blouse was silk, rather than cotton, and that her clothing had been tailored to fit her. The jewelry that glinted at her ears, neck, and wrist was platinum and diamond. "And this is Maria," as a short, dark-haired, dark-eyed girl approached. Martha lowered her voice, "Just so you know—her family's Spanish, not Mexican."

"I'm very pleased to meet you," Maria said shyly to Prudence. She turned to Martha "Is Tom here?" she asked hopefully.

Martha shook her head. "No, he wouldn't be caught dead at a YMCA dance. Or at least I hope he won't."

"Oh, Martha, don't say that! It might do him good," Maria said reproachfully.

Martha just shook her head. She turned to introduce the young men in the group—Mike, John, and Gene. Prudence hoped she would be able to remember which was which, as they all looked much the same with their long, rangy builds, crew cuts and jeans. The only difference that she could see was that Mike was a dishwater blond, John's hair was nearly black with a hint of a curl, and Gene was what was popularly called a "carrot top."

Liz sidled over to them, with a walk that Prudence was sure she had copied from Mae West. She ran her fingers down Gene's arm. "So glad you're here, Gene," she cooed.

Gene grinned and stammered, "Uh, hi, Liz. I, uh, I'm glad you're here, too."

Liz turned to stare at Prudence. "And who's this? Isn't anyone going to introduce me to the new girl?"

"This is Prudence Bates," Anne popped in before anyone else could speak. "She's staying at the Castañeda this week, and then she's going to Santa Fe to train as a Courier with the Indian Detours. That's right, isn't it?" She looked at Clara for confirmation. Clara nodded.

"Hmm," Liz looked her up and down, noting her expensive, stylish clothing. "And just where are you from, Prudence Bates?" Her glance and tone of voice made it clear that she thought Prudence was not only over-dressed, but pretentious and ostentatious.

"Cleveland," said Prudence. "That's in Ohio." She was pleased to see Liz react to the implication.

Before Liz could respond, the band started playing. Clara pushed John forward to dance the first dance with Prudence, a fox trot. She was surprised to find that he was an excellent dancer who knew how to lead. Liz had commandeered Gene, who seemed to have the proverbial two left feet, or perhaps that was due to his intense self-consciousness. Anne and Mike rocked back and forth in a one-step, seemingly more intent on conversation than on the music. Martha and Maria were also on the dance floor with young men Prudence had not been introduced to.

John thanked her for the dance, then he and Clara paired off for the next set. A young man whose name she did not catch asked her for the next dance, a Lindy Hop. As she was catching her breath after the dance was over, Martha, who was standing next to her, said, "I'll bet you know some new dance steps you could teach us."

"Maybe," said Prudence. "The latest thing I learned was the Black Bottom. Do you know it?" Martha shook her head and John and Mike, who were close enough to hear her, sniggered at the name. She ignored them, as did Martha. "It's similar to a Charleston, so if the band doesn't know the Black Bottom Dance music, we can make do with the Charleston."

Martha hurried over and conferred with the band leader. He nodded and she came running back. "He says they've been practicing it, so, let's go."

"Line up, as if we were dancing the Charleston," Prudence instructed. Everyone except Liz, Gene, and a few of the less confident dancers joined the line. The music began and Prudence demonstrated the steps, hopping, shuffling, gyrating, her arms and legs moving in syncopated rhythms. As soon as she began repeating the steps, the others began copying her, hopping and sliding and shuffling and hobbling, and it wasn't long before they were all dancing it with more or less skill and a lot of laughter.

After the exertions of the Black Bottom, they were grateful that the band played a slow waltz, then returned to the familiar Fox Trot. Liz requested that they play a tango, a dance that was somewhat beyond Gene's skill, but that Clara and John had practiced to nearly exhibition level. Mike and Anne stood on the sidelines, sipping lemonade.

Prudence, worries about being a wallflower completely banished from her mind, was rather relieved that no one asked her for that particular dance. It was just a bit too intimate to be danced with a stranger whose name she did not even know.

After an hour and a half of playing, the band set down their instruments and retired for a fifteen-minute break. Prudence, Martha, and the others joined the crowd of laughing, chattering young people at the punch bowl table. Gradually, they became aware that voices were being raised at one corner of the room. Mike and another young man were shouting and shoving each other in an increasingly aggressive manner. Maria was hovering around them, pleading with them to stop.

"Please, he didn't mean it. It was an accident—a mistake. Please, say you're sorry. I'm sure he'll forgive you." Whether she was speaking to one or both of them wasn't clear, but it hardly seemed to matter as neither was paying her the least bit of attention.

"Oh, Maria, for heaven's sake, leave him alone," Liz muttered, avidly watching the argument and smiling to herself. Prudence wondered which of the young men Liz was referring to, but guessed it wasn't Mike.

Before anyone else could intervene, the young man punched Mike in the face, and he returned the blow, and suddenly, a fistfight had broken out. Liz laughed softly to herself and took a rather large swallow of the lemonade from the cup she was holding.

Everyone moved away from the two sparring men, except for a tall, bearded older man who was easily twice their size. Prudence recognized him as Myron who had confronted the crowd that morning. He approached quietly, grabbed each of them by the collar, pulled them apart, and dragged them out the door. There was a general sigh of relief, and everyone started talking at once, although Liz looked rather disappointed. She returned to the punch bowl to refill her cup.

Maria rushed up to Martha, tears spilling from her eyes. "Oh, Martha, I tried to stop them, I really did. But, they just wouldn't listen to me."

Martha patted her on the arm. "I know you did, Maria.

It's hardly your fault."

"Still, if I'd only said the right thing..." Maria looked toward the door. "I should go after him, make sure he's all right." Martha nodded, and they watched her collect her things and walk sadly out of the dance hall.

"That idiot," muttered Martha. Prudence looked at her quizzically. "No, not Maria, although I do wonder... You'll find out sooner or later," she said. "That hooligan who threw the first punch is my brother, Tom." She shook her head in disgust. "I hoped he'd stay away like he said he would."

Prudence realized that he was the young man she'd seen arguing with Martha at the hotel. "Oh, I am sorry," she said, not knowing what else to say. She no longer felt the urge to pry information out of her about that event.

"She does realize that he's not the least bit interested in her, doesn't she?" Liz said as she walked up. "Although, he might be attracted by the challenge of good Catholic girl. What do you think, Martha?"

Before Martha could answer, Anne walked up with a glass of lemonade. "Hey, Martha," she said, "Taste this and tell me if I'm tasting what I think I'm tasting."

Martha took a sip and curled her lip. "Yeah, that's been spiked all right. Most likely courtesy of Tom."

Anne nodded. "That's what Mike said. That's why they were fighting. Mike accused Tom of spiking the punch. Then Tom called him an old maid Mormon, he called Tom something worse and..." She shrugged. "Looks like the party is over for me and Mike, anyway. Williams won't let him back in tonight." She waved goodbye to the others and left.

Martha shook her head. "Guess we'd better tell Mr. Williams about the punch."

"And spoil the party? Not much reason to stay, then," Liz said. She gestured to Gene, "Drive me home." It was not a request. He followed eagerly after her.

Martha and Prudence headed for the door. They met Mr. Williams returning from having ejected the two trouble-makers. Martha told him about the punch. He sighed and headed straight for the table.

"May I have your attention please," he said in a booming

voice, not making it a question.

"The lemonade has gone bad and will need to be replaced. Please leave your glasses on the table." He signaled to two other men who were standing at the sides of the room and the three of them emptied the glasses into the bowls, then carried the bowls outside and dumped the lemonade on the ground. They went down to the kitchen and soon returned with fresh lemonade.

By this time, the band had returned and was once again tuning up. Martha turned to Prudence and said, "I'm sorry, but I don't feel much like dancing any more. I think I'll go on home, too."

"Of course," said Prudence. She could see the tears glistening in Martha's eyes. "I understand. Would you like to go somewhere and talk about it?" She put on her "friendly, interested, and helpful" librarian face without much effort.

Martha paused. "I'd like that," she said. "Maybe we could go sit in the park." Prudence nodded. They said their goodbyes to Clara and John and left quietly.

"I don't want you to think I'm some kind of Goody Two-Shoes or Mormon, like Mike," Martha said as they walked toward Lincoln Park. "I like a nip now and then as much as the next person. I've been seen in the alley behind the Meadows," she laughed. "That's where our local speakeasy is, if you can call it that, in the Meadows. It's just that... seems like lately, Tom's drunk more often than he isn't. And I don't know where he's getting his hooch. Not from any of the locals. He sneaks out at night at least once a week and he's got way more to sell than he would if he bought it from one of the local stills. They don't produce all that much and most of it goes to their regular customers, like the Meadows. I've caught him selling to the tourists outside the Castañeda, so he's got a lot more than a pint or two."

"I saw him there earlier today," Prudence admitted. "And I saw you arguing with him about something."

"Yes," Martha nodded. "He's going to get me fired if he keeps hanging around there selling that hooch on company property. The Harvey Company is very strict about abiding by the law and about the image it projects. It would not want to be associated with any illegal activities of any kind! And..." she paused. "I think... I think he's selling it to the

Indians and, and… I think whatever he's selling them has something wrong with it, 'cause four Indians were found dead outside of town last week and three more this morning, right here in town. Not a mark on them, but they'd been drinking. And he's just got way too much money to be getting it just from selling pints to guests at the hotel. He's been talking about buying a new truck." She sniffed. "And then he pulls a stunt like this, spikes the punch just to… I don't know… get at Mr. Williams, maybe. Or may just cause trouble."

They had reached the park, and she sat heavily on a nearby bench. "I don't know what to do. I haven't been able to talk to anyone about it because… well, I don't dare. What if word got out?" She looked at Prudence as she sat down next to her. "I feel like I can trust you because you don't know anyone here to talk to," she laughed wryly, "And you'll be gone in a few days." She looked down at her feet, then back up at Prudence. "What do you think I should do? I've tried talking to him until I'm blue in the face. I'm just so worried about whoever these people are he's got himself tied up with." She dropped her voice to a whisper, even though there was no one near to hear her, "I think they are bringing it up from Mexico. I think he's mixed up with some kind of mob."

"Have you talked to your parents?"

Martha nodded. "I have, but… my mother, she got angry and told me I had an evil mind. She never has believed that Tom could do anything wrong. My father… he tried talking to Tom, but it didn't do any good. Tom just laughed at him and threatened to move out. My mother went into hysterics."

Prudence stared ahead into the dark and slowly shook her head. "I really don't know. I wish I did know what to advise you. Telling the police might be the best thing you could do for him."

Martha shook her head. "No, no, I couldn't be the one to send my brother to prison. My parents—my mother—would never forgive me." She sighed. "But, thanks for listening." She stood, "I'll be heading home now. I'll see you tomorrow at breakfast. Be sure to ask for one of my tables." Prudence watched her walk off. If only this were one of those mysteries she was so fond of. She would just call up Ellery Queen. She was certainly no Prudence Beresford and this was far more complicated than any puzzle Tuppence had solved. This mystery involved real people whose feelings she cared about. All she really could do now was go back to her room at the hotel. As she entered the building, the eastbound train—the Navajo—pulled into the station and deposited its passengers, many of whom would be leaving on a Detour the next morning.

Chapter 6

Saturday

June 1, 1929

Las Vegas, Day Two

PRUDENCE AWAKENED TO THE aroma of bread baking in the Castañeda bakery and to the arrival of the California Limited. Knowing that the restaurant would be crowded with passengers rushing to get a bite to eat before leaving on their Detour at nine o'clock, she took her time getting ready. She wondered if maybe it hadn't been such a great idea to spend a week in Las Vegas before joining a Detour. She'd already seen what Las Vegas had to offer that was within walking distance. The Montezuma was now the Southern Baptist College, not a health spa, even if she had some way to get out there. It was frustrating to be so close to the hotel that had been run as a luxury resort by Fred Harvey and not be able to at least get a glimpse of it. Well, there was always shopping. The clothes she had brought with her were most definitely not appropriate for exploring the Wild West. Even her walking shoes were starting to hurt her feet. She needed something with an even lower heel and wider toe. How Wally would have laughed at her making such an unfashionable choice.

The breakfast rush was over when she got downstairs, with only a few lingering hotel guests and a handful of locals. Martha was distant and formal when she came to take Prudence's order, which wasn't really a surprise. Librarians learned early that people often regretted revealing personal information to a practical stranger. Prudence gave her order, then said, "Martha, could I ask you something?" Martha looked wary.

"One of the reasons I stopped here in Las Vegas for a week was so that I could buy myself some more appropriate clothes. Is there a seamstress here? Or a good department store that does alterations?"

"Oh, yes!" She looked relieved and happy that the question was an impersonal one that she could easily answer. "Susan Jensen is probably the best. Not too expensive, either. She's got some nice little Mexican girls working for her. They're real fast and she always checks over their work to make sure it's good. Her shop is down on the plaza. She can run you up some dresses and skirts in no time. And then there's Ilfeld's Department Store right next to the Plaza Hotel. If you want jeans or dungarees, they're the place to go. They sell boots, too. And nice shirts. They've got some jewelry, but you can't do better than buy it from the Indians when the trains come in." Prudence was amused to note that Martha had a very good idea of what her wardrobe lacked. "Oh, there's another table just come in. Better get their order and then I can put them both in."

The "other table" was two men with crew cuts wearing the uniform of some law enforcement agency. Police? County sheriff? She couldn't quite tell. Both men were taller and broader than average. The older man was starting to run to fat, but was still solid and powerful looking. The younger man was trim and muscular. Prudence was sure that he was the officer she had seen the day before. They both hung their hats on the pegs by the door and sat at what was obviously "their" table.

Although they were two tables away, their voices carried in the nearly empty room.

"Mornin', Martha," said the older of the two men.

"Mornin', Bill. Mornin', Jim. The usual?"

They both answered in the affirmative. Martha wrote the orders on her pad and started away.

"Hear they found two more dead Indians this mornin'?" asked the one she'd called Bill.

Two more today? Prudence thought. In addition to the three she'd seen yesterday and the ones before that. It was not a coincidence or an accident.

Martha stopped and turned back. "Oh, that's awful! Was

it poisoned booze again?" she asked.

"Looks like. That makes close to a dozen now." A dozen! Prudence nearly missed what Bill said next.

"We're pretty sure we know who is sellin' it to them. We just can't figure where he's gettin' it." He glanced sharply at Martha, who looked down at her order pad.

"Wish I could help, Chief," she said. "Better get these orders in."

The two men watched her walk away and shook their heads. "That brother of hers... do you reckon she'd tell us if she did know?" asked the one called Jim. Oh, poor Martha! She was not the only one who suspected Tom.

"Prob'ly not," answered Bill. "But I doubt he'd tell her. Too dangerous for both of them. It's got to be one of those gangs based in Mexico. We'd know by now if it was one of the stills up here. Damned Prohibition." He stopped as Martha returned with their coffee. "Thanks, doll."

She smiled and moved to set Prudence's coffee in front of her, then bustled off to take the order of a table of tourists who had just been seated.

"You know we have to enforce the law," Jim was saying. Prudence wondered if they knew—or cared— that she could hear them.

"Yeah," Bill shrugged. "Don't have to like it, though. Didn't have these problems before 1920."

He sipped his coffee. "People been drinkin' since the Garden of Eden. No law is gonna stop it."

"It's always been illegal to sell to Indians," Jim reminded him.

"Uh-huh." He sighed. "It was easier to handle, though, when it was just the local boys. And they made sure not to kill off their customers— or at least not too many of them all at once. The doc figures someone is cuttin' this stuff with wood alcohol."

"Think this new federal agent will be any help? When's he gettin' here?"

"On the California Limited tonight." Bill lowered his voice as he continued to speak.

Apparently, they were aware that they could be heard. Prudence strained to hear what he said, but between his lowered voice and the increasing noise level of the restaurant, couldn't make out any words. All conversation between the two men ceased when Martha set their breakfast in front of them. Prudence also attended to her meal.

As she left the hotel later to do her shopping, she noticed several young women with dark hair, dark eyes, and brown skin wearing the uniform of maids entering the hotel. Were they Mexican? Indian? Either way, they were the first non-white people she'd seen at the hotel or even in Las Vegas, except on the train platform and among the shoppers and pedestrians in Old Town.

She took a more direct route to the plaza, as she wasn't sightseeing, and arrived within fifteen minutes. The seamstress' shop was much smaller than Prudence was accustomed to, but had all the necessary equipment, including two fitting rooms which opened onto a curtained mirrored alcove. She was relieved to see that Miss Jensen was dressed in one of the latest styles and that her marcelled hair was professionally waved. She did want to fit in with her new clothes, but she did not want to look frumpy, and like a skinny chef, a frumpy seamstress was no advertisement for the quality of her goods.

Miss Jensen herself took Prudence's measurements, showed her the fabrics she had available, asked questions about what she wanted, and recommended a few styles. The prices she quoted were far less than she expected, so Prudence ordered two skirt and blouse combinations for everyday wear in neutral colors and another set in the bright, flashy colors favored by the young women at the YMCA dance. She arranged to return in three days for fittings. As she left the shop, she realized that she had not seen anyone other than Miss Jensen. The seamstresses Martha had mentioned must work in the back of the shop, hidden away so as not to offend customers.

Ilfeld's indeed had the blue jeans she wanted, as well as ready-to-wear blouses that fit well enough for casual wear. She added several pairs of cotton knit socks to the pile. She tried on cowboy boots, but decided that they were an acquired taste, and settled for a pair of sturdy saddle oxfords. Now, it was time to choose a hat. She'd put that off until last. She simply could not wear a cowboy hat. She'd look like one of the dudes at the table, but her cloches and turbans were definitely out of place here. She finally settled on a narrow-brimmed Panama hat as an acceptable compromise, and the straw would be cooler than wool felt.

As it was now getting near lunchtime, she requested that her purchases be delivered to the Castañeda and asked if there were any restaurants in the area where she could get authentic New Mexican food. The salesclerk recommended a nearby café, "Great tamales, but you might find it a bit on the spicy side." They were and she did, but managed to finish the meal with the aid of several glasses of water and a cooling flan for dessert.

She noticed a familiar figure ahead of her as she returned to the Castañeda along Douglas Avenue. After a few moments, she realized that it was Martha's brother, Tom. He turned the corner and began sauntering nonchalantly—rather obviously so—down Railroad toward the Castañeda. About to set up shop at the corner of the hotel again, no doubt. Ah, well, as Bill had said, no law was going to stop people from drinking alcohol, but she did wish that he'd have some consideration for his sister.

On the other hand, he wasn't carrying anything. Did he have it stashed near the hotel? Was he meeting his supplier? Maybe she could find out something that would help Martha! She picked up her pace in order to get closer to him, but not so close as to attract his attention. He didn't seem to be aware of her following him, and even if he were, she was headed back to her hotel. What could be suspicious in that? She followed him as he walked past the hotel and continued toward the equipment sheds.

She stopped at the corner of the building, peering around the side of the hotel. He hadn't looked behind him and didn't seem to realize that she was following him. She climbed the few steps to the colonnade and slipped along it from one column to the next, until she reached the front corner. From there, she could see down the tracks to the sheds without being seen herself.

Tom knocked on the door of the nearest shed, then slipped inside when it was opened. She wondered how long she'd have to keep watch, but it wasn't more than five minutes when the door opened and Tom left. He stood for a moment, lighting a cigarette, then tossed the used match on the ground, crossed the yard to Railroad Avenue and headed back in the direction he had come. A few seconds later, the door opened again, and another man slipped out. He stood briefly, watching Tom walk away, then disappeared around the corner of the shed.

Prudence stood frozen. She knew that man. Jerry Begay.

What was he doing meeting with Tom Morgan? What was he doing in Las Vegas? So she hadn't been imagining things yesterday at the Plaza Hotel restaurant. He *was* the man she had seen coming out of the drug store.

She wandered back up to her room in a near daze. She knew that she wasn't mistaken. She had seen Jerry Begay and Tom Morgan together. She told herself that it wasn't her concern. He was just a stranger who had bought her breakfast on a train. But she couldn't stop thinking about what she had seen. Jerry Begay meeting with a bootlegger in secret. A bootlegger suspected of selling poisoned liquor to the Indians.

There was a knock on her door. "Delivery for Miss Bates," said a young male voice. Her clothes from Ilfeld's. That would take her mind off of things for a bit. She opened the door to accept the package of clothes tied up in brown paper and handed the boy a tip. Closing the door, she set the package on the bed and cut the string with a pair of nail scissors. She'd surprise Martha at dinner by appearing dressed as a real Western girl!

She slipped out of her dress and pulled on the jeans. They were a bit stiff, but she was sure they would soften with wear. Then one of her new cotton blouses with the top-stitched yoke and pockets. She smiled as she thought of Mary Howard on the train. Now she understood why Mary had laughed at what looked "authentic to the dudes." None of the blouses or shirts at Ilfeld's had sported mother-of-pearl, rhinestones, or fringe and certainly none were made of satin. She tucked her blouse into her jeans and realized that she'd neglected to buy a belt. And these men's jeans, with their large waistband, definitely called for a belt, although not one with a big, shiny rodeo buckle. And her little clutch purse of glove-soft leather would never do! Still… she had time for a quick trip to Ilfeld's before dinner, if she hurried. Socks and shoes and she was ready to go.

As she left the rear door of the hotel, two middle-aged women approached the entrance. One said to the other, "Disgusting!" and her companion nodded. "You be careful, my dear," the first one said to Prudence. "There's a drunken Indian stumbling around out there." Her companion nodded in agreement again.

Prudence thanked them politely and continued on her way down Railroad Avenue. She hadn't gone more than a few yards when a figure came stumbling toward her, a flat liquor bottle in one hand. He tipped it up and drank from it, then stared bleary-eyed at her.

"Well, if it isn't li'l Miss Prudence Bates," he slurred. She stared at him in shock and felt her heart drop. "Lookitchew in yer cowgirl outfit." He giggled. "Don'tcha' reco'nize me? It's Jerry... Jerry Begay, from the train." He grinned at her. "Wanna' snort?" He offered her his bottle.

"No, thank you." Prudence pushed her way past. She could smell the liquor on him.

"Awww... well, more for me." Jerry lifted the bottle to his lips once more.

She stopped and turned. "I thought you were better than this," she said sadly.

"Don' be that way, naggin' a fella' about his drinkin'" he mumbled, reaching for her, "And you so cute and all." Prudence stepped back, shaking her head, then turned and walked hurriedly away. He dropped his eyelids and stumbled over to slump against a pole. He slid down to sit on the ground, his knees bent.

"Thought I was bettern' that," he repeated. "Wimmen." He lowered his forehead to his knees and soon began to snore. His grip on the bottle loosened, and it dropped to the ground, the contents running out into the dirt.

Prudence stood on the other side of the street, staring at Jerry, tears starting in her eyes. She had read about the problem of alcoholism among the Indians and even seen the effects herself, but she had assumed that it didn't affect anyone as young, healthy, and educated as Jerry. Of course, she had seen young, healthy educated white men and even women who had had "one too many" on more than one occasion, but never on a public street in the middle of the day, and always in the context of an evening out or a party among friends. For the most part, they were loud, boisterous, and cheerful. Jerry looked so alone and friendless and pathetic. What demons were driving him?

Suddenly, she remembered that Tom was the one suspected of selling poisoned alcohol and she was sure that Jerry had bought his bottle from Tom. If she was any kind of friend… she started to cross back to him, but stopped as the two officers from breakfast wandered up to where he slumped unconscious. They stared at him, shaking their heads. One prodded Jerry with his foot. He stirred and mumbled something. Thank God! He wasn't dead, at least.

They reached down, each taking an arm, then pulled him up and dragged him to a pickup truck with an official seal painted on the doors. They shoved him into the front seat, then one got in beside him, and the other went around and got in behind the steering wheel and they drove off. Prudence stared at the truck until it turned down a side street and was lost to view. If only she had not walked past him in disgust, she might have prevented him being arrested and helped him to find some place private to sleep it off. She had thought that she was better than that.

When she returned to her room from Ilfeld's, with her new belt and tooled-leather handbag, she tried to read but couldn't concentrate. She felt restless and fretful. Why was she so upset about a man she barely knew? But, then, that was the entire problem. She barely knew him. She really knew nothing about the people of this place. She had read the books. She knew about the history of the place, the history of the native people of the place, but she knew almost nothing about the lives of those people today. And she knew nothing about them as people like herself, with hopes and dreams and disappointments, who loved and hated and despaired. Where did they come from, in their horse-drawn buckboard wagons, to sell exotic souvenirs to middle-class white people who viewed them as relics of the past? How did they feel about being put on display for the Detourists? Were they being given an opportunity to share their culture and their history, or were they being exhibited as curiosities?

For the first time, she had doubts about becoming a Courier. What had seemed an exciting adventure had been tainted by contact with reality. Well, she was nearly there now. It seemed a waste not to at least do the training and make the final decision then. In the meantime— she would learn what she could.

Martha was suitably impressed by her jeans when she arrived at the restaurant. "Well, look at you! You could almost pass for a native of these parts." She grinned broadly.

"Almost?" Prudence grinned in return.

"Well… it's all kind of new, you know, and… the shoes… not that some women around here don't wear them…" She laughed. "What'll you have?"

Prudence ordered the chicken enchiladas, wondering how they differed from the tamales which she had eaten for lunch. She then sat back to wait for her meal and observed her fellow diners. She didn't recognize any of them. Most of the people who arrived on the morning trains had booked a Detour, which left within two hours of their arrival. Those who arrived later in the day would be booked to leave the next morning. So, nearly everyone she'd had breakfast with was well on their way to Santa Fe and these people she was eating dinner with would be gone right after breakfast tomorrow. At the same time, they all looked so very familiar. The same boisterous middle-aged men and their censorious wives, wearing the same middle-class conservative clothing, exhibiting the same turquoise and silver jewelry, laughing the same laughs doubtless at the same jokes. The men called the waitresses "sweetheart" and "doll," while their wives observed them critically through narrowed eyes for any faults. She was beginning to have some insight into how locals viewed the many tourists who flowed through the hotel.

Her meal arrived and she ate it slowly, pondering what to do with herself for the next five days. Martha came with the check and to clear the table. "Say, tomorrow is my day off, Anne's and Clara's too. We're driving up to the hot springs near the Montezuma with the boys and Maria. We'll take a picnic lunch. Would you like to come with us? I can lend you a bathing suit if you don't have one." She stacked the dirty dishes as she talked.

"I was just wondering what I would do with myself

tomorrow," Prudence exclaimed. "I'd love to—and I do have a bathing suit with me. I threw it in at the last minute just in case! I'm not sure what I'll do about lunch, though ..."

"Oh, don't worry about that! Our mothers always pack twice as much as we can eat, boys included."

"I definitely want to contribute my share. I'll buy the pop if we can stop at a market."

"It's a deal. We go right past Smith's Market on the way out of town. So, we'll pick you up outside the hotel about ten, after Maria gets home from church. Oh, and we just wear our bathing suits under our clothes so we don't have to change when we get there. I'll bring an extra towel for you."

Prudence nodded. "I'm looking forward to it, and thank you again for the invitation."

Martha picked up the stack of plates and silverware and headed toward the kitchen while Prudence went back into the lobby. A tall, thin young man wearing a grey fedora and grey business suit was at the registration desk, checking in with the older man on duty as the night desk clerk. As she turned to go up the stairs, the two officers she'd seen earlier that day came in and approached the man. She walked as slowly as she dared up the stairs, making as little noise as possible and listening intently. She heard them greet him and introduce themselves, but she could not quite make out his name. They shook hands all around, the man asked for a porter to take his bag to his room, and the three of them went into the restaurant. Prudence shivered in delight. He must be the "new agent" that they had mentioned at breakfast. A genuine prohis! But what would that mean for Jerry Begay? And Tom Morgan?

Chapter 7

Sunday

June 2, 1929

Las Vegas, Day Three

PRUDENCE AWOKE TO THE sound of church bells calling the faithful to worship. She stretched luxuriously, feeling quite decadent to be still in bed on a Sunday morning. Maria, no doubt, was hurrying up the steps of Our Lady of Sorrows. If she'd been at home, she would have been dressed and ready to accompany Mother to church, but here, she felt no such compulsion. Although she enjoyed the social aspects of their neighborhood church, it had been years since attendance had meant anything more than that, not that she said any such thing to Mother. On the other hand, she was quite looking forward to the trip to the hot springs this afternoon, so she'd better get up and get breakfast out of the way. First, though, she was going to buy that Indian jewelry she had promised herself, now that Jerry wasn't there to glare disapprovingly.

She dressed and headed down to the platform. The Indians were ready with their merchandise spread out on blankets, waiting the arrival of the train. Across the tracks, several buckboards were pulled up to the bottom of the embankment. The horses casually nibbled at the weeds growing at their hooves.

It took longer than she had anticipated to select only two necklaces from among the many on display. Although they were all similar, each was slightly different, reflecting the artistry of the individual craftsman who had made it. She suspected that they also reflected the taste of their customers for something exotic, but "not too" exotic, as several of the Indians wore jewelry that was more sophisticated and original than that offered for sale. She wanted to ask them about their designs and their inspiration, but felt suddenly shy and awkward. Would such questions be appropriate? Would they think she was prying or, worse, treating them as curiosities on display?

She paid for the necklaces, smiling as politely as she could, and returned to the hotel dining room for breakfast, feeling confused and torn. Once again, she found herself doubting her decision to become a Courier. She wished that she had the courage to ask the craftsmen how they felt about selling the work of their hands in this way to middle-class white people as souvenirs, and whether they felt that they were a railroad sideshow performing for the entertainment of the passengers of the Santa Fe Railroad and the guests at the various Harvey Houses.

She put her doubts aside and got ready for the trip to the hot springs. Wearing her jeans and shirt over her bathing suit was not exactly comfortable, but she would get used to it in time. She had breakfasted and was waiting at the curb when two pickup trucks pulled up to the back of the Castañeda. Mike was driving one truck, with Anne sitting next to him, and Tom the other, with Maria in front with him. Even from that distance, Prudence could see that she looked ecstatic, and that Tom looked smug and self-satisfied. Although from what she could recall, that was his usual expression.

Clara, John, Liz, and Gene were riding in the back of Mike's truck, and Martha was in the back of Tom's. She waved to Prudence and reached down to give her a hand as she stepped up on the bumper and over the tailgate. One side of the truck bed held the picnic hampers. The towels were stacked on the other, forming a seat for her and Martha. She felt like "one of the gang" in her jeans, cotton shirt, and Panama hat. She couldn't see whether the girls in the other truck were wearing cowboy boots, but that meant that they could not see that she was wearing saddle oxfords.

"We'll stop at the store and meet Mike and the others at the springs," Martha explained.

Prudence looked at her quizzically. "I thought he and Mike..."

Martha shrugged. "Boys. They never can stay mad at each other for long."

After a quick stop at Smith's Market, they were on their way, heading northwest up the aptly named Hot Springs Boulevard. It was a beautiful day. The sky was a deep, clear blue, with just a few wisps of cloud high in the atmosphere. The air was, as usual, warm and dry. It was far too noisy in the open bed of the truck for any conversation, so Prudence lifted her face to the breeze created by the speed of the truck. The sagebrush and other shrubs and grasses along the side of the road were a mere blur as the truck sped past. The road climbed the side of the mountain, and almost before she was aware of it, they were in a forested area of evergreen trees and shrubs and green grasses. Martha nudged her and pointed up ahead to the right. There rose Montezuma Castle, with its cupola and turrets visible through the trees. Prudence thought of what it must have been like to have stayed there when it was a resort spa and sighed.

The truck slowed down and pulled in behind the other pickup off the side of the road. They scrambled out of the bed and carried the towels and picnic hampers up to the hot springs, just a few steps away. Martha and Maria quickly twisted their long hair into a bun high on the back of their heads to keep it from getting wet. They all stripped off their clothing and left it in neat piles on convenient rocks away from the water. Prudence couldn't help but notice that Liz's bathing suit was as new and stylish as her own, with one of the new loose, thigh-length tunics, while the others wore suits that had seen at least one season, if not more. Anne's and Maria's in particular were from a more modest era, with higher necklines and attached skirts, and they looked like they were made of wool. Liz also donned a bathing cap to protect her carefully waved shingled hair. She and Prudence were the only two who wore any makeup other than lipstick.

The boys removed their hats, and Prudence saw that, unlike the other three, Tom did not sport a crew cut. His thick, black curly hair was brushed back from his forehead with just a hint of a side parting. With his dark eyebrows and thick dark eyelashes, he bore a striking resemblance to the motion picture star, Ramon Novarro, a resemblance he clearly cultivated. Not for the first time Prudence found herself wondering whether the Morgans had any Spanish ancestry. She also noticed that Gene was rather more freckled than he had appeared in the dim lights of the YMCA dance hall.

There was a series of three stone and cement hot tubs rising up the slope. The mineral odor arising from them was noticeable, but not unpleasant. "These are the old tubs from when the Montezuma was a spa," Martha explained. "The hottest one is at the bottom and they get cooler going up, so we usually start at the top and work our way down."

"Not me!" said Tom. "I'm no sissy," and he plunged into the lowest pool. "C'mon, chickens," he shouted at the other boys, who shook their heads, but joined him, squawking as they entered the steaming water. The girls rolled their eyes at this adolescent display.

Prudence thought that the first pool was quite warm enough. The girls leaned back and allowed the soothing warmth to lull them into a tranquil state. They ignored the splashing and shouting from the boys in the bottom pool. Prudence felt the stress of the past day slip away as muscles she'd hadn't realized were stiff and sore began to loosen and relax. Her mental stress also seemed to lessen. She listened to the other girls chatting half-heartedly about various topics, including classes and teachers and homework.

"Are you all students at the university?" she asked.

"All except Liz," Anne said. "Right now, we're off for the summer and we're working all the hours we can to make money for the school year. We'll go back to part-time work in the Fall when school starts up again."

Prudence remembered her summers spent at a cottage by a lake or shopping and going to the moving pictures and pottering around the garden at home. She hadn't known any girls who worked during the summers and certainly none of her friends would have even thought about working during the school year.

Liz drawled lazily, "I've had enough school to last me a

lifetime. I just want to have fun while I'm young enough to enjoy it, not spend my time with my nose in a book. And I certainly have no intention of becoming an old maid schoolteacher and spending the rest of my life stuck in a classroom with a dozen snot-nosed brats. Of course, I won't have to."

The others glanced at each other but said nothing in response. Prudence sensed that there was underlying resentment, but whether due to her attitude toward teaching or something else, she didn't know. Not that her attitude toward teaching wasn't enough to explain it.

"What about them?" She pointed with her chin toward the boys in the lowest pool.

Anne answered again, "Mike and John are studying agriculture at the university in Albuquerque. They plan to work for a state department of agriculture when they graduate. Gene is studying business there. He says he's going to run the ranch from the office, not the back of a horse." Prudence noticed that she said nothing about Tom and neither did Martha.

"Clara has told me her plans, but what are yours?"

And, again, it was Anne who answered. "Once we graduate, Mike and I are getting married."

The other girls rolled their eyes. Obviously, this was something they heard regularly. "We're going to move to Arizona or Utah. Some place where there are enough Mormons that they have a real church and aren't just meeting in people's houses."

"So, you are going to convert, then?" asked Clara.

Anne shrugged. "Might as well. It will make things easier, especially when we have kids."

"Does that mean that you'll let Mike have other wives?" Prudence asked.

Anne groaned. "Mormons don't do that anymore. Not for something like forty years or whatever. Sure, there are still some around who got married back then, but they keep it quiet and they are dying out. And, no, even if they did, it does not mean that I'd agree to it! Although, an extra pair of hands to help around the house might come in handy." They all laughed at this. "Anyway, I'll teach until the kids come, then once they are old enough to be in school, I'll go back to it. It's a good job for a wife and mother and it will be easy to find a job no matter where we live, and it's a lot less messy than nursing. Martha, on the other hand..."

"I've always wanted to be a teacher, for as long as I can remember," she said. "It's more than a job to me. It's a... well, a calling. I can't imagine anything more fulfilling than preparing the next generation to succeed at life. And, yes, it's a lot less messy than nursing."

"Following in her father's footsteps, you know," Anne added.

"He's a professor," Martha explained, "At the university. But, I want to be an elementary school teacher. I'd much rather work with children than with.... well, with us." They laughed.

"But don't you want to have children of your own, as well?" Anne, as usual, asked the question that they were all thinking. "Not just spend your life working with other peoples' kids?"

"Oh, yes, I'd like to get married and have a family of my own," Martha admitted, a bit dreamily. "If I can find the right man, but, so far... he just hasn't come along."

Prudence looked at Maria. "I'm not really sure..." she seemed uncomfortable with the unspoken question.

"Ready for the next one?" Clara asked. The water now felt cool and, when they got out of the tub, they shivered at the contrast of the air on their heated bodies. They slid gratefully into the second pool. All attempts at conversation ceased and even the boys had quieted in response to the calming effect of the steaming water.

After just a few minutes, Liz climbed out of the pool. "I don't know about you," she said to the girls, "But I didn't come here just to use two out of three."

She squeezed into the third pool between Gene and Tom. Gene looked blissful. Tom looked even smugger than usual, as he leaned back and stretched his arms along the back of the pool. The other girls looked at each other and shook their heads. This second pool was quite warm enough for them and the third pool was far too crowded now, in more ways than one. Maria looked at it wistfully.

Just when Prudence thought she was starting to cook, Tom pulled himself out of the pool. "I don't know about anyone else, but I'm hungry!" He grabbed a towel and dried himself off. The other boys followed suit, with Liz languidly leveraging herself out. She trailed her fingers along Gene's back as she walked past him to pick up a towel. He turned his head to follow her with his eyes.

"Ladies?" asked Martha. The girls got out and joined the boys at the picnic hampers. The others paired off—Mike and Anne, John and Clara, Tom and Maria, and Gene and Liz. Martha grinned at Prudence, "I guess that makes us the old maids."

They sat on their towels and passed around the sandwiches, fruit, cookies, and drinks. They were silent except for the sound of chewing and the occasional murmured request. With their hunger sated, they laid back on the towels, and let the sun begin to dry their bathing suits. It wasn't long before all of them had dozed off.

Prudence was awakened by the sound of voices. She sat up. Martha, Anne, Clara, Mike and John were dressed and were packing up the leftover food and trash into the picnic hampers. Martha was saying, in a low voice, "I'm sorry. I didn't know. Why does he always have to ruin everything?" She sounded close to tears. Mike and John studiously looked away, busying themselves with cleaning up the area.

"If he's taken advantage of Maria, I'll never forgive myself, or him," Martha slammed shut the lid of a hamper. "And neither will her parents."

"It's not your fault, Martha," Anne said. "You couldn't know, and you couldn't do anything about it, anyway. Besides, even Tom wouldn't get up to too much with his sister only a few yards away."

"Anne's right, Martha," Clara agreed. "All you can do is not allow it to ruin the day." She turned to John, "Put the picnic hampers in Tom's truck. We'll all be riding back with you. We'll take the towels to sit on."

John nodded and he and Mike lifted the picnic hampers into the bed of the truck.

Prudence's bathing suit had dried as she slept, so she quickly dressed and helped to fold the towels. She wondered what the girls were talking about and also where the others were. She started to ask, when Tom and Maria came out of the trees. His arm was around her shoulders, and she was clinging to his waist and looking up at him with a vacuous smile on her face. Martha looked relieved to see that, while she looked more than a little tipsy, her clothing wasn't disarranged, so the worst hadn't happened. They were followed by Gene and Liz in much the same condition. Gene held a flat bottle in his free hand. It was nearly empty. So that was what they were talking about, Prudence thought. Tom, Gene, and Liz all held lighted cigarettes between their fingers. Tom offered his to Maria, who shook her head. He laughed and took a deep drag.

"'Bout ready?" Tom asked loudly. He laughed. "C'mon... Let's get this show on the road!" He led Maria to the truck, opened the door, and motioned her in with a wide, sweeping bow. She giggled and grabbed the door frame. She stepped up on the running board, then fell backwards. "Upsy-daisy," he said, as he caught her and shoved her into the cab, smacking her bottom, and closed the door. She giggled again.

"Let's go, Martha," Tom shouted.

"Prudence and I are going back with Mike," she replied. "Same for John and me," Clara added.

"Well, then, looks like it's you and Liz," Tom said to Gene, who pulled Liz, stumbling, to the back of the pickup. After several false starts, they managed to climb into the back, where they lay giggling on the floor. Tom started the truck and sped out, spraying dirt and gravel as he left.

As soon as Tom drove off, Martha climbed into the bed of Mike's truck, where Prudence, Clara, and John joined her. Anne passed the towels up, then got into the cab where Mike waited. After everyone had settled safely, Mike negotiated the turn and headed back down the mountain. The tension in the back of the truck was palpable, and they all breathed an audible sigh of relief and relaxed as they got down to the bottom of the road without running across a wrecked truck.

* * *

FARTHER DOWN the road, Officer Jim Phelps sat up straight in his patrol car as a pickup truck came careening down the mountain, swerving sharply back and forth. He leaned forward and switched on his siren, then pulled out and sped after the truck. The truck slid to a stop at the side of the road, the gravel piled up against the tires, whether because the driver had decided to stop or had lost control wasn't clear. The angle of the tires and the way that the bed of the truck was swung to the right suggested a bit of both.

Jim stopped behind the truck and walked up to the driver's side door. He noticed Gene Parkinson and Liz Kearney lying in the bed of the truck. Gene looked rather greenish and had his hands on his stomach, while Liz was pale and holding her head. The window of the cab was rolled down, and Jim could hear someone sobbing softly. He also heard Tom Morgan scolding, "C'mon, stop cryin'. Nothin' happened. We're fine. Yu'd think we went off a cliff, way yer carryin' on."

"Hi, Tom," Jim said. He leaned forward into the cab. "Where's the fire?"

"Huh?" Tom looked confused. "Wha'—oh, I getcha'. You mean, how come I was drivin' so fast?" He giggled.

"Uh-huh. That's just what I mean," Jim responded.

"Well, ya' see," Tom leaned forward confidentially, "I gotta get little Miss, Miss… "

"Herrera," supplied Jim. Maria squeezed her eyes shut as the tears flooded her cheeks.

"Right! Miss Her..rer…a home to her mommy and daddy. She don't wanna be late for dinner." He giggled again.

"Smells to me like maybe you been drinkin' some, too, Tom."

Tom snickered. "Well, maybe I did have a snort or two, but nothin' I can't handle."

"Uh-huh," said Jim. "How about you step out of the truck here and show me how well you can handle it?" Jim stepped back to give the door room to open.

Tom shook his head in disgust. "Cops!" but he opened the door and started to fall out. Jim caught him and eased him out, then leaned him up against the back of the truck.

"Think I'd better drive you kids back to town," Jim said. Tom nodded woozily. Suddenly, Gene shot up and leaned over the far side of the truck bed and noisily vomited the contents of his stomach. Liz moaned and retched, but didn't quite vomit.

"Chicken," Tom muttered, leaning over and looking in

the bed of the truck. "Can't hold his liquor. How you doin', baby?" he asked Liz. She moaned in response.

"We'll be callin' your folks to come pick you up from the station," Jim said to the two in the back, "And yours," he said to Maria through the open front door. "And you," he took hold of Tom's arm, "will be our guest for tonight, at least." He walked Tom to the cab door and helped him up onto the seat.

Tom slid to the middle of the seat next to Maria, who was sobbing softly and steadily. Jim looked back along the road to where he could hear another truck coming at a reasonable rate of speed.

* * *

MIKE SLOWED as they passed two vehicles pulled over to the side of the road. The one in front was Tom's pickup and the one behind was a police car. Jim was standing at the open door of the pickup. He waved at them as they drove past. They could see Tom sitting in the middle of the front seat, Maria beyond him, and Gene and Liz lolling in the bed of the truck. Martha laughed and shook her head. "Well, it could have been worse. Too bad it won't teach him anything."

Looking back, Prudence saw Jim take his place behind the wheel, and follow them down the mountain toward Las Vegas, leaving his patrol car behind. She lost sight of the truck as they curved around a bend in the road.

"Do you think they'll arrest him?" Prudence asked. The others shrugged and shook their heads.

"Who knows? Won't make any difference," Martha repeated. "I'm sorry the day had to end this way," she said to the others.

"Goodness, Martha," Clara said, "It's not as if Tom asked your permission to bring that hooch. I, for one, am not going to let his bad behavior ruin what has otherwise been a perfect day."

"It's not like it's the first time he's done something like this," John added. "We all knew the chance we were taking when we invited him. It'd have been more unusual if he hadn't brought a bottle." Clara glared at his tactlessness. He shrugged.

"He has a point, Clara," Martha sighed. "It's Maria I feel bad about. Gene and Liz knew what they were doing, but she's..." she shook her head.

"Such an innocent," Clara finished. Martha nodded.

Mike pulled up to the curb at the back of the Castañeda. Clara jumped out as soon as the truck stopped moving and headed toward the hotel, calling back to the others, "I'll phone the Herrera's so someone is there to pick up Maria when Jim gets to the station. She'll be upset enough at being brought in without having to wait for someone to come get her!"

Mike and Anne got out and came around to the back of the truck. Anne started to apologize, but Prudence interrupted her.

"It was a wonderful day," she asserted. "I'd never been to any hot springs before, and the weather couldn't have been more perfect. I feel so relaxed and calm. I wish the feeling would never end. And my skin has never been smoother. Thank you again for inviting me." She stepped over the tailgate and allowed Mike to assist her to the ground.

The others waved at her as they drove off, and she returned the gesture. She hurried up to her room to change into clean underwear and her other pair of jeans. She'd need to find a laundry soon at this rate.

There was time now before dinner to write a long, detailed letter to her mother and Wally. She only needed to write the one, as it was a given that her mother would invite Wally over and read it to him. That also meant that discretion was called for. She decided not to tell her everything about Jerry Begay, and to say nothing at all about Tom Morgan and his bootlegging, or anything else that might upset her mother. She sat down at the writing desk, removed a sheet of the hotel stationery from the pigeonhole where it was kept, and dipped the pen in the ink bottle. She thought for a moment, then began to write.

Dear Mother,

By now, you should have received the postcard I sent you with a picture of the Castañeda on it. My room is on the second floor in the back, away from the noise of the trains. You'll laugh to hear that I am sharing a bathroom with everyone on the floor! Thank goodness the maids clean and tidy it every day.

The trip out here was rather uneventful. During the layover in Chicago, I took the opportunity to explore Union Station. There is so much more to it than we have seen when we've rushed through on our way to the Palmer House! The architecture, the statuary, the shops, and, of course, the Harvey restaurants. We must have dinner there the next time we visit Chicago. I ate dinner both nights at a Harvey restaurant, and both meals were truly excellent. They are very clean and the service is impeccable. I'm sure you would enjoy it.

I know you were worried, but I felt perfectly safe on the train, with the porters and conductors always available if needed. And I met the most interesting people! Believe it or not, my companion at lunch was a Harvey Girl from the La Fonda in Santa Fe. Could it be a sign that I'm on the right track? I also met a woman rancher, can you imagine? She was wearing men's clothing on the train! And now, picture your daughter also wearing blue jeans in public! Women here wear them everywhere, along with cowboy boots and even cowboy hats. When in Rome, they say, so I headed to the local department store first chance, but I drew the line at a cowboy hat and boots. Wally won't be surprised to hear that I've also ordered several split skirt and blouse combinations from the local seamstress, as well, in order to fit in with the natives!

A very nice, older man who was on his way to Gallup, where he lives, treated me to breakfast and answered all of my no doubt annoying questions about the geography and the flora and fauna of the land we were traveling through. He provided me with a New Mexico native's view of the country.

Las Vegas is a charming little town. They have an adorable little Carnegie library that is a scale model of Jefferson's Monticello. The Old Town Plaza was built when Mexico owned this land and is quite evocative of the Southwest at that time, with the adobe buildings that surround it. I ate lunch at the Plaza Hotel, an unexpectedly elegant little gem.

The people here are so open and friendly. The first night I was here there was a dance at the local YMCA. I met some of the young women who work at the hotel over there and they introduced me around. It was such fun! I was afraid that it would be mostly square dancing and other country dances, but they all knew most of the latest dances. I suppose they learn them from the movies. I was able to teach them the Black Bottom, and they picked it up quite quickly. The band was not *bad, considering. What they lacked in skill they made up for in volume.*

The same young women invited me to join them and their boyfriends at the old Montezuma Resort hot springs this morning. The Montezuma is now a Baptist college and closed to the public, but anyone can use the hot springs. We lazed in the hot water and then ate a picnic lunch. We must plan a vacation to one of the hot springs resorts nearer to Cleveland, perhaps Hot Springs, in Arkansas. It would do wonders for your arthritis!

Wally will be interested to hear that there are HarveyCars lined up outside the hotel every morning and I was able to sneak a peek inside. The White Motor Company can be justly proud of their product.

I will write again before I leave Las Vegas. Your loving daughter,

Prudence

P.S. Please reconsider and invite someone to visit while I'm gone. I'll feel better knowing that you aren't alone in the house at night.

She felt dissatisfied with the letter, leaving out the most important people and events, but she knew that her mother would be confused and worried if she told her about the Indians found dead from poisoned bootleg, about the fight at the dance and Tom's behavior this afternoon, and, most particularly, about Jerry. Given that she would likely never see him again, there was no reason to mention him to her mother at all beyond that slight reference. She smiled to herself at her duplicity. Jerry *was* older than she by five years and he *was* a native of New Mexico. She left the letter at the reception desk on her way to the restaurant to be sent on the morning mail train.

* * *

WHEN JIM pulled up to the front of the police station, another car was turning into the parking lot. As he got out and helped Tom out, the car stopped, and Mr. Herrera jumped out. He rushed across the parking lot, past Jim and Tom walking toward the station and opened the passenger door of the pickup. He reached in and lifted his daughter out. She was sobbing and repeating, "Lo siento! Lo siento, papà! Nunca lo haré otra vez."

He embraced her and murmured, "Tranquílate. Tranquílate. No tienes la culpa, hija mia." He raised his eyes to stare across the bed of the pickup to where Tom was being led into the station by Jim. "Es ese… ese sinverguenza… que lleva la culpa. Es un diablo quien tienta los inocentes." He looked down at his daughter, whose sobs were abating. "Vamos a casa, hija. Tu madre nos espera." They walked to his car, their arms around each other. He opened the door and closed it after her, then turned to Bill, who was standing near the bed of Tom's truck. "I will take her home now," he said. "This will not happen again. I shall see to it." Bill nodded and watched as they drove off.

"All right, come on, you two," he leaned over the bed of the truck. "Let's get you out of there." He walked around to the back and lowered the tailgate. "Looks like you'll have to crawl out."

Gene and Liz both crawled forward. Bill reached in and helped Liz to swing her legs around over the edge and then slide out and down until she was standing. Gene had managed to do the same without help, clutching the side of the truck. "You'll both have to wait inside until someone comes to get you." He assisted Liz up the stairs toward the open door. Jim hurried down the stairs to help Gene, who was slowly negotiating the first step.

"I called your house and your mother's on her way," Jim told him as they made their way up the steps. "Your father said he'll send one of the hands," he called up to Liz. She nodded, then sat heavily on a chair just inside the door. Gene sat on the chair on the other side of the door.

Tom was already in a cell in the back. They could hear him shouting, "I ain't sharin' no cell with no Injun!"

"Your turn to deal with him," Jim said to Bill. "I didn't put them in the same cell, but Morgan seems to think that there should be more than bars between them." Bill nodded and went through the door in the back wall that led to the cells. He closed the door behind him. Jim walked around and sat behind his desk. They could hear the low rumble of Bill's voice punctuated by shouts from Tom, and occasional comments from some other man.

Gene sat with his head back against the wall and his eyes closed. Liz, her eyes also closed, leaned her head against the filing cabinet next to her chair. Jim lit a cigarette, then began filling out a form, inventorying a small pile of coins, cash, keys, and other small items that was in the middle of his desk.

Liz opened her eyes and watched him for a moment. She furrowed her brow. “That’s Tom’s pocketknife,” she said. “I gave it to him. Bought it in Chicago. German blade. Had it engraved with his initials. You be careful with that.”

Jim picked it up and examined it. “Nice knife.” He opened it. “Good blade. Sharp.” He turned it over. “Ah, there are the initials.” He wrote something down on the form he was filling out and laid the knife to one side, next to the coins and cash he had already counted. He finished noting the items, then put everything in a brown paper envelope, wrote on it, and slipped into his desk drawer. He ostentatiously locked the drawer. “It’ll be nice and safe in there until we return it to him.”

The door opened and Mrs. Parkinson walked in. Jim hurried around his desk to greet her.

“Thank you for coming. Sorry we had to put you to this trouble,” Jim began. She shook her head.

“I am the one who should apologize to you,” she said in a weak voice. “Thank you for not arresting Gene.” She turned to her son, who was gazing at her with bleary eyes. “Let’s go. I need to get back.”

Jim held the door open for her. She walked slowly down the steps. Gene hurried to give her his arm and walked her to an old car parked at the curb. The body was dented, the paint oxidized to the degree that the color was impossible to determine, and the fenders rusty. He held the driver’s side door open for her, then, pulling a crank out of the back seat, ran around to the front, inserted it in the engine block and gave it several turns until the engine caught. He hurried around and got in the passenger side, tossing the crank over the seat into the back. He sat with his shoulders hunched, staring at the floor of the car. His mother slowly and carefully backed the car out and then headed in the direction of their ranch. Jim shook his head as he watched them drive away. Just as he was about to return to the office, a new pickup truck pulled up to the curb.

A young cowboy jumped out, “I’m here to pick up Liz Kearney.”

Jim nodded and walked up the steps. He opened the door, stuck his head in and said, “Liz, your ride is here.”

He assisted her with descending the stairs. The cowboy was standing at the truck, holding the door open. Jim helped her into the cab and the cowboy closed the door. He nodded at Jim, then ran around to the other side of the truck, jumped in and, turning around, drove off quickly toward the Kearney property. Jim could see Liz was leaning her head against the back of the seat.

Bill was standing in the doorway when Jim turned to go back into the office. “He’ll be tellin’ that story for weeks,” he said, “How he drove her home, just the two of them.” He shook his head. “He’d better be careful not to exaggerate too much or he’ll find himself out of a job.”

Bill closed the door and walked down the stairs to where Jim was standing. “He’s quieted down now,” he said. “Looks like our other guest won’t be getting out until tomorrow. Set up a ruckus when he saw who his new neighbor was, almost like he wanted us to keep him.”

“So, what did you hold him on?” Jim asked.

“Assaulting an officer,” Bill responded. “And I will say he gave it his best shot. Good thing those bars aren’t farther apart.” He looked around the parking lot. “Seems to me we’re minus one patrol car.” Jim nodded. “It’s up there on Hot Springs Boulevard?”

“Yeah, halfway down the mountain. Maybe ten minutes.”

“Uh-huh. I think we can risk it.” He laughed and pulled his keys out of his pocket. “Give ‘em about half an hour by themselves, see what happens.”

They got in the official pickup truck and headed up the mountain to where Jim had left the patrol car.

“Simmons is out back. Had to move quick when we saw you pull up with Morgan,” Bill continued. “He’ll be able to hear everything that’s said—if anything is. I’m not sure Morgan’s drunk enough to let anything really important slip.”

“Even to his partner?”

“I doubt Morgan considers him a partner, more like a flunky. I can’t see him seein’ any Indian as an equal.”

Bill pulled over in front of the patrol car. Jim opened the

door of the truck. "I'll see you back at the station, then."

Bill nodded. "Take it slow. We want to give them plenty of time to settle in." Jim nodded, then got out and into the patrol car. Bill turned around and headed back down the mountain. Jim followed at a conservative speed.

Bill had parked the truck and was in the police station when Jim arrived. He came out to meet him as he got out of the car.

"I can hear 'em talkin' but can't tell what they're sayin'. Simmons shouldn't have any trouble, though. I'm goin' on my rounds around town, be back in time to spell you for dinner." Jim nodded and headed up the stairs to the door of the police station.

The afternoon lengthened into evening. Jim sat at the desk, filling out forms and filing reports. He could hear the murmur of voices behind the door to the cells but could not make out words. Every so often, he would hear loud, raucous laughter, but what they were laughing at, he had no idea. His tasks finished, he settled down and lit a cigarette.

Bill returned about six o'clock, and Jim left for dinner. When he got back an hour later, Bill was leaning back in the chair at the desk, finishing a cigarette. He leaned forward and crushed it in the nearly full ash tray. The front door opened, and a tall, thin young man in a grey suit with a grey fedora tilted back on his head entered.

"Get what you wanted?" Bill asked.

Simmons shook his head and shrugged.

"Well, time, place, signal, but nothing about who is heading the whole thing. Sounds pretty much like Morgan doesn't trust his partner. Not sure he even thinks of him as a partner. All he wants to talk about is women and, I have to say, he doesn't have much respect for 'em. So, I'll be heading back to my hotel, if it's all right with you two. Oh, Morgan sounds like he's sobered up enough not to let anything important slip, so, you might want to let him go as soon as you feed him."

"Someone gonna' tail 'em?" Bill asked. Simmons shook his head.

"No, not unless one of you two want to do it. I don't have the manpower to spare. Besides, if he's been telling the truth, it's a Miss Rita's. I'm sure you both know where that is." He saluted with two fingers to his forehead, "See you tomorrow," and left.

Jim lifted the phone and asked for Manuel's. "Hi, Elena. Would you send over two of your blue plates for a couple of prisoners we have here? Yeah, uh-huh, that's right. Charge it to the city." He hung up the phone.

There was a knock on the door about twenty minutes later. Bill opened it and admitted a young Mexican man carrying two trays of food, each covered with a red checkered dishtowel and stacked one on top of the other.

"Where do you want 'em?" he asked.

"I'll take 'em," Jim said.

Bill handed the young man a quarter tip. "Come back for the empties in, say, half an hour." The young man nodded, tossed the quarter in the air, caught it, and put it in his pocket, then left.

Bill opened the door to the cells. Jim went through, carrying the trays. "OK, boys, chow time." The two men stood up next to the doors and caught the trays as Jim slid them through the slots in the bars. "Careful you don't spill that coffee."

Tom removed the cloth covering his. "Awww, c'mon, not this greaser food!"

"Don't want it, don't eat it," Jim said as he turned away.

Jerry shrugged. "Looks pretty good to me. Chile verde is one of my favorites."

"You Injuns'll eat anything."

Jerry shrugged again, sat on the bed in the cell and took a forkful of the pork, rice, and beans. "Any hot sauce?"

"Should be there," Jim answered.

He looked around the tray. "Oh, here it is, in this little cup. Slid under the edge of the plate." He tasted it, then poured it over the food on his plate and took another forkful. "That's better! Nice and spicy, just the way I like it."

Tom sat on the bed and shook his head. "Guess I'll have to eat it, if this is all we're getting." He snorted. "Not gonna waste any time once I leave here. Goin' straight to Miss Rita. She knows how to treat a man right." He guffawed loudly. "On the other hand, maybe I'll try my luck with that prissy Miss Bates. She looks like she needs what I can give." He filled his mouth with food and chewed noisily.

Jerry's jaw tightened and he stared at the floor, breathing deeply. He gripped both sides of the tray on his lap.

"Whassa' matter?" Tom asked. "Thought you liked this slop. Not hungry?"

"Not anymore," Jerry replied evenly.

"You boys about finished?" Jim asked about twenty minutes later.

"Damned straight," Tom said, shoving his tray back through the bars of the cell. "Now, when are you gonna' let me go?"

"Right now," Jim replied. He carried the tray out and set it on the side of the desk, then returned with the keys and opened Tom's cell.

"Whatta' bout him?" Tom asked, looked at Jerry.

"He's not gettin' off that easy for assaultin' a police officer. He'll be here the full twenty-four hours." Tom snickered and followed Jim out to the desk.

Jim unlocked the desk drawer and pulled out the envelope with Tom's name on it and handed it to him. "Make sure it's all there."

Tom dumped the contents out on the desk, then put the pocketknife, cash, and coins in his pocket. "Oh, I trust you, officer" he said in a singsong. He picked up his key ring.

"Then sign here," Jim indicated a line on a form. Tom dipped the pen in the inkwell and signed his name with a flourish and a blot. He grinned, picked his hat up from the peg by the door and shoved it on his head, then went out the door, letting it slam behind him. A few moments later, they heard the sound of his truck starting up and driving away.

Jim returned to the cells. "You finished?" he asked. Jerry nodded and slid the tray toward him. "Can I get you anything else?"

"Just out of here," Jerry said with a wry grin.

"Sorry, but that'll have to wait until tomorrow. Unless you assault any other officers."

Chapter 8

Monday

June 3, 1929

Las Vegas, Day Four

WAS IT ALREADY THE morning of her fourth day in Las Vegas? The halfway point. And Prudence had worried that a week was too long! What would she do today? She stretched and contemplated her options. The whistle of the train as it pulled in told her that the restaurant would soon be crowded with arriving passengers. She'd better shake a leg if she wanted to use the bathroom before the new guests finished breakfast.

She passed several people going upstairs on her way down and heard the HarveyCars start up as she entered the restaurant. She'd timed it just right. The dining room was practically empty. Martha looked tired, with dark circles under her eyes.

"Is something wrong?" Prudence asked her in concern.

She nodded. "It's Tom, but I can't talk now. I get a coffee break in half an hour, though."

"Let's talk then," Prudence agreed, then ordered her meal. She ate slowly, to make the meal last until Martha's coffee break time.

After Martha had cleared the table, she returned with two cups of coffee and sat in an empty chair. "I shouldn't be sitting here in the dining room, but there's no one around, and... Tom was arrested yesterday, you know." She took a sip from her cup. "But he didn't come home when they let him out. I thought they'd kept him overnight, but the Chief told me this morning that they let him out around eight o'clock last night. My mother is frantic with worry! We don't know where he could be!"

"Have any of his friends seen him? Mike or John or Gene?"

She shrugged. "I haven't had a chance to ask them, but I doubt it. They're all at work now—they all work on Gene's father's ranch in the summer—and if he'd gone by one of their houses last night, their parents wouldn't have let him stay." She shook her head. "They don't like him much. And if they knew he'd been arrested, even just for drunk driving... Gene's mother had to drive in to the police station from the ranch yesterday to pick him up, so his parents knew, for sure..." She stared down into her cup, as if looking for answers in the coffee. "Liz's father had to send a hand in to do the same thing and Maria's father picked her up at the police station when they got here, so I guess nearly everyone knows."

"Have any of the girls seen him?"

"I asked Anne and Clara. They haven't. Maria and Liz work mornings at Ilfeld's. I could try to get over there before my lunch shift..."

"I could ask them for you. I don't have anything planned for today."

"Would you? I'd sure appreciate that. Maria works in the kids' department and Liz is in ladies' lingerie." Despite the seriousness of the conversation, Martha rolled her eyes.

"Isn't she just?" agreed Prudence with a laugh. "I know this is none of my business, but why don't you other girls like Liz?"

Martha sighed. "It's not that we don't like her, it's more that she doesn't like us. Ever since her father started making money when we were in high school, she's changed. She always did like the best of everything, but now... nothing here is good enough for her, including us. She goes to a 'modiste' in Chicago for her dresses and only buys the most expensive clothes that Ilfeld's sells and then has them altered to fit her. Her hair used to be as brown as mine. She spends half her salary just keeping it up." She laughed. "She only wears real jewelry, real stones set in twenty-four-carat gold and sterling silver—or platinum. No plate or rhinestones for her." She shook her head. "And there's something else, but none of us know what it is. She's just… different. Secretive. She always was 'daddy's little princess' and could be nasty, but now… I don't know. She can be cruel. Always making snide comments about us going to college to be teachers and working for a living the rest of our lives." She shook her head.

"But, she works at Ilfeld's."

"That's just for something to do and to get out of the house. When she feels like it. She shows up when and if it suits her. They only hired her because her father's rich and they want his business, and they only keep her because her mother's friends ask for her by name. And she does give the place a certain tone. I suspect that they get most of her salary back in purchases, as well."

Prudence nodded. "I see… Well, I'd better get on my way. I'll let you know what I find out."

There was no Jerry Begay to accost her this morning. She wondered whether he had spent another night in jail, sobering up. He was so different from the man she had met on the train…

She relived their breakfast conversation as she again retraced her steps to the Plaza and Ilfeld's Department Store and was there almost before she realized it. She paused to admire the three-story Italian Renaissance building abutting the Plaza Hotel. She'd been in too much of a rush on her previous visits. Although, like the Hotel, the store was smaller than the grand emporiums of Chicago and Cleveland, it was architecturally their equal and was larger than she had expected to find in this wild west outpost. She stopped again just inside the front door and looked around the well-lighted first floor.

"May I help you, miss?" a tall, well-groomed man in a tailored business suit asked her politely.

"Yes, I am looking for the Children's Department."

He nodded, "Ah, yes. It is on the third floor. Madam can find the elevator straight down this aisle." He swept his hand and arm in the direction indicated and bowed slightly.

"Thank you," Prudence smiled as she walked toward the back of the store, past the hardware, home furnishings, and saddlery on the first floor. The store assistant obviously assumed that she was shopping for children of her own.

The elevator opened to a floor featuring shelves and racks of children's clothing, shoes, and even a few toys. Prudence walked slowly down the aisle, looking to both sides in search of Maria. She finally found her about half-way down, tidying a display of infants' nightgowns. Maria turned at the sound of Prudence's footsteps approaching. She was heavy-eyed and moved slowly, as if in pain. Prudence suspected that she was feeling the effects of drinking the previous day. Maria smiled cautiously.

"Hello, Prudence."

"Hello, Maria." Prudence spoke softly, in deference both to the workplace and to Maria's hangover. "I'm sorry to bother you at work, but Tom is missing and Martha asked me to help find him. We're wondering if you saw him yesterday after he was released from the jail?"

Maria shook her head and winced. "

"I haven't seen him and I'm not going to. Even if my father hadn't threatened to shoot him if he came near me again—and I think he would—I wouldn't see him again. I've learned that everything that everyone says about him is true." She shook her head sadly and winced again. "I knew he had a bad reputation, but I thought that's all it was... a reputation. I thought that he just needed someone to believe in him. But, the way he drove down that mountain, he could have killed us all, and I don't think he would have cared." She looked away. "My father called him 'shameless' and a 'devil,' and I agree with that. He... he kept making passes at me and didn't want to take 'No' for an answer. I think if the rest of you weren't around, he would have forced himself on me. He... he threatened to tell Mr. Ilfeld that my abuelita is Tewa." She stopped as Prudence furrowed her brow in confusion.

"Tewa?" Prudence asked. The word was familiar, but she could not recall where she had heard it.

Maria nodded and winced. "An Indian from Tesuque Pueblo."

Prudence remembered the library program on the Pueblos and also what Jerry had told her on the train. "I've heard that some people can be prejudiced against Indians.

Would Mr. Ilfeld really have fired you?"

"I don't know. I don't think so, but maybe. Tom said he would tell Mr. Ilfeld if I didn't let him do what he wanted. I didn't let him. I told him that no job is worth a mortal sin and that I would pray for him. He laughed at me. I don't know how he found out. We've never told anyone outside the family." She stopped at stared at Prudence, "Oh, please don't tell anyone! I could lose my job. And please don't tell Martha what I said about her brother! I don't know why I even told you."

"Of course I won't say anything. It would only hurt Martha. But do you have any idea where he might have gone? He took his truck when he left the police station last night. Did he say anything... unusual?"

She shook her head. "I really don't know him all that well to know where he might have gone. Yesterday was our first date, if you can call it that. But, well... it was kind of strange. In the truck, when Jim was driving us to the station, he kept giggling and saying, "You're all a bunch of chickens. Just a bunch of chickens. And I'm the rooster." Then he'd laugh and crow like a rooster and say it again. I don't know what it meant."

Prudence shook her head in bemusement. "Neither do I. Maybe nothing at all. He was pretty drunk. On the other hand, it could be a clue, some kind of code. He must have had some reason to say it, drunk or not." Her first clue in this case! Now she just needed to decode it. "Maybe it will mean something to Liz or Martha." She looked around the floor. "I was going to speak to Liz next, anyway. Where can I find her?"

"She's on the other side of this floor, in Ladies' Lingerie." Maria gestured toward the opposite corner, then turned back to folding nightgowns as Prudence started across the floor.

She found Liz primping in her compact mirror at the ladies' lingerie counter, patting the concealing powder on the dark circles under her eyes. Prudence was not surprised to find her dressed in a silk dress in the latest fashion and wearing a diamond bracelet, dress clips, and earrings. She stared at Prudence coldly, but stopped short of outright rudeness.

"May I show you something, miss?" Liz drawled insolently, slowly closing the compact.

Prudence repeated her question about Tom. "I'm sorry to bother you at work, but Tom is missing and Martha asked me to help find him. We're wondering if you saw him yesterday after he was released from the jail?"

Liz sniffed contemptuously. "I should have known you weren't here to buy anything." She shrugged. "Not that it's any business of yours, but I haven't seen him since we left him at the police station. And if I don't see him again for another month, it will be too soon." She put a hand to her temple and closed her eyes briefly. "My head... that rotgut he gave us wasn't worth it. Next time, I'll bring my own."

"But he didn't go home last night after he was released from jail and his family is worried. Can you think of any place he might have gone?" Prudence persisted.

Liz laughed scornfully. "Listen, I wouldn't worry too much about where Tom Morgan spends the night. He's always able to find a warm bed somewhere, if you know what I mean." She gave Prudence a disdainful look. "Does that shock you?"

Prudence decided to ignore the question. "Maria said that he said something about everyone else being chickens and he's the rooster. Do you have any idea what he might have meant by that?"

Liz waved a hand in dismissal. "Oh, that. He's always saying that, even when he isn't drunk. I wouldn't worry too much about what it means. I doubt it means much of anything, really." She straightened up and looked down her nose at Prudence. "Now, if you're not interested in purchasing any articles of lingerie, I would appreciate it if you would not waste any more of my time." She pursed her lips and glared at Prudence.

Prudence briefly considered asking to be shown their most expensive silk camiknickers, but decided that she *had* wasted enough time on a fruitless endeavor.

"Well, thank you for your time," she responded politely. Liz opened her compact again and smoothed an eyebrow with her little finger as she turned her back. Prudence turned on her heel and headed toward the elevator. This detective business was a lot harder than it looked in the novels. By this point, Prudence Beresford would have tracked the gangsters to their hideaway and signaled for the police. All she had were a couple of nonsensical statements which probably meant nothing at all.

The lunch crowd was in full swing when Prudence got back to the Castañeda, which had come to feel like home now. Clara was at the reception desk, looking rather bored, so Prudence took advantage of the lull.

"Martha told me about Tom going missing," she said.

Clara nodded and looked grim.

"Maria says that when the police were driving them to the station, he kept saying that they were all a bunch of chickens and he's the rooster. Do you have any idea what he meant by that?" She doubted that Clara could cast any more light on it than the others had, but she had to ask. It was the only clue she had.

Clara pursed her lips. "Well, he has always thought he was cock of the walk, ever since we were kids. He could always make Gene do anything and he'd make sure that Gene took the blame, too, when they got caught. His parents spoiled him rotten and, when she was younger, Martha refused to accept that her 'darling big brother' ever did anything wrong. His mother still denies that he has any flaws. It's always someone else's fault or some terrible misunderstanding."

Prudence hid her disappointment and nodded, remembering her first conversation with Martha. Clara sighed. "I probably shouldn't be saying this, but it's nothing that everyone doesn't already know. It doesn't help that he's so good-looking. The girls fall for him, especially the young ones who don't know any better." She looked around to make sure that no one could overhear. "It's pretty common knowledge that he's responsible for getting at least three girls in trouble. Of course, his parents deny it and blame the girls. Two of them were Mexican, so you can imagine what they said. The really sad thing is that they won't acknowledge the children. They would rather deny themselves grandchildren than accept the truth about their son. I've even heard rumors that he's been seen with Indian girls... Anyway, no, I don't know what he meant by that." She turned to a couple who had come out of the restaurant and approached the desk, "May I help you?"

Prudence nodded her thanks and went up to her room. The restaurant would still be too crowded for her to be able to speak with Martha, and she needed some quiet in which to think. What did they know? It hadn't even been twenty-four hours since he was last seen. He'd been sober enough when he left the police station to leave under his own power. If what Clara said was true, he might have gone to Gene's and manipulated him into letting him spend the night, but why hadn't he gone home? It didn't sound as if he were afraid of his parents' disapproval. They'd brush it off and blame the police for overreacting. Had anyone visited him while he was in jail? Had he received any messages? Had he said anything while he was there or as he was leaving that might indicate where he was going? If Martha would not go to the police, she would. These were questions that needed answers.

There were plenty of empty tables when she got back down to the restaurant, several of them in Martha's section. It was also quiet enough that they could have a few words together before she placed her order.

Prudence kept her eyes on the menu as if she were deciding what to order and said, "Neither Liz nor Maria has seen him. Maria did say one thing that might be a clue. Tom kept saying that they were all a bunch of chickens and he's the rooster. Do you have any idea what he meant by that?" She didn't expect that Martha would say anything different from Liz and Clara, but she could hope.

Martha leaned over to polish the table. "He means that he's their leader and they are his followers." She sighed. "I often heard him say that he was the only man among them and could make them do anything he wanted."

"Yes, that's what Clara and Liz said," Prudence said, then turned her attention to the menu in earnest. "This Albondigas Soup looks good. I'll have that." She handed the menu to Martha. "Just a glass of water to drink."

Martha nodded and walked to the kitchen to place the order.

The soup reminded Prudence of one served in Cleveland's Italian restaurants, with its little meatballs floating in a clear broth flavored with onion and bell pepper. She thought she could taste cornmeal in the meatballs, rather than the breadcrumbs of her hometown. When Martha returned to clear the table after she'd eaten, Prudence said, "Martha, one of us has to go to the police and find out if they know anything. If you won't do it, I will."

Martha looked up from wiping the table with a clean cloth. "I can't. I just can't. My parents would never forgive me if I got Tom into trouble. But I will never forgive myself if something terrible has happened to him and I could have helped him. Yes, please, would you talk to them?"

"I'll do my best."

She went back up to her room and dressed in the most professional suit she'd brought with her, slipped on her most sensible shoes, tucked her hair into her most conservative turban, pulled on a pair of plain cotton gloves, secured her envelope purse under her elbow, and headed off to do battle with the local police.

* * *

JIM SAT at the desk, writing on a report form. A cigarette burned in an ashtray on the desk near his right hand. He looked up as the door opened and a young woman strode into the station. He recognized her as one of the guests at the Castañeda. Now that he thought of it, she'd been in the back of Mike's pickup up on Hot Springs Boulevard the day before. Then she'd been dressed like any other girl in Las Vegas, in a plaid shirt and blue jeans. Today, she was dressed like the city girl she undoubtedly was, in a matching jacket and skirt, probably silk, and a turban covering her hair. She looked like she meant business. He wondered what it was. He turned the form he was filling out face down.

"Can I help you, miss?"

She approached and said, "My name is Prudence Bates. I'm staying at the Castañeda." Jim nodded. He'd been right. "Martha Morgan asked me to talk to you about her brother, Tom. He's missing. He didn't come home last night and none of his friends have seen him."

Jim nodded. "You don't say."

"His family is very worried about him."

"I would expect so, his mother and sister, anyway, but

this is hardly the first time that Tom has taken off like this. He's got a bit of a reputation for disappearin' and turnin' up again when it suits him. Martha didn't tell you that, did she?"

Prudence was forced to admit that she hadn't.

"And by my reckonin', he hasn't even been gone for twenty-four hours."

Prudence took a calming breath. "I think these circumstances warrant more attention."

Jim smiled. "What circumstances, exactly?" He picked up the cigarette, leaned back in his chair, inhaled, and blew the smoke slowly from between his lips.

"He left after being released from your jail. He had no food and no additional clothing. He may not have had any money."

Jim leaned forward, crushed his cigarette in the ash tray, and said, "Oh, he had money, all right. He had thirty-eight dollars in bills and..." He shifted a few papers, then picked one up and read "and eighty-five cents in change. Would you like to know the denominations?"

He looked up at Prudence sarcastically. "We do require all prisoners to empty their pockets, and we give them a receipt for their property—which they get back when they leave, as long as it's not contraband. Just like in the big city."

Prudence blushed and stammered. "I..."

Jim leaned forward with both forearms on the desk, "Look, Miss Bates. I appreciate that you're concerned about Martha and her parents, and I understand you wantin' to help, but you need to leave this in the hands of the professionals."

She nodded and said conciliatorily, "I just wondered if anyone had come to see him or if anyone had sent him any messages."

He shook his head, laughing. "Even we wouldn't have missed those clues."

He stood up and walked around the desk, then put one hand on Prudence's arm and the other on the doorknob. He turned her toward the door as he opened it. "Don't you worry that pretty little head about things that don't concern you. Just leave the detecting to us professionals. I promise you; Tom will turn up sooner or later like he always does. Now, if there's nothin' else I can help you with?" He pulled her gently toward the open doorway.

"No, nothing. Thank you."

He shut the door after her, turned back to the desk, and put his hands on his hips, looking at Bill and Simmons who stood in the open door to the cells, facing him.

"Did you hear?" Jim asked

The two men nodded. Bill said, "Heard enough. Doesn't sound like they know much, though. Let's just hope she takes your advice. The last thing we need is civilians getting in the way."

* * *

IF THEY'D known Prudence better, they'd have known what a vain and futile hope that was. She marched back to the hotel, disappointed and angry and determined to beat the police at their own game. If they wouldn't bother to look for Tom, she and Martha would have to take the matter into their own hands. By the time she had reached the Castañeda, however, she realized that it would be a difficult task without some kind of motor vehicle, preferably a pickup truck.

Clara called to her as she entered the lobby. "Prudence, I was hoping I'd see you before dinner. Liz stopped by on her way home. She's giving a party tonight and has invited everyone, including you."

Prudence raised an eyebrow. "Rather short notice, isn't it?"

"Of course. That's the way Liz does things, on impulse. She likes to throw people off balance." She leaned forward and lowered her voice, "It's a cocktail party, even if it isn't until after dinner. She said something about showing us all what decent gin tastes like. Don't expect to see Mike there. Or Anne, even though she's not Mormon yet. She only pushes Mike so far. And I doubt that Maria will show up. The Kearney's can be pretty… cold … to anyone they suspect is even part Mexican. Or, worse, Indian."

Prudence stared at her. "What do you mean by that?" She didn't want to violate Maria's confidence by revealing what she knew before she was certain of what Clara meant.

"Her grandmother is Tewa. Maria thinks we don't know,

and we aren't about to enlighten her. It would just upset her. If she says her family is Spanish, they're Spanish... So, are you up for it?"

"I don't have anything else planned for tonight, so why not? What time and what should I wear? And how do I get there?"

"John is borrowing his father's car, so you can ride with us and won't have to sit in the back of his pickup." They both laughed. "Martha's coming with us, too. We'll pick you up at eight. You didn't happen to bring a cocktail dress with you, did you?"

Prudence grinned. "I certainly did. A lady never goes anywhere without a cocktail dress and I hope to have opportunities to wear it at the La Fonda."

"I'd lay dollars to donuts that Liz thinks you don't have one with you. Do us all a favor and go all out. It's time someone put Liz in her place."

After an early dinner, she took a quick bath to freshen up, then slid into her best silk camisole and panty knickers. She pulled on silk stockings and rolled them down to just below her knees. Then, the cream silk slip that matched her dress. The dress itself was a sleeveless cream crepe with wide shoulder straps and a square neck and handkerchief hem. It had a black chiffon overlay, as well as a black chiffon cape. Hand-beaded seed pearls outlined the dropped waist of the dress and the neck and front of the cape and were scattered at random over the overlay. She hung a sautoir of platinum and diamonds around her neck, the tassel reaching just past her waist, and matching dangling earrings on her ears.

She carefully applied color to her lips and cheeks, outlined her eyes and darkened her lashes. Her straight bobbed hair only required a quick brush to smooth it. She tied a beaded headband around her forehead and adjusted it so that the pearl and diamond aigrette stood above her right temple and the platinum tassel just brushed the corner of her eye. Her diamond and platinum cocktail ring slipped on her right index finger, dress clips attached to both straps, and she was dressed. A little overdressed, if truth be told. She could hear her mother's voice, "A lady only wears three pieces of jewelry, dear, in addition to her wedding ring." But, Clara had asked her to go all out, so all out she would go.

She slipped on her black patent leather dancing pumps, grabbed her beaded black evening bag, pulled on her black silk elbow length gloves, slid a pair of bangles onto her left wrist, and rushed down to the lobby. Clara was waiting for her. Prudence noted that her rayon dress, which fit her well, was at least two years out of style, and that all of her jewelry was costume. She wondered if she had overdone things until Clara exclaimed, "Oh, aren't you just the cat's pajamas! You'll put Liz to shame, and no mistake. It's about time someone took her down a peg or two. Excuse my gaucherie, but I assume that all of that is real?"

Prudence nodded. "Some of it was gifts, but most of it I saved up for." If she hadn't promised to show up Liz, she'd run back up to her room and change it all.

"I'm just thrilled be this close to the real stuff," Clara laughed. She linked arms with Prudence and led her out to the car. Prudence slid in the back next to Martha, Clara got in front with John, and they headed east toward Liz's father's ranch.

Clara turned her head toward them and said, "Won't she just spike Liz's guns, though?" John shook his head and snorted in amusement but said nothing.

Martha nodded in agreement. "She'll make her look as dowdy as… well, as us!" The two girls laughed. Prudence wasn't sure that she wanted to be their cat's paw, but, on the other hand, she wasn't wearing anything that she wouldn't ordinarily wear to a cocktail party at home. And it did seem as though Liz had only invited her in order to humiliate her, so it was only fair.

"Tell me about Liz's father," Prudence said. "I should know something before I show up at his front door."

Clara turned halfway around to lean over the back of the front seat. "He was just like all our fathers until about five or six years ago. His ranch made a halfway decent living, he was a member of the Chamber of Commerce and the Elks Club—ours is the 'mother lodge' of New Mexico, you know." She rolled her eyes. "A deacon of the local Baptist church and a Mason. Mrs. Kearney was a member of the ladies' literary society and the ladies' auxiliaries of the Elks and the church. And then... he started making money. Not a lot at first, but more and more over time. First, he stopped attending church, saying that business kept him too busy. Mrs. Kearney and Liz kept coming for a while, but now they only show up at Christmas and Easter, and not always then. He still makes donations to the church regularly, and I think he kept up his dues to the Chamber, and the Elks and the Masons. He shows up at the Chamber meetings once in a while, when they are discussing some issue he cares about, but he seems to care about less and less in Las Vegas. Rumor has it that Mr. Kearney is thinking of getting involved in state politics."

"My father says that means he's planning to start bribing officials," John added as he drove.

"John, you know we don't know that's true," Martha objected.

John murmured something that sounded like, "Don't we?"

Martha ignored him and continued, "Yes, the whole family has kind of isolated themselves from the town, but... well, it's only natural. They have a whole lot more money than any of us and... well... we just don't fit into their new life."

Clara laughed. "Martha, you are just too kind and too forgiving."

She turned back to Prudence, "Liz is their only child. Mr. Kearney has been pushing for her and Gene to get married since she graduated from high school. The Kearney and Parkinson ranches are adjoining, so if those two got hitched, it would make it the biggest ranch in the county." She shook her head. "Gene is a nice guy, but... he's got three younger sisters, so his parents have put all of their hopes on him, and he doesn't want to disappoint them. He'll probably go through with it, although I can't see that he has any particular love for Liz. He's dazzled by her, but... not in love with her. She's certainly a stronger personality. She can make him do anything she wants. That's why she was better with Tom..." She stopped suddenly. The tension was thick in the car.

"You're right, you know," said Martha. "If anyone could have straightened Tom out, it was Liz, but... I don't know what happened. They seemed to be going along just fine, and then, suddenly, about a month ago, she just dropped him. Wouldn't give him the time of day. Did she ever tell you why, Clara?

"Just that she'd lost all respect for him, but she wouldn't say why."

"We're almost there, girls," John said. Clara turned around and faced the front of the car. They turned left, through a set of high gate posts and under an arch that read "Kearney Ranch." The long drive eventually led to a large, sprawling three-story house with a sweeping gravel drive. Cars and pickup trucks lined the sides of the drive. John found a spot and pulled in.

The lights were on in all the windows on the first floor. The door was opened by a dark-haired, dark-eyed, brown-skinned man in a white jacket and black trousers. They were standing in a wide hall with a broad staircase directly in front and doors on either side. The door on the left led to the dining room, where cocktail snacks were laid out on the table and buffet. The one on the right led into a living room, where the guests were mingling.

Liz came up to them as they entered the living room. She looked Prudence up and down and her lips tightened. Although their dresses were not identical, Liz's being draped cream-colored satin with the new "hi low" hem, they were otherwise both dressed with equal style and opulence, not to say ostentation, but only Prudence recognized it as such. Liz looked their group, then said to Clara, "So, you didn't bring the little squaw this time?"

"I don't know who you mean," Clara said, coldly. Liz snorted in derision. She looked at Martha and asked, "Did Tom come with you? Or is he coming by himself later?"

"I haven't seen Tom since yesterday," Martha replied.

"Oh, yes, that's right... so he's still missing, is he? Too bad. I'd hoped he'd be here," Liz sucked on the ivory cigarette holder she held in her right hand, then gestured toward the room, "We're all friendly people," she said, looking directly at Prudence, "Just go on in and introduce yourself." She wandered away.

Martha gasped at the insult. Clara laughed. "You really got under her skin. C'mon, Martha and I will do the honors."

A white-jacketed Mexican waiter approached with a tray of martinis as they entered. They removed the gloves from their right hands and tucked them into their handbags, picked up glasses, then moved further into the room, where they stood sipping as they observed the rest of the guests, who stood conversing in small groups. Everyone was holding a martini or a gin rickey in a highball glass, and some were clearly on their second or third drink. Gene, who was standing across the room, lifted his glass to them in greeting. They lifted theirs in response. Prudence found it impossible to overlook the fact that, while all of the waiters and maids were Mexican (she doubted that the Kearneys knowingly employed any Indians), none of the guests were. Few even looked like what she had learned to call "Spanish," except Martha and one or two others.

"I'm glad that consuming alcohol isn't illegal," Prudence murmured, "Just manufacturing, selling, and transporting it—none of which any of us did, unless you count walking around holding a glassful as transporting it."

"That's what makes it hard to put a stop to whoever is selling that poison to the Indians," Clara said. "They have to be caught in the act." She sipped her drink. "We wouldn't be in any danger, anyway. We're outside the city limits here and there aren't nearly enough county sheriffs who aren't paid to look the other way." She gestured with her chin, "See that man talking to John? He's a county deputy." The deputy set his empty martini glass on a side table and picked up another one from the tray that the waiter offered to him.

A young Mexican woman in a maid's dress and cap came up with a tray of finger sandwiches. They set their glasses on handy tables and each took one. Conversation paused for a moment as they ate the little sandwiches in two bites, then they picked up their glasses again and slowly moved through the crowd, nodding to people they recognized.

Martha sighed. "I really shouldn't have come. I'm too worried about Tom. I wonder why Liz thought he would be here tonight. You told her this morning that he was missing."

Prudence finished her drink but kept the empty glass in

her hand to avoid being offered another. She nodded. "Yes, that is strange. I wanted to talk to you about what we should do. The police were no help at all. That Jim talked to me as if I were a child or a hysterical old lady." She shook her head. "I don't think they are going to do anything at all. He seemed convinced that Tom would show up when he got good and ready. I think we're going to have to take matters into our own hands and go search for him ourselves."

"Let's go into the dining room," Clara said. "It's quieter there and less crowded. We won't be overheard."

They moved through the crowd toward the hall, smiling and greeting people as they passed. The only people in the dining room were a waiter and a maid replenishing their trays of drinks and hors d'oeuvre. The chairs had been moved to the sides of the room, and there was a stack of small plates on the table, as well as napkins and cocktail forks.

Martha and Clara headed straight for the table. "We didn't get a chance to eat," Martha said over her shoulder to Prudence. She and Clara took several albondigas and deviled egg halves. They sat next to Prudence on the chairs along the wall.

"Where would we look for Tom?" Martha asked. "I have no idea where to start. And when? I'm scheduled to work the rest of the week."

"And how?" asked Clara. "We'd need some kind of vehicle."

Prudence felt frustration rising. "Can you get the day off tomorrow? Would someone trade with you?" She turned to Clara, "I was hoping that maybe John would lend us his truck. I can drive it. Or could I rent one?"

Clara laughed. "John? Let someone else drive his precious pickup truck? Besides, he needs it for work." She thought. "Matt at the garage has a couple of jalopies that he rents to tourists. You could ask him."

"I'll see if I can get someone to take my lunch and dinner shift," said Martha, "But we still don't know where to look for him."

"I have an idea about that," said Prudence. "I've been thinking about it all day and... Gallinas is the Spanish word for 'chickens,' isn't it?" She asked rhetorically. "So, what else could it mean except Gallinas Creek?" She had known all along that it was a clue, and she'd finally figured it out!

Clara and Martha looked at each other. "Yes," said Clara, "So you think Tom was referring to the creek?"

"Or the river."

"But, it still doesn't make any sense that he would call the boys that."

"It came to me this afternoon. The Gallinas flows into the Pecos which flows into the Rio Grande, right?"

The other two nodded but wrinkled their brows in confusion.

Prudence looked at Martha. "And you think that Tom is getting his bootleg from someone connected to a Mexican mob."

"I do," Martha agreed.

"What if the mob is bringing the stuff up from the border using motorboats on the Rio Grande? Tom could be meeting them somewhere along the Gallinas."

Clara shrugged. "It's as good a theory as any, I suppose, but that's hundreds of miles of open country." She opened her mouth as if to say something else, then closed it, as if she had thought better of it. She and Martha looked at each other and smiled slightly.

"I think it has to be some place fairly close," Martha said. "He sneaks out about midnight and isn't gone more than two or three hours."

Prudence nodded. "I agree. Where would be an isolated meeting place, close to the water, but also accessible by truck? One where a shipment could be stashed for picking up later, if necessary?"

Martha shook her head. "I can't think of any..." She stopped and turned to Clara. "Arroyo Pecos?"

Clara nodded. "That could be it. The Gallinas Creek and the Arroyo Pecos meet and form the Gallinas River southeast of here," she explained. "There are a lot of cottonwoods growing there, which would give them cover and there's nothing much out there except for grazing cattle." She paused, then spoke slowly, "It's on the southeastern edge of the Kearney ranch."

All three stared at each other. "That could explain Kearney's sudden increase in wealth," Prudence said, almost breathlessly. "And why he and his wife broke their ties with the more conservative segments of the community. It could explain the changes in Liz, if she knew that her father was a criminal. It might even explain why Liz had broken up with Tom, if she saw him as just a puppet of her father." The other two looked thoughtful and nodded.

"So this is where you got to," John said, poking his head around the door frame. "Liz wants everyone in the livin' room."

Liz was standing next to Gene at one end of the room. They were flanked by two older couples. "Their parents," Clara whispered. Mr. Kearney was a tall, fleshy man with thinning hair and incipient jowls. His three-piece suit had been carefully tailored to hide his growing corpulence. Mrs. Kearney stood literally and figuratively in his shadow. Her greying hair was carefully marcelled, her figure was tightly corseted, and the sleeves of her navy silk dress extended below her elbows. On the other side of the young couple stood Mr. and Mrs. Parkinson. They were the Jack Sprats of the group, both being tall and lean. Mr. Parkinson had a head of thick salt and pepper hair and wore a charcoal grey suit that had been bought off the rack. Mrs. Parkinson's prematurely white hair was pulled back into a bun at the nape of her neck. Her freckled hands and face revealed from whom Gene had inherited his coloring. Only the most charitable would not have called her washed-out, long-sleeved, midcalf-length rayon dress "dowdy." It was obvious who had the money in the group.

Mr. Kearney held up a hand for silence. "Friends," he began in a loud, unctuous voice. "Friends, as some of you may know, it has long been a dream of mine—and Mr. Parkinson's—to join our two ranches together and thus form the largest spread in San Miguel County, if not the entire state of New Mexico. Well, tonight, I have the unexpected pleasure of announcing that our dream is about to be realized. My daughter, Elizabeth, has just informed me that she has accepted Eugene's proposal of marriage."

There was a brief pause, then the guests began to applaud, and cheers of "Congratulations" rang out. Several of Gene's friends moved forward to shake him by the hand and slap him on the shoulder.

Clara murmured, "So that was why she wanted Tom to be here."

Kearney raised his hand again for silence. "And, as those of you who know my little girl know, when she wants something, she wants it now. The wedding will be at the Baptist church on the first available date, and you are all invited." There were murmurs of surprise and a few eyebrows raised. Kearney slid behind Liz and slapped Gene on the back. "Welcome to the family, son," he boomed. "Let's plan to get together soon to discuss the family business and your place in it."

Gene grinned and nodded eagerly. Kearney shook Mr. Parkinson's hand and held Mrs. Parkinson's for a brief moment. He checked his wristwatch and said, "Now, excuse me, folks, but I have some business to attend to." He waved at the guests and left the room.

Mr. and Mrs. Parkinson faded away into the background. It was impossible to tell how they felt about the announcement. Liz looked, if anything, more bored than usual, as she stood next to her mother, who had her arm around her daughter's waist and a polite smile fixed on her face.

"Should we congratulate her?" Martha asked. "She doesn't look very happy about it."

"We have to say something," Clara responded. They approached in a group, Clara leading the way, Prudence hanging back.

"Congratulations, Liz," Clara said. "Looks like you'll be the first one of us to get married."

"Hmm. Yes, I suppose I will," Liz said in a weary voice.

"Gene's a nice boy," ventured Martha.

"Hmm. Yes," Liz responded again. They stood there awkwardly.

"Well," Prudence finally said. "Congratulations again." Liz just stared at her.

"We have to be on our way," Martha interjected into the silence. "Clara and I have to be at work early tomorrow."

Liz looked away from them. Her mother said, "Thank you for coming" and looked at her daughter in concern.

Martha and Prudence left the house and wandered down to where John had parked the car, while Clara went in search of him.

"She certainly doesn't seem happy," Martha began. "I know that she's not head-over-heels for Gene, but... she's in a trance. She's acting like she thinks she's some kind of sacrifice."

Prudence nodded.

"And Gene is a nice guy. Maybe a little mercenary, but still, a nice guy," Martha continued. "He deserves better than that."

John and Clara arrived in time to hear Martha's words. As John held the car door for Clara, he said, "I couldn't agree more, but he's bedazzled. Thinks she's the bee's knees. He told me that he couldn't believe it when she dumped Tom for him."

He held the door for the other two, then slid under the steering wheel. "And he's almost as much in love with her father's millions. He can hardly wait to talk with Kearney about 'the family business.' Looks like all those courses are about to pay off."

"The Parkinson's didn't seem overjoyed," said Prudence from the back seat.

"No, they aren't," John responded. "Liz isn't who they'd choose for a daughter-in-law, and they aren't crazy about the idea of her influencing their three girls. But... well, I'm not breaking any confidences to say that their ranch is losing money. Maybe if they'd had more sons or fewer daughters... but as it is, between paying us to work it for them and the medical bills for Mrs. Parkinson and the expense of raising three girls, they're barely making ends meet." He stopped talking to concentrate on negotiating a turn, then resumed, "And Parkinson isn't really much of a businessman. He's an old-style rancher, hasn't kept up with the changing times. Still uses horses for everything."

Prudence looked a question at Martha. "Women's complaints," Martha mouthed silently. Prudence nodded in understanding.

John pulled up to the curb at the rear of the Castañeda. He held the door for Prudence, who thanked him, and said, "I'll see you both tomorrow morning," as she slid out of the car. She watched it drive off before going up to her room. Tomorrow they would go detecting!

* * *

THE NIGHT was dark, with no moon, making the stars even brighter near the confluence of the Arroyo Pecos and Gallinas Creek. Small night creatures moved amid the sage and rabbit brush, hunting for seeds and insects to eat. Suddenly, the peace of the night was shattered by the muted roar of an engine and the bright, artificial lights of a pickup truck bouncing across the range land. The small creatures ran and hid and the night birds flew toward the safety of the cottonwoods in the near distance.

The truck pulled to a stop, the engine was silenced, and the lights extinguished. Tom Morgan sat back, with his hat tipped down onto his forehead. He smiled to himself, as he leisurely lit a cigarette from the packet in his shirt pocket. He shook out the match and tossed it from the open window. He settled back to wait, casually blowing smoke out of the window and occasionally shaking ash from the cigarette onto the ground.

He didn't have long to wait. He soon heard the sound of another vehicle approaching. This one was using its low beams. Tom flashed his headlights on and off. The vehicle pulled up behind him. He heard the door open and close. Then he heard the sound of footsteps coming toward him. Tom waited until he could make out a darker shape against the night sky.

"Right on time," he said, smugly. "Nice private location, too. No one will ever know except us two. So, let's have it." He put his hand out the window, palm up.

Starlight glinted off the barrel of a revolver and the silence of the night was again shattered, this time by the explosion of the gun being fired. Tom's head jerked to the right, to rest against his shoulder. His eyes stared forward at nothing. A trickle of blood started down his left temple and flowed onto his shoulder. Blood splattered the interior of the cab, and the bullet had shattered the passenger window.

Footsteps walked away from the truck, a door opened and closed, an engine sputtered to life, there was a crunching of tires on the brush, then the sound of the engine gradually died away. The small night creatures crept out from their hiding places to begin hunting again for their dinner and the owls flew down from the trees to hunt for theirs. They all gave the strange thing smelling of gasoline and sulfur and human blood a wide berth.

Chapter 9

Tuesday

June 4, 1929

Las Vegas, Day Five

ONLY THREE DAYS TO resolve the mystery of Tom's disappearance! And discover whether he was the one poisoning the Indians. Prudence rushed through her morning ablutions in her hurry to get out of the hotel and rent a car. She dashed down the stairs to the reception desk.

"Clara, as soon as I have breakfast, I'm off to rent a car. Can you give me directions to the garage?"

Clara looked at her, somberly. "I don't think that's going to be necessary." She indicated the doorway to the restaurant.

Prudence turned to see Bill and Jim supporting Martha, who was sobbing into a napkin.

"Let us take you home," Bill was saying. "Your mother's waitin' for you. Dr. Bonheim's with her, but she's askin' for you." He looked up, "Jim will go tell your father." Jim nodded but Martha probably didn't see him. They helped her out of the building.

Prudence turned back to Clara. "Tom? He's been found?"

She nodded. "Some of the Kearney hands were out looking for stray cows and found his body this morning. He was in his pickup and had been shot in the head." She paused. "You won't be surprised to hear that he was found near Gallinas Creek where it joins Arroyo Pecos."

Prudence shook her head. "I only wish that we had been wrong. There's no satisfaction at all in being right about this. Do they have any suspects?"

Clara shrugged. "If they do, they aren't saying." She shook her head, "The problem is, it could be so many people. Some Indian whose relative died from poisoned bootleg, the brother or father of a girl he ruined..."

"Maria told me yesterday that her father threatened to shoot Tom if he came near her again."

"And did you tell the Chief?"

"No, of course not," Prudence replied. "Maria told me in confidence, but... do you think he...?"

"Shot Tom?" Clara considered this. "Not like this. If he'd done it, it would have been in the heat of the moment, if he caught him assaulting Maria. He wouldn't have planned it in cold blood like this. And he'd have turned himself in. Besides, what excuse would he have given Tom for meeting him at night at that spot?"

Prudence nodded and changed the subject. She didn't want Clara asking what excuse an Indian would have given. She was all too aware of what reason a certain Indian might have used to lure Tom to that spot. "Did the Chief say that Dr. Bonheim was with her mother?"

Clara nodded. "Yes. He's the president of the Jewish congregation. They haven't been able to afford a rabbi in years, but they still meet every week. If they need a rabbi for a wedding or something, they get one in from Albuquerque or Santa Fe. The synagogue, Congregation Montefiore, is on Columbia, across from the university. It's Reform, if you know what that means." She waited.

Prudence nodded. "Yes, there's big a Reform congregation in Cleveland. I've attended the weddings of several friends and even a few funerals there."

Clara seemed to relax. It was as if Prudence had passed some sort of test. "Their name originally was Morgenstern. Mrs. Morgan's family were Spanish Jews who came over when the Jews were expelled from Spain in 1492." She laughed. "Easy to remember that year."

Prudence realized that, for all that these young women had accepted her, she really was just a stranger from the train. There was so much about them that she did not know, and still so much to learn about Las Vegas—about New Mexico—about the Southwest—that could not possibly be learned in just a week. Thank goodness for the Harvey training course!

"How did Liz's parents feel about her dating Tom?"

"About as you'd imagine." Clara laughed shortly. "They were relieved he wasn't Indian or Mexican, not so pleased otherwise. Most of us figured that she took up with Tom mainly to irritate her parents. It didn't hurt that Tom had matinee-idol looks, of course." She shook her head. "They've been off and on since high school, right around the time that she started changing. She'd always been a bit of a daddy's girl before, had him wrapped around her little finger. Nothing was too good for his little princess, but now? If she talks about him at all... it's always contemptuous. She calls him "the old man" or "the boss," never "Father" or "Daddy," the way she used to. Going around with Tom, inviting him to the house, being seen in public with him, it really seemed like it was just another way of showing her contempt."

Prudence shook her head in commiseration. "Who can say? Some people say that it's normal for teens to rebel against their parents, but... I certainly never felt the need. Why did you say that she stopped dating Tom this time?"

"She wouldn't say. Just said that she had lost all respect for him," Clara repeated what she'd said earlier.

"You don't suppose she shot Tom, do you? Hell hath no fury, you know."

Clara considered this. "I won't say that Liz would never do such a thing, but she'd need a good reason to run the risk. She's never been one to let the law or even good manners stand in the way of getting what she wanted, but... she's got too strong a sense of self-preservation. And I didn't get the feeling from what she said or the way that she said it that she was holding any kind of grudge against Tom. To be honest, I think she was lying, just saying something that people would accept without asking questions. It was hardly my business, so I didn't press." She shrugged.

"I wonder... do you think Mike... has he really forgiven and forgotten Tom spiking the punch and mocking him because of his religion?" Even as she said it, Prudence realized how ridiculous it sounded.

Clara made an effort not to laugh. "Do you think that's

enough to justify murder? Especially a person like Mike. He has a strong moral code, you know. Yes, he'd get into a fist-fight with Tom, but murder? I don't see it. And, like Mr. Herrera, if he did, it would be in the heat of the moment for a serious reason, and he'd turn himself in."

Prudence nodded. "Well, we won't solve the mystery by standing here talking about it. And I suppose I should go get some breakfast and keep my appointment with Miss Jensen for my fittings."

In the restaurant, it was obvious from their faces that the other waitresses had heard the news. Anne had tears in her eyes when she came to take Prudence's order. Prudence was glad that she felt familiar enough with her to display these signs of grief.

"Isn't it awful?" Anne whispered. Prudence nodded. "I hate to say it," Anne continued, "But… I don't think anyone is really surprised, except maybe his mother. Everyone knew he was headed for a bad end. Well, they'll have their pick of suspects, everyone from Indians to enraged fathers to girls whose hearts he broke." She wiped her tears away and asked, "What can I get you?"

Prudence was relieved to be able to get away from the hotel after she had finished her breakfast. The seamstress' shop would provide a welcome respite from constant reminders of the recent tragedy.

"Ah, Miss Bates! So glad to see you! Everything is ready for your fittings, if you'll just follow me." Miss Jensen led her through the curtained alcove to a fitting room. "If you will just remove your outer garments, I'll be right back."

She was as good as her word. Prudence had barely hung her dress on the padded hanger provided when there was a knock at the door. She opened it and accepted the six hangers of clothes. "Just step out when you're ready," Miss Jensen instructed.

Prudence slipped on the first skirt and blouse combination and stepped out into the mirrored alcove where Miss Jensen waited. She walked and turned as directed, then stood still as a young Mexican woman knelt down on the floor and pinned the hem. No other alterations were deemed necessary, which was hardly surprising with such simple designs, but still spoke to the skill of the seamstresses. She repeated the process with the other two outfits, with the same result. The A-line skirts fit closely at the waist, then flared to the hem, swirling when she turned. The silk blouses buttoned without gaping, and the open collar created a flattering V-neckline. She might need to purchase a short pendant necklace or two to go with them.

The bell of the shop rang as someone entered. Miss Jensen excused herself. "I'll just go see who that is." She turned back to Prudence. "We have all we need, my dear. Now, if you'll just leave them in the fitting room after you've changed..." She left the alcove, pulling the curtains closed behind her. Prudence could hear the murmur of voices through the closed fitting room door and then Miss Jensen's voice coming closer.

"Just in here, my dear," Miss Jensen said. "If you'll just remove your outer garments, I'll take your measurements. Just step out when you're ready." Prudence heard the other fitting room door open and close.

She adjusted the seams in her stockings, touched up her lipstick and face powder, and settled her cloche on her head. Just as she opened the door to her fitting room, the door of the other room also opened. Liz stood there in her slip, and her condition, while still slight, was too obvious to miss in the form-fitting garment. Their eyes met. Liz's lips quirked. Miss Jensen gasped and shooed the seamstress out of the alcove. Miss Jensen turned back, her hands fluttering, but before she could say anything, Liz drawled, "It was bound to come out sooner or later," then laughed at her own joke.

Liz was the last person she had expected to see at Miss Jensen's, but if she was getting married in a few weeks, there wasn't time for a trip to Chicago to have a wedding dress made. And Liz's secret was safe with Miss Jensen. It wouldn't be the first—or the last—such secret she kept. A seamstress' reputation for discretion was paramount.

Miss Jensen looked back and forth between the two of them and fluttered her hands. "Miss Kearney... Miss Bates... I..."

"Leave us, Jensen," demanded Liz.

Miss Jensen backed away, closing the alcove drapes behind her.

Liz stared at Prudence. "I want a word with you."

"Yes?"

"Not here where everyone is listening. Wait for me outside."

"All right, but first I'm taking care of the business I came here to do."

Liz flapped a hand in her direction. "Do it, then wait for me. Just don't take too long."

Prudence returned to the front of the shop, where she paid Miss Jensen, who promised to have the skirts and blouses delivered to her room at the Castañeda. She walked up and down on the sidewalk in front of the shop until Liz came out, then suggested that they sit in the plaza.

"Good idea," Liz responded. "We'll be able to see if anyone is coming."

They seated themselves on a bench. Prudence waited quietly. Liz turned to her, "This is not my fault!"

"You mean, he forced you?"

"Of course he didn't force me. No one makes me do anything I don't want to do. No, he lied to me. He said he knew how to prevent this. I took his word for it." She sniffed in disgust. "That was my mistake. I should never have left it up to him. If you want something done right, do it yourself, I always say." She shook her head. "After all, why should he care? He's not the one who's knocked up."

Prudence flinched at her vulgarity. "Have you told your parents?"

Liz looked at her in astonishment. "What do you think? My father... His reputation is everything to him, after his money. I don't know whether he'd have shot him or dragged us off to the justice of the peace. Or both." She sighed. "I think my mother guesses, but she won't say anything to upset my father." She laughed sarcastically. "She never does."

"Does Gene know?"

"Gene? Hardly. I needed a husband, and he was available."

Prudence tried not to look as shocked as she felt that Liz's future husband was not the father of her baby. There was only one other man it could be. "Ah, then this baby is unlikely to have red hair?" she asked tactfully.

Liz laughed. "Highly unlikely. He's more likely to look like Ramon Novarro." She wrapped her arms around her body. "If only I could make people believe that's who the father really is. At least that would be romantic. This is just... common. Like any little Mexican slut." She sighed. "I had hoped that soaking in the hot springs would take care of the problem, but... no such luck. No, Gene is going to be the proud father of a premature baby. We're going to Europe for a year-long honeymoon tour. If we return with a rather large five-month-old baby, they'll just assume it's his or that they can't count." She shrugged. "He's at least as much in love with my father's fortune as he is with me, so he'll keep his mouth shut. And I don't have to worry about Tom. He made it pretty clear how he feels about marriage and fatherhood when I told him." She smirked. "Not that a woman being married would get in the way of his giving her what she wants."

Prudence went cold. Liz had not heard. She also obviously had not been the one who shot Tom. She had to tell her. "Liz... I have some bad news. About Tom."

Liz turned and stared at her. She must have read the truth in Prudence's face, because she started shaking her head. "No, no, no."

"Yes, I'm afraid so." Prudence put a hand on Liz's arm. "They found his body this morning."

Liz pushed her away. "NO! It's a mistake! It's someone else. They've made a mistake."

Prudence shook her head. "He was identified by several people who know him well."

Liz jumped up. "NO!" She shouted. "NO! NO! NO! You're lying! You're lying! You're just saying this to hurt me. You're jealous because I'm prettier than you and because a man wants me—two men want me—and you're just a dried-up old spinster of a librarian that nobody wants," she collapsed back on the bench, heaving great sobs.

If she had ever suspected Liz of murdering Tom, her reaction put those suspicions to rest. It was far too genuine and Liz had no motive to want Tom dead. Quite the reverse. She fished a handkerchief out of her bag, waited for the sobs to diminish, then quietly handed the handkerchief to Liz. She accepted it and dried her face.

"Do they know who did it?"

"Not that I've heard."

"Where did they find him?"

"I understand that he was in his pickup truck near Arroyo Pecos and Gallinas Creek."

"And it happened last night?"

Prudence nodded. Liz stared off into the distance. Her lips tightened, but she didn't say anything for several moments. Then, she took a deep breath, straightened her shoulders, and turned toward Prudence. She handed her the handkerchief. "You understand that if you say anything about any of this to anyone, I shall simply deny it. And my father will not be pleased that you tried to ruin my reputation."

Prudence nodded. "Threats are not necessary. You can trust me." She didn't add that Liz had very little reputation to protect. No one in Las Vegas would believe that Gene was the father of her child, but no one in Las Vegas would ever even hint at their suspicions in public.

"Yes, I'm sure of that. You're not stupid and, besides, you'll be leaving in a few days." She squared her shoulders, "Now, if you'll excuse me, I have a wedding to plan." She walked off toward a parked car. A man in a chauffeur's uniform got out of the front and held the back door open for her. She slid gracefully into the back seat, he closed the door, got in the front, and the car drove off.

Prudence sat on the bench, pondering what to do with the afternoon that stretched ahead of her. She did not want to intrude on the Morgan family's grief. Obviously, she was not about to rush back to the Castañeda and share the news about Liz with Clara and Anne. She'd love to investigate Tom's murder, but didn't have any idea of where to begin. As Anne had said, she had her pick of suspects. Was it a rival bootlegger? The only person she knew who might fit that description was Jerry. She was sure that he was not the only possible suspect, but had no idea who else might fit the bill. Was it related to selling poisoned liquor to the Indians? Again, the obvious suspect was Jerry. Was it some father or brother defending his daughter's or sister's honor? They'd ruled out Mr. Herrera and she didn't know who any of the other girls were, or even how many of them there were. Was it some girl he'd ruined? Again, they'd ruled out the only girl she knew of for certain. And those were only the categories of suspect she could think of. There were bound to be others. At least she could cross Liz off of the list. If only she could do the same with Jerry.

Well, it was lunch time. That was something to do. She could eat at the Plaza Hotel restaurant again. As she crossed the plaza, she suddenly turned on impulse and headed for the drug store on the corner. A sandwich or blue plate special at their lunch counter was more suited to her mood. She didn't feel up to examining a menu and making choices and the elegance of the Plaza Hotel felt smothering rather than stimulating today. She didn't admit the real reason even to herself.

The lunch counter was in the front of the store, with booths running along the windows opposite it. There were a few white faces, sitting together at a couple of the booths, but most were the brown of Mexicans and Indians. She walked down the length of the lunch counter to slide onto the vacant stool next to the dark-haired man at the far end, ignoring the glances of the other customers.

He looked up from his plate of rice, beans, and enchiladas. "Hello, Prudence," he said.

"Hello, Jerry," she replied. There was now no doubt in her mind that the man she had seen coming out of the drug store that day had been Jerry, He had lied about staying on the train to Gallup. "What are you—"

He interrupted. "Here for lunch?"

"Yes, but, I thought you said—"

Again, he interrupted. "I recommend the special."

"Is it… very spicy?"

He grinned. "It doesn't have to be. Just ask for it 'poco picante.' They're used to white people here."

Clearly, he was not going to tell her why he was here and not in Gallup. Did it have something to do with Tom Morgan and bootlegging? She pushed the thought to the back of her mind and gave her order for the blue plate special and a Coca Cola to the young woman behind the counter. She waited until the waitress had walked away before she turned to Jerry and said, "You're looking better than you were the last time I saw you."

He took a forkful of food, chewed and swallowed and said, "I should hope so. I was blotto the last time you saw me." He picked up his glass, "Just water this time," grinned and took a large drink.

"Yes, well… I much prefer you this way."

"A man has the right to relax once in a while, don't you think?"

She pursed her lips. "You were a little more than relaxed. You admitted it yourself."

He shook his head. "We all have our vices, Prudence. Even you." He laughed, "Don't be so high and mighty self-righteous. Don't tell me you've never set foot in a speakeasy."

"Of course I have, but," she lowered her voice and hissed, "I've never been so drunk that I passed out on a public street."

He looked at her appraisingly. "No, I don't suppose you have, but what about your friends?"

She opened her mouth to protest, then shut it. He stared at her, one eyebrow raised quizzically. "Yes, some of them. But I don't approve of them doing it, either, and at least they don't do it in the middle of the day, all alone."

"Ah," he responded. "So that makes it all right, as long as it's at night among friends?" He continued to stare at her, his face set.

The waitress set her Coca Cola in front of her. Prudence again waited until she had walked away. She did not want to argue with Jerry, and she had to admit that he did have a point. Why was it acceptable for her white friends in Cleveland? It wasn't, but, more than to the point that wasn't the issue. She took a deep breath and looked directly at him. "I'm worried about you."

His face softened and he smiled. He reached out and squeezed her hand where it rested on the counter. "That's sweet of you. I appreciate it. But you don't need to be. I know what I'm doing."

What was he doing? Before she could ask, her meal arrived, and they both spent several minutes eating the spicy, flavorful food. This time, Prudence didn't feel the need to take a drink between every bite and was able to appreciate the melding of chiles, corn, and chicken in the enchiladas, complemented by the earthy flavor of the mashed and fried beans, and the savory rice with onions and tomatoes. It was comforting and sustaining and very different from the food of the same name served at the Harvey House.

She decided to drop her inquiries and just enjoy Jerry's company. He obviously wasn't going to tell her what he was doing here in Las Vegas, and she didn't want to waste what little time they had together arguing.

"This is just what I needed," she said. "It has been a trying day, and it's barely noon." Jerry looked a question at her. "I heard this morning that Tom Morgan had been found murdered. Did you know?"

He nodded. "Word gets around. How do you know him?"

"I don't really know him. I know his sister, Martha, from the Castañeda. She's a waitress there. She and some of the others invited me to go to the hot springs with them on Sunday and he was one of the party. That was the day that he was arrested. Martha was worried when he didn't come home that night or yesterday. But the police refused to do anything."

He shrugged. "What could they do?"

"Something. Anything would have been better than just brushing it off."

"Do they have any idea who did it? Or why?"

Prudence shook her head. "I haven't heard, but," she looked around to make sure that no one was close enough to hear what she said, "we have some ideas." She wondered as she said it whether she was putting herself in danger, but now that she was with Jerry, she found it difficult to picture him as a murderer or, at least, as someone who would murder an innocent person. She felt slightly guilty at even suspecting him, but... how well did she really know him?

"We?" asked Jerry.

"Martha and Clara and I. She works the front desk at the Castañeda. You know that Tom was involved with bootlegging?" She blushed as she recalled why she knew that he knew, but Jerry just nodded. "Well, we think that he was getting his liquor from one of the Mexican mobs." Jerry nodded again. "We think that they came up the Rio Grande to the Pecos and then the Gallinas in motorboats, and Tom met them there where it meets the Arroyo Pecos."

"Really?" Jerry sounded amused. "That would make quite a plot for a moving picture."

"Oh!" Prudence shook her head in frustration. "But that is exactly where he was found. And," she looked around again and lowered her voice even further, "he was always calling the other boys 'chickens' and saying that he was the 'rooster,' and," she said in triumph, "Gallinas means chickens in Spanish."

"Uh-huh." Jerry took a drink of water. "So, who killed him and why?"

"Well, we're not really sure. It might have been rival bootleggers." Jerry nodded. "Or maybe it was because he was selling poisoned liquor to the Indians."

"Was he?" Jerry interjected.

"Someone has been, and we think it was him. Oh, Jerry, you must be careful. I know you bought that bottle from him."

"How do you know that?"

"I happened to see you with him that day and… I hate to think what might have happened."

Jerry squeezed her hand again. "Well, it didn't. Now, getting back to who might have murdered him. Any other candidates?"

"Well, it might have been some father or brother of a girl he… got in trouble. Or maybe one of the girls herself."

"More than one?" He again raised a questioning eyebrow.

Prudence nodded. "Yes, several. And he was trying to force Maria…"

"Is there anyone who didn't have a motive?" He laughed. "So, what are your plans for this afternoon?"

"I'm at loose ends. I had a fitting at the seamstress' this morning, but… no other plans."

"Ah, so that's why you're not wearing your blue jeans." She nodded. "Well, I just so happen to be free myself and I have… my friend's pickup, if you'd like to go for a drive?"

Her eyes widened. "Could we go to where Tom's body was found? Do you know the way?"

He sighed and shook his head. "I have an idea about the

general area, yes, but why would you want to go there?"

"To look for clues, obviously!"

He signaled to the waitress. "All right, if only to put this idea of yours to rest." He stood and pulled his wallet out of his back pocket. "Por los dos," he said.

"Jerry, I can't let you keep paying for my meals," she protested.

"Yes, you can," he replied as he steered her toward the door, then down the street to where his truck was parked. They were both aware of the stares and murmurs that followed them as they passed, but neither said anything to the other.

Jerry helped her into the cab of the truck, then got in on the driver's side, started the engine, shifted into gear, and drove off in the direction of the Arroyo Pecos. The paved street eventually gave way to a gravel road, then a dirt track, which ultimately ended at the arroyo itself.

"Well, this is as far as it goes. We'll have to go off-road now," he said. "Where, exactly, was his truck found?"

Prudence waved a hand. "Out there… somewhere." She sighed. "You're right. It's hopeless."

"We might as well get out and look around since we're here." He got out to help her to step down from the cab. "Which way?"

She stood for a moment, breathing in the scents of sage brush, creosote, and juniper. "Over there, where those trees are? They would provide cover for the exchange and could make a hiding place for a drop." She indicated a stand of juniper in the distance.

They headed across the uneven ground, Prudence holding onto Jerry's arm for support. "You and your flimsy city-girl shoes," he said.

"I wasn't expecting to be hiking through the brush when I got dressed this morning." She didn't add that it gave her an excellent excuse for holding tightly to his arm. He certainly did not seem to mind. He reached over and covered her hands with his and smiled at her.

They reached the trees but saw nothing that indicated that a truck had been parked there. "Let's head that way, toward the creek and those trees." She pointed to where a line of cottonwoods signaled the presence of water.

Jerry smiled indulgently and led her in the direction she indicated. Still no clues. After wandering around for another ten minutes or so, Prudence said, "You're right. It's hopeless. He could have parked anywhere. I don't even know what a clue would look like, to be honest." Her face dropped. "I just wanted to be able to give Martha some news, some hint as to who killed her brother."

"I know," Jerry said. He slipped his arm around her shoulder and pulled her close in a hug. "You're being a good friend to someone you just met and that's nothing to be ashamed of."

Prudence moved closer, laid her head on his shoulder, and slipped her arms around his waist. Jerry wrapped his other arm around her and rested his cheek on the top of her head. After a moment, he said, "Prudence, we can't do this."

"Why not? I think we can. I think we are." She raised her face to his. "You're not married, are you?" He shook his head. "Engaged?" He shook his head again. "Neither am I, so why not?"

He put his hands on either side of her face and stroked her cheeks with his thumbs. "You know why not. You've seen the looks people have given us just for having a meal together."

She slid her arms up his chest and around his neck. "Show me what it is we can't do, Jerry. Show me now."

She stretched up and touched his lips with hers. He lowered his head and pulled her closer. She ran her fingers through his hair and grasped the back of his head. They kissed hungrily, releasing the tension they both had been feeling since they first met on the train. Jerry began slowly kissing down her cheek toward her neck. His hands explored her body, caressing her curves. She sighed and leaned back in his arms, pressing her hips into his. She bent her knees and leaned farther back, trying to pull him down to the ground with her.

He pulled her back upright, both hands on her back for the moment. "Unfortunately," he breathed as he nibbled at her earlobe, "This is not the place for that." He chuckled deep in his chest. She flicked her tongue around his ear and whispered, "Do you have a blanket in that truck? There's no one around to see."

"Sadly, no." His hands continued their explorations, pausing now and then to give special attention.

"Mmm. That's nice," she murmured. She took a deep breath, stretched back with her arms around his neck and, looking deeply into his eyes, said, "Then let's go back to my room at the hotel."

He shook his head and brushed her cheekbone with his thumb. "Leaving aside the fact that there are plenty of people there to see, including… is it Clara? I'm not a cad. This can't work, Prudence. We live in two different worlds." He paused. "That's not really true. You live in your world. I… well… I've lived your world and…" He smiled wryly. "In college, there were girls… it didn't take me long to realize that most of them were just attracted to some kind of romantic idea of an Indian brave." He stopped and smiled at her. "You were, at first."

She dropped her eyes and nodded. "Until I saw you…"

"Until you saw me drunk." She nodded. "And then, you weren't disgusted. You were worried."

She lifted her eyes. "Well, I was rather disgusted, too."

He laughed. "And you were worried. About me. The others lost interest pretty quickly when they found out I wasn't a medicine man or a warrior, but just another poor college student. They were disappointed that I didn't have a bow and arrow stashed under the bed or a feather headdress in the closet—and that I spoke English as well as they did."

"I did not think that you had a feather headdress," she protested. "I do know more than that. But I was a bit disappointed by your hair style." She reached up and touched the hair at his temples.

He laughed again. "Give me time to grow it out." He paused. "There was one girl… my second year in college… but, then, she introduced me to her parents and that put a stop to it. They made it pretty clear that it was them or me. And by them, they meant their money at least as much as they meant their love."

He shook his head and grimaced. "And she was not willing to give up either one."

"It's not the same situation now," Prudence said. "We're

not kids anymore. We're not financially dependent on our parents. We're both adults, trained for professions. I don't know how my father would have reacted, to be honest. I was only fifteen when he died, so the question of... boyfriends... hadn't really come up. My mother?" She smiled. "I'm not sure she'd quite understand, but... family is everything to her. She'd do her best to be welcoming."

He hugged her. "I'm sure she would, but it's more than that. I used to think that I had a foot in both worlds, but I don't. I don't fit into either. I make a pretense of living in the white man's world, but I've come to realize that it's more that I live in some kind of limbo between the two worlds. I don't know if I ever can fit into one or the other, but I know which one I would choose to live in, if I could. And it isn't yours."

"And I don't suppose that I would fit into... the one you would choose?"

He shook his head. "We'd be more likely to be accepted... barely. Most of my family already has doubts that I can live as a Navajo, and to bring home a white wife..."

Prudence placed her hands on his chest and pushed back so that she could look up at his face. "Wife?" she said, "Aren't you jumping the gun a bit?"

"Isn't that what we're talking about? At least the possibility?"

"I just hadn't..." she laughed nervously. "But now that you mention it..." She looked up at him again. "Yes, it is at least a possibility." She searched his face. "And the thought of it doesn't make me feel trapped the way it does every time Wally brings it up."

He raised his eyebrow in a question. She shook her head. "He's the boy I left behind, I suppose. No one important. Certainly no one for you to be worried about." She slipped her arms back around him and rested her head on his chest. He kissed the top of her head. Her cloche had long ago fallen to the ground, unnoticed.

"Sweetheart, I know what I'll be giving up and I know what I'll be gaining by leaving the white man's world. You don't. Could you really give up the life you know—the life that this Wally could give you—to live in a completely different world, one that doesn't begin to have the material advantages of yours? There's no running water or electricity on most of the reservation, no paved roads, nothing but a trading post for shopping, and certainly no restaurants, no seamstresses, and no libraries, Prudence."

"I... I could learn to live without restaurants and without seamstresses, and I could create a library where there isn't one, but... I wish that I could say that electricity and running water don't matter, but... they do." she said, sadly. "And they would matter more and more over time. I'm sorry to say that just having to share a bathroom at the hotel this past week has been a trial, and it isn't getting any easier." She looked up at him. "But, those things will be available eventually, surely? You said your house already has them."

He nodded. "I don't intend to keep living in that house, Prudence." He sighed. "Yes, there's running water and electricity in a few of the areas on the borders and places like Window Rock. We'll likely get cafes, grocery stores, the kinds of services that grow up in small towns, in some areas in time, but I don't plan to live in one of those areas. Of course, if I have anything to say about it, there will be schools and there will be libraries, but..."

"But not today." She made it a statement. He shook his head. "And probably not tomorrow. And not where you plan to live."

He nodded. "But my world—the world that I want to be mine—has advantages that yours doesn't for those who are part of it. There's this land of course," he paused to look around at the vast, spreading landscape, "and more than that—what we call 'the Navajo Way.' It's family and traditions and history and culture. It will take me the rest of my life to regain what was taken from me in the white man's schools, if I ever can." He held her closer. "I wish that you could be a part of it... but..."

"But I'm a white woman, and worse, a middle-class white woman from the city who has run off and left her aged mother alone." She put a finger on his lips to stop his protest. "No, you're right. I don't know what it would mean, and I'd be more of a hindrance than a help to you." She stroked his cheek. "You need someone who does know and who can help you regain what you've lost, not someone who would need you to support her."

He kissed her palm and said harshly, "Why can't what I need be what I want and what I want be what I need?"

Prudence held him quietly. There was no answer. Finally, she said, "Let's go back." They walked to the truck with their arms around each other's waist. Prudence felt drained emotionally.

"It's strange," she said. "Since the first moment we met, I've felt that I've always known you."

He nodded. "I've felt the same, seeing you standing there in that observation car in your silly little shoes. I told you things that I have never told anyone other than a few close friends. It just felt so natural," He laughed. "Some people believe that our souls are reincarnated life after life and we really are meeting people we've known before." He shrugged. "It's not a Navajo belief."

"Nor a Methodist one." She laughed. "I prefer to think that it's because I'm a librarian. People trust us, you know, with all their most intimate problems and, even more importantly, with their dreams and fantasies. I know which women who patronize our branch—and which men, for that matter—read erotic romances, for instance. And they aren't always the ones you would expect. But they know that their secret is safe with me and that I would never judge their choices."

They reached the truck and drove back in a companionable silence, reaching out occasionally to touch each other, but saying nothing, as there was nothing left to say. Jerry dropped her off at the Castañeda. He offered to walk her to the door, but she shook her head and stood watching as he drove away. So much had happened in less than a week.

Clara called to her when she entered the lobby. "Tom's funeral is tomorrow morning at nine o'clock. I've got the morning off to go to it. You're welcome to ride with John and me, if you'd like to go." Prudence nodded. "We'll pick you up outside at eight thirty and go straight to the cemetery. The service will be at the grave side."

"Thank you. I appreciate that. How is Martha?"

"Better than her mother. I don't think either Martha or her father is really shocked by this. Saddened, of course, but not shocked. They both knew that Tom was involved with some dangerous people. His mother, though…" Clara trailed off. They both knew what she was going to say.

"I'll be ready in the morning," Prudence said and headed up the stairs. She had no appetite for dinner and needed privacy and quiet to sort through her feelings. Had she just kissed a murderer—and not only enjoyed it, but come away wanting more?

Chapter 10

Wednesday

June 5, 1929

Las Vegas, Day Six

PRUDENCE AWOKE FEELING DEPRESSED, but she didn't know why. Then she remembered her conversation with Jerry yesterday and Tom's funeral today. She was sad about Tom, but heartbroken about Jerry. He was right, of course, that there was no future for them, given what he wanted for himself, but that didn't make it any easier to accept. She wondered whether she should have tried harder to convince him, but she knew that she hadn't because if she had succeeded, they'd both live to regret it in time. So, it was better to end things now, before it was more than an infatuation. She had no doubt that it had the potential to be more. And, she reminded herself, he might very well be a murderer or maybe executioner was the correct word, if he had killed Tom in order to stop him from murdering any more Indians with his poisonous alcohol.

Enough of that. She had to get ready for the funeral. Her navy-blue dress would do, with the matching cloche (thankfully not the one she had left out on the range yesterday) and her black shoes and minimal jewelry. She knew she wouldn't be expected to participate, simply stand quietly and respectfully in the background with the others who were not of the faith, so she dressed as inconspicuously as possible.

Anne took her order. "Just oatmeal and fruit? Are you sure?"

She nodded. "I don't have much appetite, considering."

"Oh, that's right. You're going to Tom's funeral, I guess. I can't go. We're shorthanded since Martha isn't here, so I couldn't get the morning off." She stopped. "Listen to me. I wouldn't need the morning off if Martha were here." She shook her head. "This thing has discombobulated everyone. Even though no one is really surprised, it's still a shock. No one really expected him to be killed this way! Well, give my condolences to Martha and her parents when you see them, please. I'll over to the house as soon as I can to do it in person, too."

It was a good thing that she was going with John and Clara, as the Montefiore cemetery was on the western outskirts of the Old Town, next to the Masonic cemetery. The mourners were lined up on both sides of the newly dug grave, with Dr. Bonheim and a group of other men standing at the head, each wearing a dark suit and a black skullcap. Martha had her arm around a woman with a heavy, black veil draped over her face. Prudence assumed that she must be Mrs. Morgan and that the man on the other side of her was her husband. The coffin, a simple pine box, rested on boards laid across the width of the grave, with ropes running underneath, ready for lowering it when the time came.

John, Clara, and Prudence quietly moved to stand on one side near Maria and her parents. Maria murmured a quiet introduction, "My parents, Mr. and Mrs. Herrera, Prudence Bates." They nodded at each other in acknowledgment. It was not the appropriate setting for much more than that.

Prudence was surprised to see Mr. and Mrs. Kearney standing on the opposite side, with Liz and Gene next to them and Mrs. Parkinson next to Gene. She and Clara looked at each other. It would have caused more talk if they hadn't come, Prudence supposed.

The service began with the recitation of several psalms in English. Everyone joined in reciting the twenty-third Psalm. "The Lord is my shepherd, I shall not want," they began. Mrs. Morgan's voice began to break as they progressed through "Yeah, though I walk through the valley of the shadow of death," and she had stopped even trying to recite the words when they reached the end, "I will dwell in the house of the Lord forever." Prudence reflected cynically that the words hardly seemed to apply to Tom, that the best anyone could hope for was that mercy would follow him. Out of the corner of her eye, she saw the Herreras unobtrusively crossing themselves and kissing the rosaries they held inconspicuously in their hands.

Dr. Bonheim then gave a brief eulogy, which was designed more to comfort Tom's parents than to provide an accurate portrait of his life and character. The coffin was then lowered into the ground. Mrs. Morgan collapsed, weeping, into Martha's arms. Mr. Morgan poured a shovelful of dirt into the grave, then added two more, one each for his wife and daughter. The Jewish mourners then recited a final prayer in Hebrew. They lined up in two parallel lines leading away from the grave, and Dr. Bonheim motioned for the rest of those in attendance to join one of the lines. As the Morgan family passed between them, friends offered their condolences in a word, a grasp of a hand, a touch on an arm.

After the Morgans had driven off, Clara said, "Let's give them a few minutes to get home and get ready for visitors. I expect that some of the ladies of the Sisterhood will be there to help." Prudence nodded, distracted. She hadn't been surprised to see Bill and Jim there, as they were members of the local community, but she wondered why the prohis was also in attendance. Did they expect the murderer to make an appearance? Assuming, of course, that the murder was related to Tom's bootlegging activities.

They started to walk slowly toward John's car. The Herreras approached them, and Mrs. Herrera leaned forward and touched Clara on the arm, "Tell them that we forgive him and that we are praying for them and for his immortal soul."

Clara nodded and replied, "Thank you. I know they will appreciate it."

Maria stayed behind as her parents moved off to give her a few moments of privacy with her friends. "You asked me what my plans for the future were the other day," she said to Prudence. "I have been contemplating a certain path, and Tom's death has made it clear that it is the right path for me." She took a deep breath and looked at Clara and John to include them in the conversation. "I am going to become a postulant of the Sisters of Charity while I finish my education, and then I will enter the novitiate."

Clara embraced her quickly. "I am not at all surprised, Maria. You will make a wonderful sister." She stepped back and held both of Maria's hands in hers. "Have you told your parents?"

"Yes." She nodded. "Last night. Like you, they were not surprised." She smiled. "Apparently, I was the only person who was." She turned to where her parents were standing a few feet away. "I'd better go. They are waiting for me."

"Congratulations," said Prudence. "It's so satisfying when you discover your calling."

Maria smiled and nodded, then hurried to catch up with her parents.

Clara shook her head as she watched her go. "We didn't meet Maria until we started college. She went to a Catholic school in the Old Town, of course. It didn't take us long to see how important her religion is to her. The only surprise was when she started chasing after Tom, but… I suspect it's that she's so good in herself that she was determined to prove us all wrong about him. Well, at least it forced her to recognize what her own values are."

"Is she their only child?" Prudence asked, as they continued their walk toward the car.

"The Herreras? No," Clara shook her head. "She's got two older sisters and an older brother, and two younger brothers. And before you ask, no, I don't think any of them murdered Tom. The younger ones are too young, and the older one is too much like his father."

John laughed at the idea.

"So, why didn't they come to the funeral?"

"They didn't know him and don't really know the Morgans. Remember that they live in Old Town and went to school there. Maria is the only one who had any reason to come to Tom's funeral, and that's because she met Martha in college."

"How do you think her parents will feel about her becoming a nun? She said that they weren't surprised, but do you think they are pleased?"

"Oh, I imagine so. They are very religious and the older kids are all married, with kids of their own, so they have plenty of grandchildren already. I wouldn't be surprised if that youngest boy becomes a priest, as well. Or a monk. Something religious. I've always suspected that Mrs. Herrera had hopes along those lines for that oldest boy, but..." She laughed. "Let's just say that his vocation did not lie along those lines."

John snorted as he held the door open for Prudence. "Not by a long shot."

"His firstborn—charitable people say he was a seven-month baby." Clara laughed as she got in the car. After the door was closed, she leaned over the seat and added, "The same thing they'll say about Liz's. Only this one won't look like its father."

Prudence stared, open-mouthed. "You know?"

John slid behind the wheel and started the car. He snorted in amusement again. "The only person who doesn't know is Gene, and that's because he doesn't want to know." He steered the car toward the cemetery exit.

"As if Liz getting married as soon as possible isn't all the evidence anyone needs," Clara added.

"And she swore me to secrecy. I hope she doesn't think I've told you."

"Oh, no one will say anything to her. Say! How did you find out?"

Prudence told her about the incident the day before. "Poor Gene," she ended.

"Poor Gene?" John laughed. "Poor Gene is getting exactly what poor Gene wants—the unattainable Liz Kearney, along with the Kearney money and lands. If it means acceptin' a cuckoo in the nest... ow!" he said as Clara punched him lightly on the shoulder.

John pulled up at the Morgan's house. "I'll have to just drop you girls here and get off to work," he said.

"Parkinson wasn't happy about giving me and Gene the time off for the funeral, as it was, but his wife insisted."

"Don't bother to get out," Clara said, giving him a peck on the cheek. "We can manage the doors ourselves." They waited until he had driven off to walk up to the house. "We won't stay long," Clara said. "Just long enough to give our condolences."

It was a modest, two-story family home near the university where Mr. Morgan was a professor. The patchy grass and struggling rose bushes gave evidence of an attempt to establish a lawn in this arid climate. The front door was opened by a middle-aged, dark-haired woman who welcomed them quietly and led them into the parlor, where the family was seated. Several men and women were seated on chairs ranged around the room, conversing in low tones.

Clara and Prudence approached the Morgan family. Prudence was struck by Martha's resemblance to her mother. Tom had also inherited her dark hair and sultry eyes, although Mrs. Morgan's were now red and swollen from weeping. She had stopped crying and sat, looking dazed, as if she were wondering why she was here in this room with these people and why everyone was so sad. Martha sat on one side, holding her hand and Mr. Morgan on the other, his arm around her shoulders.

Martha looked up at them. "Thank you for coming," she said softly.

"We are so sorry," Clara said. She reached out and took Martha's free hand and held it briefly.

Prudence did the same and added, "Our deepest sympathies."

Martha nodded. "Mother," she said, "Here's Clara."

Mrs. Morgan smiled sadly and reached for Clara's hand. "Little Clara. You remember my Tom when he was a boy."

"Of course, I do."

"He was a good boy, my Tom." She smiled nostalgically. "And so very clever and so handsome always. All the little girls chased after my Tom, even you, Clara."

"Yes, I did," Clara answered, with a smile. "But, that was a long time ago, Aunt Sarah."

Prudence looked at her in surprise.

"He was such a beautiful baby. Such big dark eyes and that smile... it would melt your heart. And he only got more handsome and more clever as he grew up," his mother insisted. "Like a film star. All the girls said so."

Clara nodded. "And he was good to his mother," she changed the subject.

"He was, always," his mother agreed. "And to his little sister," she turned to Martha and squeezed her hand.

Martha nodded.

"He was taken from us too soon," her face crumpled, and she began softly sobbing. Martha took the wet handkerchief from between her fingers and handed her a dry one. Martha looked up at Clara and said, "Thank you for coming," again.

Clara squeezed Martha's hand and nodded. She stepped over to Mr. Morgan and leaned forward to kiss his cheek. "I am so sorry, Uncle Dan," she said.

He nodded. "As are we all." He looked at Prudence.

"This is our new friend, Prudence Bates. She's been staying at the Castañeda." He nodded.

"I met Tom on Sunday when we went to the hot springs," she explained, "and I wanted to express my sympathy to all of you. I know he will be a great loss."

Mr. Morgan quirked his lips. "It is kind of you to say so." He sighed. "I loved my son, but I was under no illusions about him. Maybe if I'd been a sterner father..."

Clara shook her head. "Uncle Dan, you were—you are—a wonderful example of a good man and a good father. Martha is proof of that. No, Tom made his own choices, for his own reasons, as has Martha."

He nodded. "Yes, we still have Martha. She is our great comfort." He stared ahead. "And we have three grandchildren whom we have never acknowledged. That is something that is going to change just as soon as this week is over. I do not know if their mothers can forgive us, but I will make every effort to convince them of our sincerity."

"Oh, Father," Martha leaned across her mother, who seemed to be in a world of her own. "I am so happy to hear you say that. I've so wanted to be a real aunt to them."

He smiled at her. "You go talk to your friends for a few minutes, now." He then turned back to Prudence and Clara, "Thank you both for coming."

"Oh, before I forget, Uncle Dan, the Herreras asked me to tell you that they forgive Tom and are praying for all of you and for his immortal soul."

He nodded. "I appreciate their concern and their consideration. Now, you girls go have a little talk. I am here for my wife." He looked at her with tears glistening in his eyes and pulled her closer. She looked up and smiled at him, then looked around the room again as if confused.

Martha slipped her hand from her mother's and moved with Clara and Prudence to the other side of the room.

"We are so sorry—" Clara began.

"I feel so guilty," Martha interrupted. "If only I had taken your advice," she said to Prudence, "and gone to the police with my suspicions, this might have been prevented. It's all my fault."

Tears flooded her eyes and ran down her cheeks. Prudence looked at Clara in dismay.

Clara put her arms around Martha. "Hush, now. Of course it isn't. Tom was an adult. He knew what he was doing and the kind of people he was involved with." She looked at Prudence for confirmation.

"Clara is right, Martha. Tom is the only one who is responsible for the consequences of his choices. And, we don't know who killed him or why. It may have nothing to do with the bootlegging."

Martha giggled, a little hysterically. "You mean, it could have been one of a dozen people?" She sobbed harder. "How many people wanted my brother dead?"

Prudence and Clara looked at each other helplessly. "Hush, now," Clara repeated. "It is not your fault. We all know how much you loved him. No one could have forced him to change his ways. Even Mr. Williams gave up." Prudence could see that she couldn't think of anything more to say. Prudence quietly put a hand on Martha's back, even more at a loss for words. The sobs slowly diminished.

Martha took a deep breath. "I know you're right. He wouldn't listen to Father or Mother, let alone me. I just..." She shook her head. "Thank you for coming." She squeezed their hands, then turned and walked back to sit by her parents, the three of them united in their grief.

Prudence and Clara moved quietly through the room and out the door. When they had reached the sidewalk, Prudence looked at Clara. "Aunt Sarah? Uncle Dan?"

Clara smirked. "You never asked me my last name." She turned and began walking down the sidewalk toward the Castañeda.

"I guess I didn't. So, it's Morgan? You're Jewish, too?"

"Yes, it's Morgan, and, no... technically, I'm not. My

father was Uncle Dan's brother. My mother was a nice Baptist girl. Jewishness is inherited from the mother, you know."

"Don't tell me she was a Kearney! Or a Parkinson."

Clara laughed. "No, not a Kearney or a Parkinson. This isn't quite that small a town! And, no, as far as I know, I'm not related to Anne or Maria or Mike and definitely not related to John... yet. Although, I wouldn't be surprised to find that Aunt Sarah and the Herreras are related somewhere along the line."

"You said "was." Have both of your parents passed?"

Clara nodded. "Mother died not long after I was born. My father raised me, with the help of Aunt Sarah and Uncle Dan. Tom and Martha were more like siblings than cousins. We all went to Saturday morning services together and on Sundays, Grandma Turner hauled me off to Sunday School. When I was sixteen, they said I could choose whether to be confirmed a Jew or baptized a Christian. I told them I chose to remain a heathen."

She stopped as they came to a cross street. "I live just down this street. Would you like to come over for lunch? I can't promise anything fancy—probably just sandwiches—but I'm sure I could scrape something together."

"That would be wonderful," Prudence responded. "To tell you the truth, I would love 'just a sandwich.' The food at the Harvey House is excellent, of course, but after nearly a week of it... I'm longing for something plain and simple."

"Well, plain and simple is my specialty," laughed Clara.

They turned the corner. "How did your family react to your announcement that you were choosing to remain a heathen?"

"I think they were just relieved that I hadn't decided to become a Mormon. Mike had certainly been giving it his all, but there was never any chance of that. This is my house here."

They went through into the kitchen. Clara tied an apron around her waist.

"Have a seat," she said, indicating a chair at the kitchen table. She got a loaf of bread out of the bread box and set it and a bread knife on a cutting board. "Would you mind cutting bread for sandwiches?"

"Not at all." Prudence pulled the cutting board closer and started sawing at the bread. "Do you mind if I ask how your father died? My father died when I was almost fifteen from a lung disease."

Clara dug around in the ice box and placed a butcher paper package of sliced ham and one of cheese on the table.

"Mine died two years ago, when I was eighteen." She added a tomato and some lettuce, along with a jar of mustard and a pitcher of iced tea. "He just went to bed one night, and in the morning, I found him dead. Heart attack, they said. He was older when he and Mother married and even older when I was born, so... it wasn't entirely unexpected."

"Still, it must have been a shock to find him like that! I am so sorry."

"Yes, it was. I don't know that we're ever really prepared. In any case, it was several years ago, time's a great healer, as they say and as I'm sure you know."

Prudence nodded. "Would you like me to slice this up?" she asked, indicating the tomato.

Clara nodded. "Just use the bread knife and leave it on the cutting board. Less to wash later."

She got two plates and two glasses down from the cupboard and set them on the table, along with two table knives and two napkins, and sat in the chair facing Prudence.

"He was a professor at the university, like Uncle Dan. They used to call it the 'family business.' So, as the child of a faculty member, I get free tuition. It's part of my legacy. This house is most of the rest of it."

Prudence put two slices of bread on each plate. She spread hers liberally with mustard, then passed the jar to Clara. Each added as much ham, cheese, lettuce, and tomato as she wanted and poured a glass of the cold tea.

Prudence felt compelled to try to narrow the gap between herself and Clara. "Mine was an accountant for an automobile company when he died. He never went to college. He'd worked his way up to accountant from a clerk. That's why he left us so well-provided for when he died, though. As an accountant, he knew about planning ahead. He left enough insurance to pay off the house and left

Mother an annuity for her lifetime and enough in a trust fund for me to pay for my college education. Actually, it was more than enough, since I qualified for scholarships every year. That's how I have enough to take these months to train as a Courier."

They each took a bite of their sandwich and chewed it in silence. Prudence swallowed and asked, "So, tell me about John. How does he feel about being with a heathen?"

Clara finished chewing the bite in her mouth and responded.

"He's the one who suggested it. He was never baptized into any church." She drank some tea. "His father works for the Santa Fe. They moved around quite a bit when he was a child, so his religious upbringing was kind of... erratic. They've been here since he started high school. They stayed because they wanted him to finish school in one place, and then he started at the university in Albuquerque, so they just stayed on. Like me, he's an only child. I get the feeling that his parents would have liked more kids, but it just didn't happen for them. We met in high school, discovered we have a lot in common and..." She shrugged and ate more of her sandwich.

"Are you planning to...?"

"Get married?" Prudence nodded. "Eventually, when we've both finished college. What we do after that... we'll decide when we get there. We're just taking it as it comes. One thing we do know is that neither one of us wants the conventional married life."

Prudence chewed thoughtfully. "Tell me about the Navajo Indians."

"The Navajo? Why the Navajo? They live over to the west of here, mostly in Arizona."

Prudence blushed and looked at her plate. "I met someone... on the train."

Clara leaned back. "Prudence Bates! You are a dark horse. You tell me about the Navajo."

She shook her head and tried unsuccessfully to smile. Clara leaned forward and touched her hand.

"What's the matter? I'm sorry, I didn't mean to..."

"Oh, it's not your fault. You have nothing to apologize for." She sighed. "I barely know him. As I said, we met on the train. He bought me breakfast. We talked. He made me laugh. He's a teacher on the reservation. He said he was going on to Gallup. I never expected to see him again, but... there he was at the lunch counter in the drug store at the plaza yesterday. We talked some more. I... we're so comfortable together. It's as if we've known each other for years. He drove me out to where Tom was killed," Clara looked at her in surprise. Prudence shook her head. "We didn't find any clues, but... we did kiss."

"Oh? You did, did you?"

"Um-hmm. The way I've always wanted to be kissed." She smiled in remembrance. "Then, he told me that he does care for me, but he wants a traditional Navajo life." She shrugged.

"And a traditional Navajo wife to go with it," Clara finished. Prudence nodded. "In that case, he should never have kissed you."

"Oh, I insisted that he kiss me. I didn't really give him much choice," Prudence admitted. "I more or less kissed him first."

"Really? Well, in that case... I do have to give him credit for taking you out on your wild goose chase. But, to be frank, it sounds to me like he doesn't know what he wants. Or, he wants to have it both ways. He is right about one thing—you could never live a traditional Navajo life. I doubt I could, and I grew up here, but you? Definitely not. No, it's best to forget him. There are plenty of other fish in the sea."

"Yeah, like Wally." She laughed ironically.

"Wally?"

"The boy I left behind. We've known each other since, oh, we were five years old. He's hardly my only boyfriend, but the others moved on and so did I. He's been after me to marry him since we graduated from college, but... I don't want to get married right now and, even if I did..."

"It wouldn't be to Wally," Clara finished for her.

"No, and it isn't just because he doesn't send me. He kisses me like I'm his sister and he calls me 'Pru.'" She glared at the memory. "That was my childhood nickname. My mother still calls me that, but no one else does, except Wally. I've stopped telling him not to because it does no good. It's as if he can't see that I'm no longer that little girl in short skirts and pigtails."

Clara laughed. "You call him "Wally"."

"He likes it! That's something else about him that bugs me! Seriously, though, we just don't want the same things out of life. He wants a nice little wife and nice little kids in a nice little house behind a nice little white picket fence. He wants to go off to the office every morning for forty years, leaving the wife home to take care of the house and kids, then to spend the rest of his life gardening and playing with his nice little grandkids."

"That's some women's idea of heaven," said Clara. "Not mine, of course, but it's pretty much Anne's idea of what she wants out of life."

Prudence nodded. "And I hope Anne gets it. Seems like she will with Mike. But it isn't mine, either. I want to travel, to see new places, meet new people, experience life for as long as I can. And I want to spend it with someone who wants those same things."

"You've certainly made a good start with these Indian Detours!"

"Well, I hope so... but it's not certain they'll accept me into the training program." She sighed. "I'm a college graduate and I'm the right age, but they 'prefer young ladies who have the personal knowledge that comes from having lived in the Southwest,' and I'm beginning to realize that one week in Las Vegas is hardly adequate."

"I don't really know much about them, other than what I see when they meet the tours, but it seems to me that what really matters is enthusiasm and a pleasant personality. I can't see that you'll have any trouble learning the material and there are plenty of young ladies here in the Southwest who know nothing beyond the town they grew up in."

"I hope that they agree with you. I'll certainly do my best to convince them."

Clara nodded toward the clock. "I'd better get to work before I'm late."

"Oh, I am sorry! Let me clean up while you change." Prudence quickly cleared the table, put the remaining food into the ice box, and had the plates and cups draining on the drain board when Clara came back downstairs in her hotel uniform.

As they walked toward the hotel, Clara said, "Did I understand you correctly? Did you say that your Navajo told you he was going on to Gallup? What was he doing here in Las Vegas yesterday?"

"He's not 'my Navajo.' His name is Jerry. Jerry Begay," Prudence protested, "and I don't know. Every time I tried to ask him, he would change the subject." She said nothing about seeing him with Tom or drunk on the sidewalk.

"Hmmm," murmured Clara. "Maybe Jerry suddenly found Las Vegas more attractive than Gallup."

"I can only hope," Prudence responded. They were laughing as they entered the lobby of the Castañeda but stopped as they remembered why Clara had been given the morning off.

Clara took over from the clerk who had been substituting for her. Prudence went up to her room, wondering as she went what the answer to Clara's question really was. What *was* Jerry doing in Las Vegas, not just yesterday, but all this week?

In her room, she kicked off her shoes in relief, stepped out of her dress, and lay down on the bed in her slip to think. Why was Jerry in Las Vegas? Why had he met with Tom at the train yard? Had he shot Tom in revenge for Tom's poisoning his people? He certainly seemed to know where Tom's pickup truck had been parked or at least said he did. Not that they'd found actual evidence of it, but, then, he'd have been careful to steer her away from any clues, if he'd been the murderer. How did she know if the place he'd taken her was even close to the right place?

Maybe he'd been drunk when he'd done it? Maybe he wasn't aware of what he was doing? Maybe he didn't even remember doing it? No, that made no sense. Tom had been shot in the head at close range by someone they assumed he was meeting. It was obviously a deliberate act.

She had no evidence of any kind that he was the murderer, either. There could be any number of reasons that Jerry was in Las Vegas. It would be nice to think that Clara was right and that he had... what? Got off the train at the last minute? Come back from Gallup?... because of her. But if that were the case, why hadn't he made any effort to get in touch with her? He knew she was staying at the Castañeda.

As these and similar thoughts spun their way through her mind, she slipped off to sleep. She'd been up early and it had been an emotional day. When she finally awoke from confused dreams of Jerry carrying a rifle to Tom's funeral in the scrubland near the Arroyo Pecos, it was dark and she was hungry. It had been hours since the sandwiches at noon.

Clara had already left for the day, and she was relieved not to recognize any of the waitresses in the dining room. She could just order her meal, eat it, and leave. She ordered the special, without asking what it was, and scarcely noticed what she was eating. She refused coffee and returned to her room, still immersed in her thoughts.

Back in her room, she realized that, due to her late nap, she was not in the least bit sleepy. Going to bed would be pointless. She was also too restless to settle down with a book or to write a letter. Maybe a walk would help. She'd never have gone out this late at night alone in Cleveland, but what could happen in a sleepy town such as Las Vegas? She changed into her jeans and saddle oxfords, and quietly left the hotel. She headed south along Railroad Avenue and soon was beyond the lights of the hotel and the city.

The sky was thick with stars. She stood amazed at the wide glistening band of the Milky Way. She had read about it in books and even seen some artists' renderings and some photographs, but they were a pale reflection of what was in the sky above her. She tried to pick out constellations, but the only ones she could ever reliably locate were the Big Dipper and Orion, and even they were lost in this multitude of stars.

The sidewalk eventually ended in a dirt track well beyond the railroad yard. The ground was too rough to navigate without some form of light, so, after stumbling around on the uneven ground for several minutes, she turned to head back to the hotel. As she got closer to the edge of the railroad yard farthest from the hotel, she could hear the throb and purr of automobile engines off to the east, coming closer across the open desert. Was it the bootleggers? Were they coming to meet with Tom? What would they do when he didn't show up? She was seized with curiosity. She started creeping carefully and quietly past the outbuildings that dotted the railroad yard.

Suddenly, a hand was clapped across her mouth and a strong arm around her waist, and she was dragged into the deeper shadow behind a train shed. She struggled and attempted to scream. A low voice said in her ear, "Hush, Prudence. You white people are so noisy. It's a good thing I'm the one who heard you coming." She froze in astonishment. She knew that voice. In fact, she knew those hands and those arms, and that chest. Her heart skipped a beat and then began racing, but not in fear.

"That's better. Calm down. Your heart's going a mile a minute." She cursed her traitorous heart for betraying her heightened emotions.

"Now, don't make a sound and don't move. Do you understand?" She nodded. "Good." He sighed. "My dear Prudence, I don't know what I'm to do with you. I simply cannot allow you to destroy six months' worth of work." He paused. "I don't have anything to tie you up with, but I wouldn't if I did. I'm just going to have to trust you. Will you remain here quietly and wait for my return?" She nodded. "Because, believe me, Prudence, these people who are coming would not hesitate to kill both of us." He removed his hand from her mouth.

"You can trust me," she whispered.

"That's my girl," Jerry said. He released her, took her face in his hands, kissed her quickly, and said, "Wait for me right here. Not a sound and not a movement."

She nodded. Her heart sank. So this is what he was doing in Las Vegas instead of Gallup. He was a bootlegger. A charming, lying, roguish bootlegger. And he had killed Tom in order to take over his territory. Why did it have to be that? Why couldn't it have been to stop him from selling poisoned alcohol? But she wouldn't betray him. At least, not now, when it could mean his death—their deaths. Her conscience would force her to turn him over to the prohibition officer, but she would wait until it was safe to do so.

The car engines were now silent. Jerry slipped along toward the equipment sheds along the train tracks.

When he reached the tracks, he pulled a flashlight from his pocket and turned it on and off twice in succession.

Car doors opened and closed. Voices carried through the still night air. "That you, Morgan?"

"Morgan couldn't make it. He sent me."

There was the sound of guns being cocked. "Yeah? And who're you?"

"Name's Begay. I'm an associate of his." Prudence suppressed a sob.

"How do we know you're not a copper? Or a prohis?" There were murmurs of agreement.

One voice asked, "Want me to bump him, boss?"

"I'll let you know." There was a pause. "So, answer the question."

"You ever see an Indian cop?"

Prudence could hear mutters of "No, nope, never did."

"And I knew the time, the place and the signal, didn't I?"

Further mutters of "Yeah, that's true, sure did."

Prudence shook her head and bit her lips. The evidence was undeniable.

"You don't sound like no Injun."

"Yeah, well, white man's schools, you know."

Suddenly, Jerry's face was lit up by a blaze of light from a flashlight pointed directly at his face. His eyes squeezed shut and he averted his face. "Injun, all right," said the voice. Again, murmurs of agreement.

"Why would Morgan send you?"

"I'm his agent to the Indians." Jerry shrugged. "I can sell the stuff in places where a white man would attract too much attention."

Now, there were murmurs of agreement to this statement.

It was all Prudence could do not to cry aloud. She leaned back against the wall behind her and put her hands to her mouth. Her worst fears were coming true. There could be no question now that he had killed Tom in order to take over his territory, which included selling to the Indians. Oh, that couldn't be right. She was absolutely certain that Jerry would not do anything to hurt his people. She simply could not have been that wrong about him. If he was lying about selling alcohol to the Indians, and she was sure that he was, maybe he was lying about the rest of it? But, then, what *was* he doing here?

"Hmmm..." The voice contemplated this. "Gotta give Morgan credit for that idea. Well, we drove all this way. Hate to haul it all back again. And you did know the time and the place and the signal. OK, I'll risk it. You got the cabbage?"

"Right here."

"Let's see it."

"Show me the merchandise first."

"What? You don't trust me?" The voice laughed sarcastically. "No dice. First, we see the color of your money."

There was a pause, then the rustle of paper being removed from a pocket, then the glimmer of light from a flashlight held low. Again, the rustle of paper being quickly counted.

"Not enough."

"That's all Morgan gave me."

The voice chuckled. "Won't be the first time Morgan came up short. That explains why he sent you. I told him what he'd get the next time he tried to stiff me. OK, this will get you six crates. Tell Morgan he'd better have it all next time—and that goes for any agent he sends. I'm not in this business to do him any favors."

Prudence could hear car trunks opening and men grunting, then the clash as crates of bottles were dropped to the ground. Suddenly, the train yard was ablaze with light from the headlights of half-a-dozen cars parked in a semicircle.

"Hands up, boys," a voice shouted. "This is Agent Simmons with the Bureau of Prohibition. Put the guns down. You're surrounded by armed officers."

There was the sound of multiple guns being cocked. Prudence peeked around the edge of the shed. Light glinted off the barrels of shotguns and rifles pointed toward the bootleggers. They looked at each other in astonishment and disgust. A few muttered something to those closest to them, but they all eventually began to lay their weapons on the ground and put their hands in the air. Prudence counted at least six men, possibly a few more, and two trucks. She felt as discombobulated as the men looked.

One of the goons started to raise a Tommy gun he was holding close to his side. Prudence heard Bill's voice, "Drop the gat or you'll find out what a twelve gauge can do to a human head." The gangster slowly lowered the gun and laid it carefully on the ground.

"Wilson," Bill called, as he slowly walked forward, keeping the shot gun trained on the man with the Tommy gun. Prudence saw a man in a suit move into the light. He pulled the man's hands behind his back and fastened them with handcuffs, then picked up the gun and headed back toward the car lights, pulling the goon along behind him.

Bill, Jim, and other men she recognized from around town directed their rifles and shotguns toward the gang, while Wilson and several other men in suits holstered their handguns and moved among the bootleggers, handcuffing them and picking up their weapons. They pushed them towards the waiting police cars and vans and shoved them inside. They handed the guns to a waiting officer who stowed them in the back of one of the cars.

Prudence searched frantically for Jerry in the crowd of gangsters and officers. It took her several seconds to find him. He had moved to stand next to Agent Simmons and the two were quietly conversing. Several of the handcuffed men spit in his direction as they walked past and more than one muttered "Dirty Injun." He just smiled. Prudence felt lightheaded. He wasn't Tom's agent. He was an agent of the Bureau. He was under cover as part of a sting operation. She wanted to laugh out loud. She also felt ashamed for ever having doubted him and wondered if he would ever forgive her. She wasn't sure that she would ever forgive herself for even imagining that Jerry would be party to Tom's deadly schemes.

The leader of the gang stopped and, staring directly at him, said, "I won't forget this, Begay."

Jerry smiled again and replied, "I'm not worried. All us Indians look alike to you."

Bill pulled on the gangster's arm and led him off. It suddenly occurred to Prudence that, if things had gone otherwise, Jerry would be lying there dead on the ground, filled with lead. Once again, she felt dizzy and lightheaded.

Jerry said something to Agent Simmons, who shook his

head in bemusement, then nodded. Jerry turned and motioned to Prudence to come forward. She half-ran toward him and threw her arms around him.

"I knew you couldn't be a bootlegger or a murderer," she whispered. She couldn't decide whether to laugh or cry.

"A murderer?" He sounded puzzled and shook his head. "It's late. You may not be tired, but I am. I'm going to take you back to your hotel now. You can meet me at the police station at ten o'clock tomorrow morning and I'll explain everything. And you can tell me who it is I didn't murder and why you would have imagined that I'd be capable of such a thing."

He nodded toward Agent Simmons, who tipped him a wave and walked over to where the police cars were lined up. He spoke briefly with Bill and Jim, then slid into a car and started it up. Bill got in the lead car, and the others followed him out of the train yard, toward the police station. Jerry shook his head.

"I don't know how they are going to get all of those gangsters into those two cells. They won't spend a comfortable night, that's for certain."

He looked down at Prudence. "Now, let's get you home." They walked to the remaining pickup truck parked in the shadow of a shed. He opened the passenger door and helped Prudence up, then walked around and got behind the wheel. He drove the short distance to the Castañeda and parked against the curb. He turned slightly to look at Prudence. She could just make him out in the dim light from the lobby of the hotel.

"Well, I guess I'll see you in the morning, then," he said softly

She turned to face him and stared at him silently. She reached out and grasped his hands and pulled him toward her.

"Prudence," he began, huskily.

"Hush," she said and tugged slightly harder. He slid across the seat and gathered her into his arms, swinging her legs around until she was sitting on his lap. She leaned forward to press her lips on his and her body up against his. His arms came up almost without his volition and drew her closer to him and his lips responded to hers. After several seconds, he pulled away and stared into her eyes.

"You're like a bad habit I can't seem to break."

She smiled. "Those are the best kind of habits. Now, kiss me again." He obeyed her command with pleasure, then pulled back again and shook his head.

"We shouldn't... you know that nothing has changed."

She stroked his face. "I know. But we both get a say in this and if all we'll have are memories, then they should be memories worth having. So, kiss me again."

After several seconds, Jerry reached up and touched her face. "Are these tears?" he asked. She nodded and buried her face in his neck. "Shhh," he stroked her hair and gently rocked her. His eyes glistened and he swallowed hard several times.

"I'm sorry," she murmured into his shoulder. "I wanted to... to tempt you... to... with no strings and no regrets... but..." She looked up at him. "I care too much."

He nodded and, lifting her hand from his shoulder, he kissed her palm and nuzzled it. She stroked his face.

"You know I want you?" he asked. She nodded. "And once would not be enough?" She nodded again. "It would be like that first drink of alcohol, that just leaves me thirsting for more, so..."

There was no analogy he could have drawn that would have had a greater impact. "So, I'd better go." She slid off his lap and, kissing him softly, opened the door and stepped down. She turned, "Do you forgive me?"

"For what?"

"For thinking that you were a bootlegger or a murderer?"

He laughed. "I'd forgotten all about that. We'll discuss it tomorrow, but, yes, I forgive you."

She nodded and walked away.

* * *

JERRY SAT and watched until he saw her cross through the lobby. He slid back under the steering wheel, folded his arms across the top of it, and rested his forehead on his arms. After a minute, he leaned back and took several deep breaths. He grasped the steering wheel and shook it in frustration.

He jumped slightly when there was a knock on the cab window. He turned to see the face of Agent Simmons grinning at him. He rolled down the window.

"So, get the little lady home all right?"

"Were you spying on us?"

"Nah." Simmons shook his head and smirked. "I'm staying here, remember? Just on my way back from the police station. She's a winner, that one. And, for some unfathomable reason, she seems mighty taken with you. If she looked at me the way she looks at you… I wouldn't let her get away." He glanced shrewdly at Jerry.

"You know how it is."

"Yeah, yeah, I know. Traditional life, traditional wife." He shook his head. "Well, it's your funeral. Catch ya' tomorrow." He slapped the side of the truck and headed for the hotel.

Jerry shook his head, turned the key, put the truck in gear, and drove off toward Old Town and the Indian boarding house where he had a room.

Chapter 11

Thursday

June 6, 1929

Las Vegas, Day Seven

LIZ KNOCKED ON THE door of the den. Her father opened it and motioned her inside, then closed the door after her. The early morning sun was streaming through the eastern windows, lighting the massive desk that dominated the room and the almost throne-like chair behind it. Her father said, "Have a seat."

Liz sat on the large, overstuffed leather sofa facing the desk with calm and poise. "What did you want to see me about?"

Mr. Kearney walked over to the desk and sat in his chair. He took his time lighting his first cigar of the day, then shook out the match and placed it carefully in the large glass ashtray on his desk. He leaned back and examined her through slitted eyes.

"Doesn't show yet," he said. Liz lifted an eyebrow. He leaned forward and tapped the ashes off the end of his cigar in the ashtray. "I have been informed," he said slowly, "that you have a bun in the oven and it wasn't put there by your husband-to-be." He leaned back and puffed on his cigar, while waiting for her response.

"And who told you that?" she asked coolly.

"The man himself. Came to see me on Monday. Came up the back way so he wouldn't be seen. Left the same way." He tapped his cigar on the ashtray again. "Funny thing. He knew about your engagement to Eugene before it was even announced. Now, I wonder who could have told him?"

Her jaw worked and her breathing became more rapid, but she said nothing.

Her father again leaned forward to tap ash from his cigar. "Seemed to think his news was something I'd pay to keep quiet—over and over again."

"Did you kill him, or did you order one of the men to do it for you?"

He smiled. "You're like me, Liz, you go straight to the point. As to that, as I always say, if you want something done right, do it yourself."

He stood and walked to the window, still carrying his cigar. "He brought it on himself. He was becoming a danger to the business, selling that poison to the Indians and drawing the attention of the feds. There was one at his funeral, you know, just making sure that I knew he was here. And he was getting too drunk too often. Couldn't trust him to keep his mouth shut." He drew on the cigar. "And then, trying to blackmail me with this? It was one thing when you were just having your fun with him, I could look the other way, figured you'd get him out of your system. But, blackmail? No, he had to go. I can't have him holding this over my head for the rest of my life. And I had to make sure that it didn't happen again. I've got plans—big plans—and no two-bit kike is gonna throw a monkey wrench into them."

He turned and pointed the cigar at her. "And neither are you. Don't think I don't know what you were planning. Planning to have your cake and eat it, too, playing the dutiful wife during the day, and out catting around with lover boy at night. And catting around is the word for it. Morgan had the morals of an alley cat. His parents did better than they knew naming him 'Tom.' Not that yours are any better." He drew on the cigar again. "Neither are mine, for that matter, but it's different for a man." He paused. "Like I said, you're like me, which is why I knew that if he were around we'd never know who the father was, except maybe by hair color. Parkinson is too weak to stop you or take Morgan out, that's for certain, so I had to do it for him."

He crossed the room in a few quick steps and leaned down, his face close to hers. "Now, you listen to me, you little slut. I won't have any cuckoos in my nest. You'll get rid of it as soon as you're married to Parkinson. Chicago, Los

Angeles, San Francisco, there are places a woman with enough money can go to deal with these little problems. And then you'll be a good and faithful wife to Parkinson and you'll give him a whole raft of kids with orange hair and freckles, you hear me? No half-breed Jew bastard is going to inherit the Kearney land and money."

She nodded, saying nothing, her face a mask. Her father patted her awkwardly on the shoulder. "Just do as you're told and everything will be fine, Princess. You'll see. You'll get over it. Don't I always know what's best? And you'll get your reward when your old man is sitting in the governor's chair in Santa Fe." He walked back to his desk and set his cigar in the ash tray. He stood, facing away from her, staring down at the papers on his desk and breathing hard.

"Daddy?" Liz finally spoke and called him by the name she hadn't used since she was a teen. She walked up behind him and put her hand on his arm. "I'll do what you want, but first, can I just say goodbye to him? Please, Daddy?"

Her father looked at her, puzzled. "We went to the funeral. I did that for you. Thought you'd want to."

She nodded. "Thank you for that, Daddy. But, take me to the place where... it happened. I want to see for myself where... where it happened. I want to know where he breathed his last."

"Bit morbid, isn't it?" She just looked at him, tears glistening in her eyes. "But, if that's what you want."

She nodded. "It is, Daddy. I just want to know... And this will be the last you'll ever hear of it from me. Can we go now?"

He shrugged. "Might as well get it over with." He shook his head in bemusement at the ways of women.

She nodded. "We'll take my truck." She started toward the door, then turned, "Bring one of your shotguns. If anyone sees us, we'll tell them we're going rabbit hunting." He nodded. "I'll meet you outside." She left the office and headed for the garage where the family vehicles were kept.

A few minutes later, she had pulled her pickup truck up to the front doors. Her father came out, holding a shotgun broken open over his arm. He set it in the bed of the truck and climbed into the cab. Liz started off toward the spot where Tom had been killed. They drove in silence until they came near to the place, then her father gave her directions and finally told her to stop.

"This is it?" asked Liz, "This is the place?" Her father nodded. There was nothing to mark the spot, but she knew her father well enough to know that he always remembered such details. "Show me exactly where the truck was parked." He looked at her. "Please, Daddy? I just need to know."

He sighed, got out of the truck and started walking forward. She reached up and took her shotgun from the gun rack across the back window, then got out of the truck, took two shotgun shells out of her pocket and loaded the gun. She closed the breech.

"You shouldn't have done it, Daddy," she muttered. "He was mine. Nobody takes what is mine. And this baby is mine and I'm keeping it." She raised the gun, aimed, and fired. Her father fell forward onto his face and lay there, blood flowing from the wound on his back and staining the back of his jacket. She stood for a moment, then deliberately shoved her foot into a rabbit hole and fell forward onto the ground, scratching her face and hands and scuffing the knees of her jeans. Getting up, she reloaded the gun and looked for the telltale ears that signaled the presence of a jackrabbit. She aimed and fired, reloaded, aimed, and fired, half-a-dozen times. She returned to the truck, pulled a box of shells from under the seat, loaded her father's shot gun, and repeated the process, sometimes aiming for a jackrabbit, sometimes aiming for a prairie chicken or pigeon or some other bird scared into flight by the sound of the shots. Finally, satisfied, she walked forward and dropped his loaded shotgun near his right hand. She then returned to the truck, threw her gun into the bed, and drove off to the ranch to report the "accident".

* * *

IT WAS exactly ten o'clock when Prudence walked up the few steps to the door of the police station. She was wearing one of her new A-line skirts and silk blouses and her saddle oxfords with her new Panama hat. She had spent far too much time getting her hair and make-up just right, but she did want to look her best at this last meeting with Jerry. She had debated wearing one of her new silver and turquoise necklaces, but ultimately decided against it. She wasn't sure how Jerry would react, and she didn't want anything to spoil this day.

The door opened just as she reached out her hand to turn the knob. Jim stood back and waved her in. He closed the door behind her and walked around to sit at the chair behind the desk. He picked up a cigarette that was burning in the ash tray.

Bill was leaning against the back wall, with a cigarette in his hand, Agent Simmons was sitting in a chair near the desk, and Jerry was perched on one corner of the desk.

Jim began, "Sorry I had to give you the brush off the other day, Miss Bates, but, I think you can understand now why we didn't want anyone lookin' into Morgan's disappearance. We didn't yet know what had happened to him, but we did know that he was mixed up with these Mexican bootleggers. We couldn't keep it quiet here in Las Vegas, but we were tryin' to keep word from gettin' to them."

"Let's start at the beginning," Jerry said. "About six months ago—"

"Wait a minute!" protested Prudence. "I thought you were a teacher. Are you telling me you're a prohis?"

Jerry laughed, "No, I *am* a teacher. That part is true. If you'll let me explain. About six months ago, the amount of bootleg being sold to the Indians around here suddenly increased. The Bureau was aware of it and stepped up their investigation. They were able to identify Morgan as the probable source, but had no hard evidence. Then about six weeks ago, Indians started dying from it. Someone had started selling poisoned liquor to the Indians here and it was making its way to the pueblos. It wasn't all poisoned—there were plenty who were drinking but weren't dying, so—"

"We reckoned it was someone tryin' to make a little extra on the side for himself by cuttin' just a few bottles of hooch at a time. And we were pretty sure it was Morgan. He suddenly had far too much money," Jim interrupted, "but we had no way to prove it."

"Right," said Jerry. "So, that's where I came in. Bob here," he indicated Agent Simmons, who nodded at Prudence, "knew me from college. He had put together a sting, but needed an Indian to make it work. I made contact with Morgan as a customer—"

"Oh!" said Prudence. "So, that time..."

"I was pretending to be drunk," Jerry said.

"Why didn't you tell me?"

He shook his head. "Believe me, it was the hardest thing I've ever done, not telling you then or later, at the lunch counter, but I couldn't risk someone overhearing and I didn't want to involve you in this. It was too risky."

"But, I was so worried about you."

"I know, and I'm sorry." They gazed at each other, ignoring the grins from the other men.

Jerry continued, "The truth is, I don't drink at all." Agent Simmons coughed. It came out sounding like "Anymore."

Jerry glared at him. "That stereotype about Indians and alcohol is true, in my case at least. One drink and I can't stop." He and Prudence glanced at each other and then away. "So, I'd buy the hooch, then wander off to "drink in private." There was nothing but water in that bottle. That day you saw me was the day that Bob arrived. We all needed to meet, but it would have looked suspicious for me to walk into the police station. On the other hand, no one would have thought twice about a drunken Indian being hauled in to sleep it off in a cell. I've seen enough people in that condition to do a pretty good impersonation."

Agent Simmons coughed again. Jerry glared at him again. Simmons smirked.

"But you smelled like..."

He nodded. "I'd spilled enough on my shirt to give the impression before I dumped it out and refilled the bottle with water."

"What would you have done if I'd taken you up on the offer of a 'snort'?"

"I knew that there was no chance of that," he laughed. "Anyway, I managed to set up a buy of a crate of booze from Morgan. We figured that he'd cut the hooch with wood alcohol in order to maximize his profits and minimize the risk. He knew that he was under suspicion and was looking for a way to divert it. He'd sell it to me, then I'd sell it to the Indians, and if anyone traced it back, it would come to me.

And I'd probably be dead from sampling my own wares. He'd be free and clear. And if he didn't cut it, we'd still have him for selling alcohol to an Indian. A judge might look the other way at a bottle, but not a crate."

Prudence shuddered. She was suddenly glad that Martha wasn't here to learn how evil her brother had been.

"But then," Bill took up the story, "Morgan ends up dead." He shook his head at a look from Prudence. "We still don't know who's responsible for that. He was shot in the head at close range by a handgun, so we figure it was someone he knew well enough to let them get that close. Doc puts his death at around midnight, so some one he trusted enough to meet out there in the middle of nowhere in the middle of the night. Kind of hard to imagine he was there for any other reason than to meet someone in private. The cowboys who found his body tore up the ground pretty bad ridin' over it and destroyed any tire tracks that might have been left."

"Do you have any idea where he was for a day and a half before that? He left here Sunday evening and was found dead Tuesday morning. Where did he go on Sunday night, and where was he all day Monday?"

Bill shrugged. "All we know is where he wasn't. He wasn't at home, and he wasn't here."

"On Monday, when I asked if she knew where he might be, Liz said that he, in her words, 'had found a warm bed somewhere,' but she didn't say with whom," Prudence repeated with distaste.

"Sounds about right. Could be any of a half-a-dozen… ladies," Bill responded. "Anyway, Tuesday he's dead and we have to do some fancy footwork. The hooch is already on its way up from Mexico… by truck." He looked at Prudence and shook his head. "You were right about the meetin' place where they divide up the cargo to go out to their agents, but by motorboat up the Rio Grande to the Pecos and then the Gallinas? You've been readin' too many mystery stories, missy, and not enough about the geography of New Mexico. There are places where those rivers are so shallow, they'd have to get out and carry the boats." The other men snickered. "You were also wrong about Morgan's standin' in the organization. He was basically a foot soldier, if that, not one of the lieutenants who would be trusted with the cargo. No, he paid for what he got, and he only got what he paid for. Anyway, we figure the big boss, whoever he is," the three men exchanged glances, "won't be able to get in touch with the gang at such a late date, so if we can just convince them that Jerry here is Morgan's agent… it won't be a total loss."

"And we finally had enough manpower, thanks to Bob," Jim added. Agent Simmons touched two fingers to his temple in a mock salute. "As Jerry said, we'd had our eyes on Morgan and the train yard for a while, but we never knew when a delivery would be made or how many guards they'd have, and with just the two of us…"

"We were also banking on them wanting their money enough to take a risk on me," Jerry continued. "But we didn't know how much Tom paid for a shipment. We just guessed… and guessed wrong." He laughed. "Still, it all worked out. Lucky for us that he'd been short in the past."

"You could have been killed!" Prudence exclaimed. "And for what? Tom was the one poisoning the liquor and he was dead. That put a stop to it. What if the big boss had sent another agent of his own to meet them? Why did it have to be you? Why couldn't it be one of them?" she indicated the other three men. "It's their job, not yours!"

"Feisty little thing, isn't she?" Agent Simmons spoke aloud for the first time. "But, then, you always did like 'em like that, Jer." Prudence blushed furiously.

"Helping my people is my job," Jerry said softly. "If this means less bootlegged liquor in the pueblos for even a week, it was worth it." There was silence for a moment.

"Just as a matter of curiosity," she asked, turning to Agent Simmons, "Why were you at Tom Morgan's funeral?"

"Once again, Miss Bates," he said smugly, "You're making much ado about nothing. Small town like this, it just seemed like the right thing to do. Paying my respects to his family. Getting the lay of the land. Letting everyone know that the feds were on the case. I didn't expect his murderer to show up and give himself away or to see the gang of bootleggers among the mourners, if that's what you're thinking."

He stood. "Well, gentlemen," he said, "It's been great working with you. I have a van full of prisoners to escort to

Santa Fe, so if you'll excuse me," he shook hands all around. When he came to Prudence, he held her hand a moment and said in a low voice, "Jerry's a fool, but give him time. He'll be able to tell a hawk from a handsaw, once the wind has changed." He placed his grey fedora on his head and, turning the doorknob, said, "Thanks again for the assist, Jerry. I'll be sure to keep your name out of the papers," and left.

Jim lit a cigarette and broke the silence. "The big boss did send another agent. We picked him up before they got there, but he's not talkin'. Claims he was just out 'takin' the night air.' Has no explanation for that wad of cash we found in his back pocket." He laughed. "Says he must have forgotten that it was there." He shrugged. "He's right about one thing. We can't prove anything, so we'll have to give him back his money and let him go."

"Do you know who the big boss is?" Prudence asked.

Bill answered. "We have a good idea, but no proof. On the other hand, while we haven't put him out of business, we've hurt him. This operation will have shut him down for several weeks and may have damaged his connection with the Mexican mob. Our immediate concern though is who killed Tom Morgan. It would help if we could find the bullet, but it went straight through his head and out the window. It could be anywhere out there, and since they were all out there on their horses, cuttin' up the ground." He gave a shrug. "On the other hand, even if we did find it, we'd still have to find the gun. At least we'd know what kind of gun to look for, but it could be at the bottom of the Gallinas or it could have been cleaned and returned to the gun cabinet. We'd need more than vague suspicion to confiscate someone's guns."

"It could be so many people," Prudence mused. "It could still be a rival bootlegger, maybe that man you picked up," the men all shook their heads.

"He's just a flunky," Bill said, shaking out the match he had used to light another cigarette. "And anyone wantin' to take over would have to bump off someone higher up than Morgan was."

Prudence looked unconvinced. "It would have been a start, though. It could have been revenge for selling poisoned liquor to the Indians, but it would have to be someone he'd agree to meet at that place at that hour, someone he trusted at least that much." She carefully did not look at Jerry.

"Is that why you thought I was the one who killed him? More importantly, do you still think that?"

She shook her head. "Yes, it's why I thought that and, no, I don't think that anymore. I know I was terribly wrong, and I don't know whether you can forgive me..."

They gazed into each other's eyes.

"Of course I can. At least you ascribed it to noble motives. I've never been accused of being a righteous avenger before." Prudence caught the other two men grinning at each other.

"Maybe you won't when you know that I also thought you might have bumped him off to take over his territory."

Jerry laughed. "And continue selling liquor on the rez? Make up your mind, Prudence, it had to be one or the other. No, I'd much rather have seen him standing trial and publicly convicted of his crimes."

She blushed and looked embarrassed. "Well, if not a rival bootlegger or a righteous avenger, then, the father or brother of a girl he got in trouble or even one of the girls."

"Or a husband," Bill said casually, as he lit another cigarette. Prudence looked shocked, but then she remembered what Liz had said at the Plaza.

"Could be any of those," Jim leaned back in his chair. "From what I hear, there are plenty to pick from. But, which one? What reason would they give him for meetin' at that time and place? And why would he agree to it? Just doesn't seem likely. No, it has to be someone he trusted enough and who could give him reason enough."

Prudence said, slowly, "It was Mr. Kearney."

Jim sat up straight in his chair. They all stared at her. "What makes you say that?" Bill asked.

"The way Liz looked when I told her where Tom was found." She held up a hand as the men looked skeptical. "I know that's not evidence. Consider this: he's someone Tom would agree to meet that late at night in that spot and he's someone that Tom would allow to get close enough to shoot him, if he really is the big boss and Tom his agent.

And," she held up a hand again, "he has the most motive. Revenge for getting Liz in the family way," the men looked at each other, "and Tom was becoming a danger to his bootlegging operation. Selling poisoned liquor to the Indians was drawing the attention of the Bureau and, from what I saw, he was becoming too fond of the merchandise. He couldn't be trusted to keep his mouth shut. I was wrong about what he meant by calling them all "chickens" and saying that he was the "rooster." It wasn't nearly as complicated as I wanted it to be. He simply meant that he was their leader, and they were his followers. And, of course, that he was their source of hooch and that gave him power over them. Who knows what he would have said next? Bragged about his connection with Kearney, maybe? Told the world who the father of Liz's baby really is?"

Bill stood up from against the wall. "That's kind of how we figure it, but we didn't know about Liz. Just one more reason, then." He looked down at the floor, then back up. "But how do we prove it? Like you say, the middle of the night in the middle of nowhere. And on Kearney land, so if anyone saw him comin' or goin' he wouldn't need a reason and it wouldn't even look suspicious."

"As I say, Liz suspects, but I don't think she has any real evidence."

"She'll never roll on her father, in any case," Bill said. "It's a cinch his wife knows somethin', but she's too loyal—or too scared."

"What we don't know," Jim said, "is who set up the meetin' and why. We all assumed it was Kearney, but what if it was Morgan? Cashin' in by threatenin' to go public about Liz?"

"Blackmail?" Jerry asked. "We hadn't thought of that, but, now that we know about Liz... from what I hear, her father would do anything to preserve the family's reputation, especially now with his political ambitions. Word is that he bought her a husband. And I wouldn't put much of anything past Morgan."

"Could be," Bill agreed, "Problem with that is—why would Morgan be such a sap as to meet Kearney at that hour in that place? He had to know Kearney wouldn't take blackmail lyin' down."

"From what I've heard, Tom thought he was leading a charmed life," Prudence said. "His parents—well, his mother—had always covered for him and blamed others, and he had always been able to hide behind some patsy like Gene. I don't think it even occurred to him that Kearney would rather murder him than pay him off. He thought he had the upper hand."

Jerry sighed and stood up from the corner of the desk. "This is all just speculation. It's getting us nowhere."

"It's getting us closer to the truth. What I don't understand is why I didn't see it before," Prudence said. "It's obvious when you think about it."

"You were too busy suspecting me and working out convoluted means and motives," Jerry laughed, and the other two men joined in. Prudence blushed.

She changed the subject, "It's just about time for lunch. Join me at the hotel?"

"The Castañeda won't serve me."

"They will if you're with us," Bill said as he firmly seated his hat on his head. "The damned city oughta' be givin' you a medal. The least it can do is stand you lunch." He opened the door.

Jerry picked up a small duffel bag resting against the wall. He, Prudence, and Jim walked out and Bill closed it behind them. He jerked his chin at Jim, and the two of them preceded Jerry and Prudence down the sidewalk, leaving them to walk alone together.

Neither said anything for a few moments. Then, Prudence asked, "Why did you tell me that you were going on to Gallup?"

He laughed. "It seemed like a good idea at the time. I couldn't think how to explain why we couldn't see each other again, even though I was getting off here. Of course, I hadn't counted on running into you and certainly not outside the Castañeda while I was doing my act. I think I carried that off pretty well, by the way."

"Too well. If teaching doesn't work out, you could always try the stage or moving pictures." They both laughed.

"And it never crossed my mind that you'd even enter that drug store."

"Well... I have a confession to make... I saw you leave the store on Friday afternoon when I was having lunch at the Plaza Hotel... so... well... I went there hoping that you would be there."

"Did you, really?" He sounded inordinately pleased.

"So, are you leaving for Gallup for real this time?"

Jerry nodded. "On the afternoon train." He hefted the duffel bag. "I'll just wait at the station after lunch."

"Would you like some company while you wait?"

"I would." He reached out and squeezed her hand. She squeezed his back and both forgot to let go.

"That reminds me," said Prudence. "Where were you coming from when I met you on the train? Shouldn't you have been going east, not west, if you live near Gallup?"

"Always the detective," Jerry laughed. "I was coming back from a meeting in Denver with Bob and the other agents. I boarded that train at La Junta." He gave the city its proper Spanish pronunciation.

Prudence smiled to herself. It really was too much to expect that he would have taken Mary Howard's vacated seat and bunk.

When the four of them entered the hotel lobby, Clara looked up and her eyes got big. "Uh, Miss Bates," she called. "Could I have a word?"

"I'll meet you inside," she said to the men and went over to the counter.

"Is THAT your Jerry? I can see why you don't want to throw him back. He's the cat's meow, if you don't mind me mixing my metaphors."

Prudence shook her head. "I told you, Clara. He's not MY Jerry."

"Honey," Clara leaned over the counter, "I know you're from the big city, so maybe you haven't heard of making hay while the sun shines, but I'm damned sure you know that you should gather ye rosebuds while ye may."

"'While I may' is until the afternoon train. On the platform. In full view of the public."

Clara shrugged. "So they are tiny rosebuds. You'll still have them to cherish."

Prudence nodded. "You're quite wise for an undergrad."

Clara smirked. "It's all that reading I did in the library.

Oh, before you go, here's a letter for you from Cleveland."

Prudence laid the letter down next to her plate when she sat down at the table. It provided an obvious explanation for why Clara had called her. She ordered at random from the menu and listened to the men talking without hearing what they were saying. She couldn't stop thinking that, in just a few hours, she and Jerry really would part for the last time. It was all she could do not to cry.

She also couldn't help noticing that he kept pressing his knee against hers. She looked at him out of the corner of her eye to catch him looking at her the same way and twitching his lips in amusement. Well, if he liked 'em feisty... she pressed back against his knee. He coughed into his napkin, then pressed the side of his foot against hers. Two could play at that game, although it wasn't quite the same when he was wearing cowboy boots. She had just slipped her foot out of her shoe and started to run her toes along his instep, when a young cowboy rushed into the restaurant.

"Chief," he shouted at Bill. "Shootin' at the Kearney ranch. Come quick."

Bill and Jim stood up. "Who's been shot?" Bill asked. It wasn't in their jurisdiction, but they'd sort that out with the sheriff later.

"Old man Kearney. They say... his daughter. Accident... I don't know," the young man was breathless with excitement.

Bill motioned to the waitress and handed her several bills. "This should cover the meal.

These two," he indicated Prudence and Jerry, "can stay as long as they want. Right?"

Anne nodded and looked offended. "Of course. Paying customers are always welcome to stay as long as they like."

The fun had gone out of the afternoon. The pressure of Jerry's leg on hers was now comforting rather than stimulating. She slipped her foot back into her shoe. They quietly finished their meal, then walked out to sit on a bench on the platform.

"I suppose it's a kind of justice," Prudence finally said.

Jerry shook his head. "It's no kind of justice. It's just a perpetuation of the same... sickness. More people have been hurt. His daughter is a murderess, no matter what the charge is. His wife is a widow. His grandchild will always be known as the child of the woman who murdered its grandfather. Even her fiancé is harmed by this if he marries her or if he doesn't. Where will it end?"

"And the Morgans will never really know why Tom was murdered or who murdered him," she added.

"Do they know he's the father of Liz's child, their grandchild?"

"I don't know. I'm fairly sure that Martha does, but even if they do, they'll never be able to acknowledge it. Poor Mrs. Morgan, she won't even have Tom's child as a comfort to her—and she's already rejected the others."

"And so it spreads—the Kearneys, the Parkinsons, the Morgans. What does your Bible say? To the third and fourth generation?"

She nodded. "Some people read that as a curse. I've always thought that it was a description of the impact of parents' actions on their children and subsequent generations."

"My people would agree with you." He stopped as the Indians pulled up to the train tracks in their buckboards, and then started spreading their blankets and merchandise in anticipation of the arrival of the train from the east. "The once proud people of this place, Navajo, Zuni, Hopi, Pueblo pandering to tourists, playing the exotic curiosities, their history and mythologies reduced to quaint folktales and legends."

"Is that why you hate the Indian Detours?"

"When did I say that I hate them?"

"You didn't have to. It was written on your face."

"I don't know how I feel about them—or about this. On the one hand, we are 'the colorful natives,' performing our 'primitive ceremonies' to entertain the white man; on the other, it allows us to make the money we need to live in this new white man's world while preserving our traditional way of life. And maybe a handful of your Detourists walk away with a new appreciation of and respect for our history and traditions."

"I'm beginning to feel the same way. I wanted to become a Courier for the adventure and, yes, the exoticism. But after this week… I'm not sure whether I want to continue, but at the same time, I want to experience this land and people myself and learn about their history and traditions. And, maybe… if I can help even one Detourist gain that appreciation and respect… well, then, I'll have achieved something. I guess we're both educators, in different ways."

They heard the train approaching in the distance. They stood and walked down the platform.

"Seems like we're always saying goodbye at the train station," Jerry tried to laugh. Prudence nodded, then flung her arms around him. "People are staring."

"Let them."

"Let's give them something to stare at, then," he said, as he tipped her chin up so that her lips met his. After several long seconds, he pulled apart just enough to murmur, "We'd better stop. It's one thing to give them something to stare at. It's another to get arrested for public lewdness."

Prudence giggled.

"I have places to go, you know. I can't be wasting time sitting in a jail cell," he said, "And, besides, two nights in that cell were enough for me."

Prudence looked at him quizzically. He shrugged. "After they 'arrested' me, they kept me the allowable twenty-four hours so that there wouldn't be any suspicion. Then, just as Bill was about to let me go, Jim showed up with Morgan. We had to move fast to get me back in my cell and Bob into the Chief's office. I thought that his confidence in me as a partner would be strengthened if he thought we were both victims of the police and maybe I could get some more information out of him. So, when Bill came in later, I punched him through the bars and he rearrested me for striking a police officer." He laughed. "Bill got right up in my face and said, 'What'd you do that for, boy?' and I muttered back, 'I wanna talk to my partner.' I could see that he understood. I didn't know until later that he stationed Bob outside the window." He shrugged. "Tom talked plenty, but not about bootlegging. Mainly, he bragged about his conquests. Anyway, I spent Sunday night in the pokey, as well."

"So, you were there when I talked to Jim about Tom?"

"Yep. I was just about to leave when you opened that door. I heard every word." He laughed. "So did Bob, for that matter. He had just arrived for a confab. We both scrambled for the cells when we heard the knob turn."

"So you already knew about my theories when I was telling you about them at the lunch counter?" She pulled back and tried to look angry but failed.

He grinned. "Uh-huh. Of course, I couldn't let on, and it was the perfect excuse to ask you to go for a drive."

They smiled at each other, remembering. "I don't mind telling you that we were all concerned that you'd throw a monkey wrench into the works. And you almost did last night. But, all's well that ends well, and if it convinced you that I wasn't a murderer or an avenger, it was worth it." He looked down at her, "And if anyone has a bone to pick, my sweet… who was it who suspect whom of murder?"

Prudence blushed and hid her face against his chest. "I've said I'm sorry."

The train squealed to a stop. Passengers began disembarking, some heading toward the Castañeda, others walking down the platform, examining the jewelry spread out in front of them and asking to inspect specific pieces. None of them attempted to engage the sellers in conversation, merely asking "How much?" More than one of the men added, "Chief" to the question.

"Well, this really is goodbye," Jerry said at the bottom of the steps up to the train car. "I really am going on to Gallup this time." He held her hand. "I…"

Prudence nodded, then stepped back, withdrawing her hand from his. "I know." He stepped up into the vestibule. "If you're ever in Santa Fe, look me up," she said, this time with tears in her voice. He nodded.

The conductor called "All aboard," and the train wheels started turning. Jerry waved and walked into the train car. Prudence watched through the windows as he passed down the corridor, toward an empty seat. He sat and stared straight ahead. She watched until the train had left the station.

"Good lookin' man, that one," said a female voice in her ear. She turned to see one of the older women who sold jewelry on the train platform, her hair in a traditional bun and her skirts sweeping the ground. She nodded in agreement.

"Navajo?" Prudence nodded again.

"Thought so. Good people, Navajo. Maybe not so good as Pueblo people," she laughed, "but good. So how come you let 'im go?"

Prudence's lips quivered and she felt tears starting in her eyes. "I didn't let him go. He let me go." She stared down the tracks. "He wants to go back to his people, live a traditional life."

"Humph," the woman sniffed. "Won't work. Seen it too many times. These young ones… Old people know there's no going back to what was, only way to move is forward. These young ones, the ones they took when they were little, they got to find their own way, make their own place. Not easy, finding the middle way between the Indian world and the white man's world."

"That's why he wants… someone else. Someone who can help him with that."

"That man?" she laughed. "That man wants you. And you want him. Besides, not too many girls his age want to live that kind of life. They're all moving to Window Rock and Gallup, places like that, places with electricity and running water, that sort of thing. And the ones who do want to stay, live the traditional life… they want a man they can rely on, not one they have to train."

Prudence nodded. "But it doesn't matter. He has to try."

The woman nodded. "Yeah, he has to try. Only way to find out. But… we'll see." She nodded again. "We'll see."

An older man sitting in the lone buckboard still waiting at the tracks shouted something at her in a native language. She shouted back in the same language. "I got to go, but you remember what I said. Sooner or later… he'll find his way and it won't be what he thinks it will be. I've seen it, many times, now those kids they took away are grown up and tryin' to come back. And if you're still around…" She paused. "I like to see people happy, you know?" She patted Prudence on the arm and crossed the tracks to the waiting wagon. The man lifted the reins and turned the horses. They headed off across the desert, sitting stiffly upright next to each other on the wagon seat.

Prudence watched them leave. Once again, she wondered where they had come from and where they were going. There were no pueblos in this area and as far as she knew, no towns or villages in the direction the wagon was headed. Where did they live? How had they come here? Had the Harvey Company moved them here? Was there anyone here whom she could ask? Was there anyone here who even gave it a second thought? She walked sadly back to the hotel.

Clara gave her a sympathetic look. "He's gone, then?" She nodded. Clara held an envelope out to her, "You left this in the restaurant."

Prudence took it. "It's from my mother." She laughed. "No doubt Wally has written a few words or given her a message for me. Poor Wally."

"So, what gives? What were you doing with the Chief and Jim?"

"I can't possibly begin to tell you all about it here and now."

"I'm off at five. Meet me here and we'll go to the Meadows for tea" she winked, "and you can tell me all about it."

"It's a date. In the meantime, is there any place I could get my laundry done today? I know… I've left it to the last minute!"

Clara nodded. "If you're willing to pay for express service, Swanson's guarantees they'll have it done in two hours. They'll even pick it up and deliver it." She reached under the counter for a large brown paper bag with "Swanson's Laundry" emblazoned on it. "Just fill this up and bring it back down and your clean, pressed clothes will be delivered by five o'clock."

Prudence grabbed the bag and rushed up to her room. She quickly sorted through her clothes and filled the bag, then returned it to the desk. Clara handed her a form to fill out, then picked up the phone and called the laundry service. Prudence thanked her and went upstairs to finally read the letter from her mother.

My Dearest Daughter,

What a wonderful, exciting time you are having! I so enjoyed the picture postcard you sent me of the Castañeda Hotel. I hope I spelled that correctly. Your train trip sounds like such an adventure, and you met so many unusual people. Thank you for wiring your old mother and putting her fears to rest.

I've suggested to my ladies' club that we take up the American Southwest as our next topic of study and they think that's a fine idea. They were all very interested to see your postcard and asked for you to send more with scenes of the land and people. They are particularly interested in pictures of the Indians in their native dress. Have you seen any Indians yet? Wally assures me that they are perfectly peaceful these days, but I can't help but worry that some of them might go on the warpath.

No, Mother, she thought. The warpath is not what you need to worry about in regard to Indians. That's not where the danger lies, at least in regard to one Indian.

The ladies were also very interested to hear of the hot springs. Old Mrs. Richards actually spent a week at the Montezuma when it was still a resort hotel and regaled us with her memories of the place. I can't help but wonder, though, whether they are still properly hygienic. How very kind it was of those young people to invite you to accompany them. It doesn't surprise me. You always made friends so easily. I imagine that you will miss them when you leave Las Vegas.

Mrs. Jacobs had her baby on Thursday, the day after you left. It was a boy. Her mother will be coming down to help her when she gets home next week. I don't know how Mr. Jacobs is managing, but I suspect he is eating at diners and restaurants. I imagine that the first thing his mother-in-law will have to do is give the entire house a good cleaning. Men are so helpless when it comes to household tasks.

I saw the Lewis twins at the beauty parlor this week. You wouldn't believe how they have grown! It seems like only yesterday that they were roller skating down our sidewalk, and now, they are having their hair bobbed and marcelled! And wearing just a little too much makeup, if you ask me, but I suppose that's the new style. Do the women there wear makeup?

Johnny is coming over this week to weed the flower beds and generally tidy the yard. He says the maple tree needs trimming, as well, and he suggested that it's time to repaint the picket fence. It is look-

ing rather weathered. Do you remember the summer that you helped Father paint the fence? You got more paint on yourself than on the fence, but, oh, how you had fun "helping Daddy."

She paused, remembering. Yes, she remembered that summer. Her father had praised her skills highly and rewarded her for helping by taking her for an ice cream soda at the drugstore down the block. She also remembered the subsequent summers, when she gradually took on more and more of the responsibility for painting the fence and weeding the flower beds and pruning the roses and generally assisting her father with other outdoor chores. She had taken over completely those last few years, when his physical condition began to deteriorate. She remembered, but did her mother? Or did she only remember her as a little girl, when her father was alive and they were a complete family? She'd often wondered why her mother had never been interested in marrying again. Was she living in that idyllic past?

Higbee's was showcasing the new summer "tennis dresses" and other daytime sportswear for women. It would look lovely on a young woman such as yourself, but this old matron won't be wearing them. I noticed that hemlines are dropping again on daywear otherwise. You'll have to update your wardrobe when you get back.

The city is promising to go all out for Independence this year, with several parades at different locations and concerts and fireworks in all of the parks. The Carvers have invited me to join them at a picnic in the park. Mrs. Carver is making fried chicken and I'll be taking my famous potato salad. You must write all about the celebrations in Santa Fe or wherever you are on July 4.

Well, dear, that's the news from Cleveland. The house is so empty without you, but I keep myself busy with my chores and other activities. You'll be pleased to hear that I have invited my cousin, Mildred, to stay for a few months! I learned that she was recently widowed, so I suggested that the two of us keep each other company. I remember how lonely I was in the first months after your father left us.

She *was* pleased and relieved at this news, not only because it meant that her mother would not be lonely and alone, but because it also indicated that she had finally come to accept that Prudence was not going to be returning to Cleveland in the near future. And it was just like Mother to reach out to someone who needed comfort and care.

I invited Wally over to read your letter and he stayed to supper. He's going to add a few words to this, so I'll sign off now,
Your loving Mother

She could hear her mother's voice in her head as she read it, as if from a distance. It was at once familiar and foreign, after only a little more than a week, and so very parochial, concerned only with people and events within a few city blocks. She felt as if she were rereading a favorite novel about fictional people in a fictional world. Already, she had changed and her relationship with that world had changed. The people and events of Las Vegas were now an indelible part of her and always would be, even when she returned to Cleveland. Miss Freeman, Miss Eastman, the woman on the platform, they were all right. Travel changed you and you couldn't go back to what you were before or even to where you had been. It would all be different because you would be different, looking at it through different eyes.

She turned over the last page, and there was Wally's postscript.

Dear Pru,

Ma let me read your letter. Thanks for the mention! Good to hear the old buses are doing the job. Sounds like you're having a bang-up time there in the Wild West, running around to hot springs and whatnot with your new friends. Just don't forget the ones you left behind! The old man called me into his office today. Seems he's had his eye on me for some time. By the time you get back, someone will have been promoted to staff accountant. I might even have traded in the old jalopy for a new crate. I'll take you out to dip the bill and trip the light fantastic at some gin mill when you get back to civilization, if you're a good girl and play your cards right. Haha! Great idea for Ma to invite a guest. I know she's lonely and missing you.

Don't take any wooden nickels, kiddo, Wally

Had Wally been reading P.G. Wodehouse? She had mentioned to him that he was her favorite humorist. She shook her head. Poor Wally, she thought again. He was stuck in a dream of her that he'd first had when they were… children? Teens? Much younger, in any case. She felt a surge of irritation, as well. He refused to see her as she was today, to see that they had very little in common other than childhood memories. She sighed. Wally, Jerry, her mother, all of them clinging to a dream of the past, trying to return to a time and a world that had never really existed. She, on the other hand, was moving forward. First, she'd answer her mother's letter, then she'd join Clara at the Meadows for "tea."

She sat at the writing desk and quickly dashed off a formal note of condolence to Cousin Mildred on the loss of her husband, Harold. It was a fairly easy note to write, as she had only the vaguest memory of her mother's cousins, who lived in Michigan somewhere, and could resort to the formal phrases. She did add that she was glad that Mildred would be keeping her mother company and expressed her hope that the visit would be a pleasant one.

Then, she sat, pen in hand, struggling to know what to say to her mother. This letter was even more difficult to write than the last one. She certainly could not tell her mother about Tom's murder or the full story of the arrest of the bootleggers or of Mr. Kearney's death. And, once again, she would have to refrain from any direct mention of the person who was uppermost in her mind.

Dear Mother,

It was wonderful to get your letter. I am pleased to hear that Cousin Mildred is coming to stay. I am enclosing a note of condolence to her with this letter. Please give it to her with my love. I am also pleased that the Carvers have invited you (both?) to join them for their Independence Day Celebrations, and I will be sure to give you all of the details of the local celebrations. It's difficult to believe that this is my last night in Las Vegas, but I am eager to move on to Santa Fe.

You ask whether I have seen any Indians. Yes, they meet every train that comes in to Las Vegas to sell their jewelry and other hand-

icrafts to the passengers on the train. They arrive in their horse-drawn wagons shortly before the train is due and spread out their wares on blankets along the platform. The quality of their work is easily the equal of anything you'd find in a fine jewelry store in Cleveland, and I bought two silver and turquoise necklaces my second morning here. They go perfectly with my new western wear. Would you like me to purchase something for you? A necklace, ring, or bracelet? Please ask Cousin Mildred if I can buy anything for her, as well. They also sell pots and handwoven blankets and rugs. I will have many opportunities to buy items, as the Harvey Company has agreements with the Indians at every station where there is a Harvey House. I will send you some picture postcards of the Indians and their houses when I see them.

You asked if women here wear make-up. They do and they style their hair in the latest styles, as well. I'm sure that it's due to the influence of the moving pictures. There are two picture palaces here in Las Vegas and they show the latest pictures, so everyone is quite up-to-date in that regard.

So much has happened in the past few days! On the mundane side, I picked up my new clothing, so I'll be able to show up to the La Fonda in Santa Fe dressed like a native. I just hope it will convince them that I'm what they are looking for in a Courier.

In some happy news, one young couple, Liz and Gene, announced their engagement at a party at Liz's parents' home the other night. The wedding will be held after I'm gone, of course, but I was able to wish them well. Both families seemed to be pleased by the match. Tragically, her father was killed in a hunting accident just this morning. It has cast quite a pall over their engagement, but at least he lived to see it.

Also sadly, the brother of one of the young women I mentioned before—Martha—passed away unexpectedly a few days ago. I attended the funeral with Clara and John and expressed my condolences to the family. It is so sad when someone so young passes away. I wish that I could have done more to ease their grief.

There was quite a bit of excitement in town this morning, as we learned that last night the local law enforcement and agents of the Bureau of Prohibition broke up a bootlegging ring that had been operating out of Las Vegas and selling alcohol to the Indians, who are particularly susceptible to its effects. They arrested at least half-a-dozen bootleggers, who were taken off to Santa Fe this morning.

She paused, chewing on the pen. What more could she write? She wondered if the gaps would be as obvious to her mother as they were to her, but she had to be careful not to say anything that would worry or frighten Mother. Although she had said nothing that was not strictly true, she felt guilty at deceiving her mother by omission and disingenuous comments. And even if her mother could understand about Jerry, she felt incapable of putting her feelings about him onto paper. She sighed. This was the first time in her life that she had not been completely honest with her mother about something of importance.

Should she add a message for Wally? She was fond of him, but she didn't want to lead him on and give him false hope. When she compared how she felt about Jerry with how she felt about Wally, she knew that, regardless of what happened between her and Jerry, she could never settle for Wally. Better to remain a spinster with her memories. It wasn't fair to him, either. He deserved someone who would feel about him the way that she felt about Jerry. If only she had a younger sister she could introduce him to or even a female cousin who lived closer to Cleveland. Now that she thought about it, he and Martha might be perfect for each other. She seemed to be just the kind of nurturing homebody he was looking for.

As she sat there, reliving every moment with Jerry and pondering how to end the letter, there was a knock on the door. She left the letter on the desk and hurried to answer the door.

"Yes, who is it?" she asked.

"Swanson's laundry," said a male voice.

She opened the door and accepted the bundle of clean laundry. "That was fast!"

"We aim to please." He grinned cheekily, copied no doubt from some character in a movie.

She laughed and handed him the tip she had ready on the bedside table.

Closing the door, she opened the bundle and sorted the clothes. She set her suitcases on the bed, and in preparation for leaving in the morning, she packed what she considered her "Cleveland clothes" and anything else she didn't expect to need on the Detour in the largest, which she would have sent on ahead of her to Santa Fe. Her new "Western clothes" and other necessities she packed into the smaller of the two, with her jewelry safely stowed in the bottom. It would go with her on the Detour. Her pajamas and toiletries would go in that bag in the morning. She stood the two bags on the floor at the foot of the bed. It was just a few minutes after five o'clock when she arrived downstairs to find Clara ready to leave.

* * *

CLARA LED the way around the Meadows to the door in the alley that led to the cocktail lounge. The interior was as streamlined and modern as the exterior. The lights of the chandeliers glinted off of the gold and silver accents on the intricately carved tables and chairs, with their elaborate stitching and upholstery. Prudence was surprised to see Anne, Maria, and John sitting at a large corner booth with drinks in front of them. John put his arm around Clara as she slid into the booth next to him and she kissed him in greeting.

"What a coincidence," Prudence said, as she slid into the booth next to Clara. A waiter came up and took their orders.

The others laughed. "No coincidence," John said. "We couldn't let you leave Las Vegas without giving you an appropriate sendoff."

"And we all want to know what you were doing with the Chief and Jim," Anne added. "And I want to know who that hotsy-totsy was you were playing footsie with, the one who looked like a Navajo."

Prudence blushed.

Anne grinned. "Next time, make sure the tablecloths go all the way to the floor."

"Isn't Mike here?" Prudence changed the subject.

"Goodness, no," Anne replied. "He wouldn't be caught dead in here." She rolled her eyes. "I told him he could just have club soda, like me, but he believes in 'avoiding the appearance of evil.' I told him that he's not Caesar and I'm not his wife, yet."

"Martha's still sitting shiva, of course," Clara added, "but I know she'd be here if she could." She shook her head. "I'm worried about her. She's wracked with guilt over not turning Tom into the police earlier. She thinks it might have prevented him from being murdered if she had. Nothing that I or anyone else can say seems to make a difference."

"Oh, she can't think that!" Maria exclaimed. "Tom made his own choices." The others murmured in agreement. "We don't even know why Tom was murdered, do we?" She looked at Prudence.

"No, the police have some suspicions, but no firm evidence."

They paused as the waiter returned with their drinks. John and Anne asked for another. Maria shook her head. She was nursing hers.

"So, give," said Clara. "I've been waiting all day for this."

"Well, it all really started about six months ago," Prudence began. She related the story that she had heard from Jerry and the others that morning, then told them about meeting Jerry on the train from Chicago and of the events of the night before. It was a carefully edited version. Certainly nothing was said about a kiss on the range or about the episode in the pickup.

John leaned back. "So, this Jerry was an undercover agent all along." She nodded. "Getting back to the original question, who does the Chief think murdered Tom and why?"

"I'm not sure whether I should be telling you this.... but... we believe that the evidence points to Mr. Kearney." They all looked at each other. No one seemed surprised. John nodded as if it confirmed what he was already thinking. "They don't know for certain, but it may have been because Tom was becoming a danger to his bootlegging operation. His selling poisoned hooch to the Indians was drawing the attention of the feds, and with his own drinking, he could no longer be trusted. It may also have been revenge for getting Liz in the family way," again, no one seemed surprised. "They also wonder if Tom were trying to blackmail Mr. Kearney about Liz."

"Now, that I can believe," John said. "Tom always had an eye on the main chance and he'd have seen this as a continuous source of income."

"There's something I've never told anyone," Anne said, looking down into her drink. "Back when I first started working at the Castañeda, Tom tried to sweet talk me into helping him steal the Harvey silver service or at least part of it. I've never said anything because it would only cause trouble for Martha."

"The Harvey silver service?" Prudence asked.

The others nodded. "It's worth about, what would you say, Clara?" Anne asked.

"Something around two hundred thousand, I've heard."

"It's used whenever a Harvey House is hosting some kind of bigwig," Anne continued. "We have to polish it up before it's sent out on the train to whatever House needs it. Then, we polish it again before it goes back into the locked vault when they return it. Tom wanted me to pocket a piece here and there and give it to him to sell. Where, I don't know, as it's all got the Harvey House monogram on it. Maybe he planned to melt it down first." Anne took a gulp of her club soda. "And it never seemed to occur to him that every piece was counted as it was put away, and if any had been missing, we girls would have been the first to be suspected. It wasn't that he was a mug so much as he'd always been able to find someone else to take the blame or soft soap his way out of it. He seemed to think that he was so irresistible to women that all he had to do was whisper a few sweet nothings in my ear and I'd be his to do with as he liked." She grimaced and Maria nodded in agreement. "He was good-looking, I'll give you that, but... I don't know... there was just something smarmy about him." She shook her head. "I'll take an honest man who's a bit of a prig any day."

Clara laughed. "And that's what you've got." Everyone, including Anne, laughed at this. "It's a good thing Prudence didn't know about this before, or she'd have suspected you of murdering Tom. She already suspected Mike."

"Mike?!" Anne exclaimed. "What reason would Mike have to bump off Tom? I was certainly never one of his chippies."

"She thought because he spiked the punch and called Mike an 'old maid Mormon.'"

Everyone laughed, and Prudence joined in. It did sound ridiculous when put that way.

"If he were going to murder him for that, he'd have done it ages ago," Anne said. "No, it would take a lot more than that to get Mike to break one of the big ten."

"The person I really suspected was Jerry," Prudence admitted. "I was afraid that he was exacting revenge for the poisoned liquor. I mean, he did lie to me about going on to Gallup... I just kept hoping that someone else would have a stronger motive." She looked at Maria, "I even tried to pin it on your father or your brother."

Maria smiled and shook her head. "That would have been a last resort, only if all else failed, and they'd have admitted it, after going to confession." She laughed, "They'd have been much more likely to lock me away in a convent. I'm saving them the trouble." She smiled again.

"So, we were wrong about the Gallinas?" Clara asked.

Prudence nodded. "By the way," she asked suddenly. "Why didn't you tell me that those rivers are too shallow for motorboats?"

Clara smirked. "You were having such a great time with your detecting and your deducing and your theorizing, I didn't want to spoil it for you. Besides, it was something you could have found out easily enough, if you'd stopped in the library and looked in a reference book. Or just asked me." Prudence had the grace to look ashamed. "And, at the time, it was as good an explanation for what he meant about chickens and the rooster as any other. So, given that wasn't what he meant, why was he shot where he was shot?"

"Most likely because it was an out-of-the way place on Kearney land where they wouldn't be disturbed. Probably nothing more significant than that. And he probably meant nothing more than what he always meant—that he saw himself as their leader and them as his followers. Or saw himself as the only real man among them."

John nodded. "Most likely both. Clara told me what you thought he meant. Bit elaborate, don't you think? Simplest answer is usually the best, as they teach us in our science classes. Principle of parsimony." Clara poked him in the ribs. He grinned.

"And Liz shooting her father?" Maria asked. "Was it really an accident?"

"I don't know," Prudence answered. "I'm certain that she at least suspected that her father was somehow involved with Tom's death, but I don't know any more than that."

"She'd do it, if she thought her father had killed him to stop them from seeing each other," Clara declared. "She and her father... they may not have looked alike, but they had the same personality. They both put themselves and their desires before anyone else—and anything else. But only if she thought she could get away with it, so I'm sure it will have been carefully staged to look like an accident. What I want to know is whether she'll still marry Gene and whether Gene will still marry her."

"She'll have to, won't she?" Maria asked again. "I mean, with the baby and all." The others nodded in agreement. "And, he needs the Kearney money, doesn't he? To pay for his mother's medical treatments and to help his sisters?" Again, the others nodded.

"I still want to know why you were playing footsie with that Jerry," Anne demanded. The others laughed.

"Enough, Anne," Clara said, looking at Prudence's face. "Haven't you ever heard of two ships passing in the night?"

"Oh, I'm sorry," Anne reached over and touched Prudence's hand. "I didn't think..."

"It's all right," Prudence smiled with an effort. "It was just one of those things that didn't work out. And you're right, we should have paid more attention to the length of the tablecloths." This time her smile was genuine and nostalgic. "And if he weren't wearing cowboy boots! Nothing ruins a good game of footsie like cowboy boots." She laughed and the others laughed with her.

Maria suddenly sat up straight and pushed her drink away from her. "I have something to tell you all," she said in a firm voice. "You know I'm going to enter the Sisters of Charity as a postulant soon." They all nodded, wondering where this was going. "I can't do that with a lie on my conscience." They all looked at each other. What dreadful secret could Maria have? "So... I want you all to know that... my abuelita is Tewa, not Spanish." She finished in a rush.

There was a long silence. Prudence could see that no one knew quite how to respond. They obviously didn't want to embarrass Maria by telling her that they already knew.

Finally, Clara reached out and touched her hand, "Thank you for trusting us, Maria." The others nodded in agreement and Anne also put out a hand to her.

"And what you said about Tom maybe trying to blackmail Mr. Kearney, I can believe that because he tried to blackmail me into… into… well, you know." She paused and looked around the table. "No one is to tell Martha or her parents!"

Everyone shook their heads. "Of course not—it would only hurt them—it will be our secret."

Maria relaxed for the first time that evening. "That's my big announcement out of the way. Now, Clara, I think you have something to tell Prudence."

"Oh, let me tell her," Anne insisted. Clara smiled in agreement. "Well, we don't know if this will do any good, but we figured it couldn't hurt."

"Get on with it, Anne," Clara interjected.

"OK, ok. Well, Prudence, yesterday, Clara and I got together and we wrote a letter to the head of the Indian Detours in Santa Fe. Well, Clara did most of the writing, I just told her what to say and signed my name," she laughed. "Anyway, we gave you a glowing recommendation as a Courier." She beamed at Prudence. "So, what do you think of that?"

"The three of us who work at the Castañeda signed it, including Martha," Clara added.

"I honestly don't know what to say." Prudence grasped Clara's hand next to her and reached across the table for Anne's and then Maria's. "Thank you, thank you all."

John finished his drink and called for the check. "I've got this, ladies," he said as he counted out some bills and placed them on the table. "I don't know about the rest of you, but I have to be up before sunrise to get to work, so I'm going to be calling it a night."

"Same here," said Anne. "I'm on the breakfast shift."

"And, as usual, I'm on the morning shift at the desk," Clara added.

At the door of the Meadows, Maria gave Prudence a quick hug and said, "I'm so glad that I got to know you. I will keep your name in my prayers." She blushed slightly, "That you'll be accepted as a Courier and also that you and

Jerry..."

Prudence returned her hug. "Thank you, Maria. I appreciate it. If anyone has influence with the powers that be, it's you."

She turned to Clara and Anne. "I guess I'll see you in the morning?" They both nodded.

There were quick hugs all around, then they headed off in different directions, the others to their homes and Prudence back to the hotel.

She saw the letter lying on the desk when she turned the light on in her room. She knew just how to end it!

The most wonderful thing has happened! My friends here took me out to the local speakeasy for a farewell drink tonight, and, the ones who work for the Harvey company have written a letter of recommendation for me to the Southwestern Indian Detours in Santa Fe. I don't know whether it will influence their decision, but it certainly cannot hurt, and, regardless, it was a lovely gesture. So, tomorrow morning, I join the Southwestern Indian Detour as a Detourist. And four days after that, if all goes well, I'll be in Santa Fe, training to be a Courier.

You can write to me at the La Fonda, in Santa Fe. I'll write to you once I get there. I'll be on the road with the Detour and have no time to write or way to post a letter before that, so do not worry when you don't hear from me for a week or so.

All my love, Prudence

Chapter 12

Epilogue

Offices of the Las Vegas Optic

THE EDITOR AND REPORTERS of the biweekly *Las Vegas Optic* were arguing over the lead story for their Friday issue. The murder of Tom Morgan, which they had reported on the third page of the Wednesday edition, suddenly became front page news when rumor linked it to the arrest of eight bootleggers on Wednesday night and to the killing of Randolph Kearney on Thursday.

"No, we can't lead with 'New Evidence in Morgan Murder.' There's no evidence, just a lot of rumor," declared the editor, in response to his cub reporter's suggestion. "And we can't lead with 'Kearney Revenge Killing,' either. It's only speculation that Liz murdered her father in revenge for him killing her lover. Hell, it's only speculation that Morgan was her lover, for that matter, and that Kearney murdered him because of it. Do you want to set us up for a libel suit? Unless she is found guilty of the murder by a jury of her peers, Liz will still have the Kearney fortune and won't hesitate to use it. She's as careful of her reputation as her father was, maybe more, being a woman."

The cub reporter protested, "But everyone knows that she and Morgan were an item."

The editor glared at him. "Hardly what you'd call evidence of murder. And everyone knows, or should know, that 'everyone knows' is not evidence in a court of law. So, what else have we got?"

"Well, there's always 'Feds Arrest Bootleggers at Railroad Yard,' offered the lead reporter. "According to Federal

Agent Simmons, Morgan had been the Bureau's man on the inside, and the mob killed him when they discovered it. That ties the Morgan murder into the arrest. On the other hand, Simmons wouldn't say whether the Feds think that Kearney ordered the hit on Morgan or possibly even carried it out himself. They won't even say if they think Kearney's involved with the bootlegging." He turned toward the cub, "no matter what 'everyone knows.' And Liz wouldn't hesitate to sue if we were to link her father's name to criminal activities so we'd damned well better have harder evidence than that. And without the Morgan-Kearney link," he shrugged, "the story is definitely page two."

"What about the rumor that Morgan was the one selling poisoned liquor to the Indians?" asked the cub, in desperation.

The editor shook his head. "Even if we had evidence that's definitely a page three or even page four story. And that rather takes the shine off of him as an undercover agent, if it's true. Better to just steer clear of it or report it as 'unidentified member of the gang.' Besides, it would only bring more pain to the Morgan family, and Mrs. Morgan's pretty near the edge as it is, from what I hear." Everyone in the room nodded.

"So that's it?" The cub responded in disgust. "They just get away with it? SHE just gets away with it?"

The editor shrugged. "Kearney's out of it, however you figure it. Even if we could pin Morgan's murder on him, what difference would it make? And, unless you have a witness that the police haven't been able to find or some hard evidence... yes, she gets away with it." He shook his head. "At least as far as the law is concerned, but, as they say, old sins cast long shadows, so... who knows? The real question now is whether she takes over her father's bootlegging operation."

"You mean, whether Parkinson takes it over," the cub corrected him.

The other three laughed. "No, I mean exactly what I said," the editor responded. "Parkinson will do exactly what his lovely wife tells him to do, if he wants a long and even moderately happy life. My guess is she'll leave the running of the ranch to him and handle the… side business… herself." The others nodded in agreement.

The cub reporter tried again. "What about this undercover agent? Anyone know who it is? Any story there? Didn't someone say there was a woman there? Could the agent be a woman?"

The lead reporter shook his head. "The only thing I know for sure is that it's a man. I tried to pry the name out of him, but Simmons wasn't saying and neither were Bill or Jim. Just kept repeating that 'his identity is being kept confidential for his own safety.' My guess is it's someone local whose life wouldn't be worth a plugged nickel if the Mexican gang found out who he is. They didn't say anything about any woman. I doubt that rumor has any truth to it."

The editor of the society pages asked, "What am I supposed to do with the announcement of the Kearney-Parkinson engagement? Liz says that the wedding is still planned for the next couple of weeks, but running it in the same edition as the news of her father's death? Looks a little insensitive, at best." She shrugged. "On the other hand… she wants an announcement in this edition." She lowered her voice. "From what I hear, she doesn't have the luxury to call it off or even to move it forward." The cub started to speak. She silenced him with a sharp glance. "Yes, that's only rumor. So, for that matter, is the identity of the father." The editor and lead looked at her quizzically. "Oh, haven't you heard? Well, far be it from me to slander a Kearney, but, as everyone knows," she grinned at the cub, "it won't be a surprise to anyone if the kid doesn't have red hair and freckles. That's all I'll say."

The editor made his decision. "We run with the Kearney tragedy on page one. And I said 'tragedy.' End with the news that the wedding is going ahead as planned because it's what Kearney wanted. Everyone knows he's been pushing for this merger with the Parkinson ranch for years, so Liz will be 'honoring her father's wishes.' That'll make her happy and she's the Kearney we have to worry about now. 'Bootleggers' arrest on page two. Morgan was the inside man and was murdered by an 'unknown member of the mob.' That makes him the hero, so not a word about him selling poisoned liquor to the Indians. That's 'an unknown member of the gang,' as well. If he really was Liz's lover, this will just make her happier. And don't forget to mention Taylor and Phelps. It never hurts to put a little shine on police-press relations when we can. Run the engagement announcement, but soft peddle it. You know the language," he waved a hand at the society editor.

She nodded, "Mrs. Randolph Kearney and the late Mr. Randolph Kearney, etc."

"All right, I want the stories on my desk before five o'clock. Let's go, people."

Las Vegas Optic Friday June 7

TRAGIC ACCIDENT AT KEARNEY RANCH

San Miguel County was deprived of one of its leading citizens by a freak and tragic accident on Thursday morning. Randolph Kearney, local rancher, businessman, and philanthropist, was killed while practicing his marksmanship by hunting jackrabbits with his daughter, Elizabeth. She had stopped to reload, while her father walked on ahead, scouting for prey. She started after him, stumbled over a rabbit hole, and the gun went off, the pellets striking her father in the back. There were tears in her eyes when she told this reporter that she considered that the accident had been her fault. Like all Western girls, she had been raised to always carry a shotgun broken open and to keep her finger off the trigger of any firearm until she was ready to shoot. Her voice broke as she explained that her mind had been distracted by thoughts of her upcoming wedding to Eugene Parkinson, son of neighboring ranchers. After rushing forward to her father's aid and determining that there was nothing she could do, she drove back toward the house in search of assistance. She came upon some of the Kearney hands working not far away and they followed her back and respectfully lifted her father's body into the bed of the truck. She picked up his shotgun herself and placed it next to his body in an act of filial respect. She then sent one of the hands to town for help and sent the others on ahead of her to prepare those at the house, while she drove the body home as fast as possible, but they all knew that it was too late. Las Vegas Police Chief Taylor and Officer Phelps were the first to arrive at the Kearney home and determined that Kearney was deceased. They immediately called for medical assistance for Mrs. Kearney and Miss Kearney, who were hysterical with grief. Both women have been placed under a doctor's care and confined to bed for the next few days. The county sheriff does not contemplate filing charges in what is so clearly a case of accidental death. The staff of the *Optic* offers its sincere condolences to the Kearney family in their time of bereavement. The recently announced Kearney-Parkinson wedding, being one of Randolph Kearney's fondest wishes, will take place as planned at a time and place to be announced here later.

FEDS ARREST BOOTLEGGERS AT RAILROAD YARD

A major bootlegging distribution ring associated with a Mexican mob was broken up last Wednesday night in a successful "sting" operation conducted under the expert leadership of Bureau of Prohibition Agent Robert Simmons. In an interview with this reporter, Simmons revealed that Tom Morgan, victim of a murder by an unknown assailant on early Tuesday morning, had been the Bureau's man on the inside. He felt certain that the mob had killed him when they'd discovered his undercover status. However, with the expert assistance of Las Vegas Police Chief William Taylor and Officer James Phelps and an undercover agent whose identity shall remain confidential for his own safety, the Bureau was able to carry out a successful operation that resulted in the arrest of eight of the gangsters and the confiscation of nearly twenty cases of illegal alcohol. The Bureau is keeping the details of the case confidential until after charges have been filed and the case comes to trial. There is some speculation that this mob was also responsible for the adulterated liquor that has caused the deaths of a dozen or so Indians in the past month.

Kearney-Parkinson Engagement

Mrs. Randolph Kearney and the late Mr. Randolph Kearney announce the engagement of their daughter, Elizabeth, to Eugene Parkinson, son of Mr. and Mrs. Richard Parkinson of this county. The date of the wedding has not been fixed.

* * *

FRIDAY EVENING, John flipped a copy of the *Optic* across the reception desk to Clara. "You read this?" he asked, leaning on the desk and pointing to "Tragic Accident at Kearney Ranch."

She nodded. "If it weren't for the names, I wouldn't recognize the story. Liz out traipsing around the open range rabbit hunting with her father? I wouldn't have believed that even if I had seen it, and I'm not sure the reporter does, either. 'Filial respect?' Not that Liz isn't a good shot…"

"Almost too good. I've never known her to miss anything she aimed at with a rifle, let alone a shotgun," John said. "But, she doesn't have to prove her innocence. It's down to the law to disprove it, and with no witnesses…" He shrugged. "I hear there were even a dozen or so rabbit corpses out where she says it happened. I also hear that it happened pretty close to where they found Tom's body."

"Poetic justice, do you think? The bootlegger story makes Tom out to be a hero," Clara said in disgust. "I'm not surprised that Jerry isn't mentioned by name. He was undercover, after all, but to make Tom into a hero, a martyr even? Prudence would be livid."

"It'll make Mrs. Morgan happy and maybe Martha."

"There is that to be said for it. I doubt that it will fool Mr. Morgan, and Martha will only believe it because she wants to, but if it helps her to not feel guilty… You and I both know that this had nothing to do with the Morgans, though. It's all about keeping Liz Kearney happy, now that she's inherited the Kearney fortune."

"You noticed the last line?"

"You mean, the wedding going ahead as planned? Yes, and the engagement announcement is on the society page. It's like Maria said, she's got no choice on that one."

John shrugged. "Why not? With her money, what would it matter?"

Clara shook her head. "Raising a kid without a name? Liz is too name-proud to do that. Besides, she'll want Gene around to run the ranch. It will be cheaper than hiring a manager and safer, too. He'll have a vested interest in its success."

"Are we going to the wedding?"

"Will we be invited?"

"I thought everyone at the party the other night was invited."

"They were, but that was before. Things might be different now. Liz does love to be the center of attention, but only the right kind of attention. If she thinks people are coming only to watch a murderess get married…"

* * *

AT THE staff meeting on Sunday, the editor of the *Optic* assigned his lead reporter to cover the Kearney funeral. "I know that I can trust you to give it the correct treatment," he said, glaring at the cub reporter.

The lead nodded. "Leading member, loss to the community, etc. Got it." The cub looked disgusted.

The editor turned to the society editor, "And I know that I can trust you to give the correct treatment to that little private event you've been invited to."

She nodded. "Somber, dignified, understated. Did they ask for a photographer?"

The editor shook his head. "Even Liz Kearney wouldn't go that far."

Las Vegas Optic Wednesday June 12

KEARNEY LAID TO REST WITH MASONIC RITES

Randolph Kearney, late of this county, was laid to rest in the Masonic Cemetery in Las Vegas on Monday morning with full Masonic Rites. The leading members of the Las Vegas community gathered at the ceremony to honor Kearney and offer comfort and support to his widow and daughter. A native of Las Vegas, Kearney was a prominent rancher who had turned a small holding into one of the largest and most profitable spreads in San Miguel County. He expanded his business interests to include partnerships in hotels, restaurants, and other retail concerns. A longtime member of the Las Vegas Baptist Church, and a founding member of the Las Vegas Elks Club (the mother lodge of New Mexico) and the Las Vegas Chamber of Commerce, he was known as a philanthropist who donated to such worthy causes as the Church building fund, the recently created Elks National Foundation for charitable causes, and to the Chamber of Commerce boosterism campaign, which has done so much to promote our fair city. He is survived by his wife of 25 years, Evelyn Kearney, his daughter, Elizabeth (Kearney) Parkinson, and his son-in-law, Eugene Parkinson.

Kearney-Parkinson Nuptials

In deference to her father's wishes, Elizabeth Kearney and Eugene Parkinson were married Sunday at a private ceremony conducted by the justice of the peace in the parlor of her family home, attended by the bride's mother and the groom's parents. Due to their recent personal tragedy, the couple will postpone their honeymoon trip for the foreseeable future.

Las Vegas Optic Friday June 14 Society Pages

Mrs. Evelyn Kearney, widow of the late Randolph Kearney, is leaving Las Vegas next week for an extended stay at the world-renowned Rockhaven Sanitarium in Glendale, California, where she will receive treatment for the emotional devastation resulting from the recent accidental death of her husband. The staff of the *Optic* wish her a speedy recovery and extend their condolences to her daughter and son-in-law in their time of trouble.

Fried Chicken, Castañeda

Created by Chef Dan Tachet, Hotel Castañeda, Las Vegas, New Mexico

Fry an onion, chopped very fine, in butter, add flour, mix and pour in one quart chicken broth and one half pint cream. Stir and let come to a boil. Let it cook about ten minutes. Add two egg yolks and parsley, and remove from the fire. This sauce must be quite thick. Dip thin slices of one three pound hen in the sauce so that it adheres to both sides. Lay them in a pan sprinkled with bread crumbs and also sprinkle the chicken with bread crumbs. When cold, dip them in beaten egg and crumbs and fry in deep hot grease. Serve with tomato sauce and French peas as garnish. If handled properly, one three pound hen will make ten to twelve fair-sized orders.

For modern cooks:
1 large onion, minced
3/4 cup unsalted butter or olive oil
3/4 cup flour
1 quart chicken broth
1 cup heavy cream (do not substitute low fat dairy)
2 egg yolks, beaten
2 tablespoons chopped parsley
6 chicken breasts (3 lbs.), pounded to an even thickness
1 cup plain breadcrumbs
2 whole eggs, beaten in a shallow dish
Neutral oil, such as canola, sunflower, or vegetable oil
Marinara sauce or your favorite tomato sauce
Green peas

Sauté onion in butter until soft. Add flour and stir for 1-2 minutes, until incorporated into the butter. Gradually add one quart of chicken broth, whisking until smooth. Add heavy cream. Mix well. Bring to a boil. Reduce heat and simmer about 10 minutes until thick. Remove from heat. Temper beaten egg yolks by beating a few tablespoons of the hot mixture into them, then add all to the pan and mix well. Add parsley.

Spread a layer of breadcrumbs over the bottom of a rimmed sheet pan. Dip each chicken breast in the white sauce and lay it in the pan. Repeat with each breast. Sprinkle the chicken with additional breadcrumbs, pressing lightly to adhere. Let set until cool.

Heat several inches of oil in a frying pan. Spread additional breadcrumbs in a shallow dish. Dip each chicken breast in the beaten egg, then dredge in the breadcrumbs and fry until golden brown.

Serve with marinara sauce and green peas.

Author's Note

The Fred Harvey Company really did offer Southwestern Indian Detours from 1926-1941, when World War II put an end to them. There was a brief revival from 1947 to around 1968, when Grey Lines bought the rights to the name and the routes, but the heyday had ended. There really was a Miss Anita Rose and she really did make a marketing tour of the U.S. in 1929 and really did visit Cleveland that year. She used lantern slides (now held by various university library and museum special collections in Arizona, including the Heard Museum in Phoenix) and motion pictures in her presentations, although the actual text as presented is recreated based on brochures and other marketing materials. The Castañeda Hotel was restored and reopened to guests in April 2019. There is an Amtrak station just south of the Hotel where the Southwest Chief stops twice a day, once eastbound from Los Angeles and once westbound from Chicago.

The Meadows hotel continues to do business today as the Historic El Fidel hotel. Although it no longer houses a speakeasy, there is a room on the first floor with an exit into the alley behind the hotel.

While there is plenty of information to be found online about the Detours, the definitive work is D. H. Thomas' *Southwestern Indian Detours: The Story of the Fred Harvey/ Santa Fe Railway Experiment in "Detourism"* (Hunter Publishing, 1978). Additional information about the Fred Harvey Company and the Harvey Houses can also be found online (in particular https://fredharvey.info/ and their Fred Harvey History Weekend) and in Stephen Fried, *Appetite for America: Fred Harvey and the Business of Civi-*

lizing the Wild West–One Meal at a Time (Bantam, 2011) (see also his blog at https://www.stephen fried.com/blog/), Lesley Poling-Kempes *The Harvey Girls : Women Who Opened the West* (Da Capo Press, 1994), and George H. Foster & Peter C. Weiglin, *The Harvey House Cookbook: Memories of Dining Along the Santa Fe Railroad* (Taylor Trade Pub., 2006).

Linda Eastman was the director of the Cleveland Public Library from 1918 – 1938, the first woman to head a major metropolitan library, and Marilla Waite Freeman was Head Librarian (assistant to the director) from 1922 to 1940. A quick search of the internet will reveal more information about both women, including extensive Wikipedia entries as well as Suzanne M. Stauffer (2019) Marilla Waite Freeman: The Librarian as Literary Muse, Gatekeeper, and Disseminator of Print Culture, *Library & Information History,* 35:3, 151-167, DOI: 10.1080/17583489. 2019. 1668156.

About the Author

After 20 years as a librarian and another 20 as a professor of library science and library historian, Suzanne Stauffer is moving on to her third career as a novelist. She was inspired by an exhibit on the Harvey House Couriers at El Tovar at the Grand Canyon and her research in women's history. When not writing, she can be found reading, baking, gardening, and binging t.v. westerns. She has lived and worked in Utah, Puerto Rico, Texas, Oklahoma, Spain, New York City, Los Angeles, and Baton Rouge. She now lives in Albuquerque with her Australian husband and brown and white spotted rat terrier dogter.